THE
LOST
YEAR

ALSO BY KATHERINE MARSH

Nowhere Boy
The Door by the Staircase
Jepp, Who Defied the Stars
The Twilight Prisoner
The Night Tourist

THE
LOST
YEAR

KATHERINE MARSH

ROARING BROOK PRESS

NEW YORK

To my grandmother, Natalia, and her homeland

Published by Roaring Brook Press
Roaring Brook Press is a division of Holtzbrinck Publishing Holdings
Limited Partnership
120 Broadway, New York, NY 10271 • mackids.com

Our books may be purchased in bulk for promotional, educational, or
business use. Please contact your local bookseller or the Macmillan Corporate
and Premium Sales Department at (800) 221-7945 ext. 5442 or by email at
MacmillanSpecialMarkets@macmillan.com.

Library of Congress Cataloging-in-Publication Data is available.

First edition, 2023
Book design by Samira Iravani
Printed in the United States of America by Lakeside Book Company,
Harrisonburg, Virginia

ISBN 978-1-250-31360-7 (hardcover)
7   9   10   8   6

*You may not be at a point where you have fully
recovered all your power or all your memories . . .
But courage need not be remembered . . .
For it is never forgotten.*

—The Legend of Zelda: Breath of the Wild

1

MATTHEW

Leonia, New Jersey, USA
2020

Dark Beast Ganon charged. I aimed the Bow of Light at the monster's glowing core and jumped. I shot off one arrow, then another.

"Yes, yes!" Zelda encouraged me. "Ganon's power is weakening!"

A few more direct hits with the Bow of Light, and I'd finish off the biggest, baddest boss of all and unlock the ending to the entire game. But I was down to half a heart. I needed food—fast!—before I ran out of lives to fight.

"Matthew?"

I searched my meal inventory. I'd eaten all my steaks and almost everything else.

"Matthew!" Mom shouted. She was standing right over me.

"Coming," I said, without making a move from the couch, where I was curled in a ball around my Switch.

"Time to go outside."

Wait! I still had a mushroom skewer.

"You've been playing *Zelda* for five hours," Mom said.

I selected the skewer. "I know! I did my homework this morning."

I wasn't even lying. For an entire month now, since Covid had closed all the schools, I'd been doing "online learning" in my bedroom, but I usually polished off my homework while the teachers barked at kids to turn on their cameras or stop goofing off in the chat. Everyone else was stuck at home, too—school, sports, birthday parties were all canceled—but most of my friends could at least hang out in one another's backyards and spend an hour feeling normal. I wasn't even allowed to do that because a few weeks earlier, Mom had moved my great-grandmother out of her nursing home and in with us. Her name is Nadiya, but we call her GG (for great-grandma, obviously). She's one hundred years old, which means we can't take *any* risk when it comes to Covid, including inviting a friend to the backyard.

"It's not about that," Mom said. "You need to come back to Planet Earth."

"No thanks," I said.

Planet Earth was the last place I wanted to be. I was basically under house arrest with Mom and GG. Don't get me wrong—I love GG. When Mom and I used to visit her in the nursing home, she'd always slip me 3 Musketeers bars. She'd never been a big talker even before her stroke, but I didn't mind; we'd smile at each other while Mom asked the nursing home aides a million annoying questions to make sure they were treating GG right. Her moving in with us hadn't made her any more chatty and she didn't smile much anymore. She spent a lot of time in bed watching TV or staring off into space with a gloomy expression. When she had a work Zoom, Mom sometimes made me deliver GG's meals, weird stuff like oatmeal with stewed prunes. It was always a relief to get back to the living room couch and *Zelda*. Link, my avatar, had woken up after one hundred years and was on a quest to regain his lost memories so he could free the kingdom of Hyrule from Dark Beast Ganon. He was constantly on the move, traveling around Hyrule collecting magical objects and fighting monsters, not living the same depressing pandemic day over and over.

I scarfed down the mushroom skewer, and Link's energy level shot up. I was back in business. *I'm coming, Zelda!*

I raised the Bow of Light, aimed . . .

And that's when Mom grabbed the Switch out of my hands.

I hollered and jumped to my feet. But since I'd been lying there for so long, my ankle gave out and I stumbled.

Mom sighed. "Your muscles have all atrophied."

"No, no, no! You can't do this! I'm almost done with the *entire* game!"

Her expression didn't change. Why did I think this would mean anything to her? Dad was the one who used to play video games with me at his place—but that was before he left for his big, important job in Paris.

Mom pointed to the back door. "Out."

As the feeling came back into my lower legs, I thought about trying to grab my Switch and making a run for it. But Mom looked even more ready to fight than Dark Beast Ganon.

"Just let me save my game," I pleaded.

Mom wasn't about to hand over the Switch. "Tell me what to press."

There was nothing more nerve-wracking than watching Mom poke at my tech. I was terrified she was accidentally going to erase the whole game. I made her hold up the screen to make sure she'd done it right.

"How long do I have to go out for?" I asked.

I expected she'd start with a half hour, and I could negotiate her down to fifteen minutes. But she already had it all figured out.

"I need to do a quick grocery run before Jack calls to nitpick this story." Mom was an editor at a weekly magazine run by some guy named Jack who she was always complaining about. "GG's napping, so I want you out till I come back."

"Or I could just stay inside with *Zelda* and be totally quiet?" I said.

"Nice try." Mom held up my Switch. "Oh, and I'm taking this with me."

"That's child abuse!" I said.

I was only half joking. What was I supposed to do outside all by myself? I pulled out my phone to text my best friend Josh for moral support—SOS Mom took my Switch

"And no phones outside, either," Mom said, holding out her hand to confiscate it. "I want a screen-free visit to the great outdoors."

Mom suited up in mask, face shield, and gloves, and marched me deviceless out the door. At that moment, I really hated her. But it wasn't like I could run off and live with Dad. He had taken this newspaper correspondent job in Paris, and because of stupid Covid, the borders had closed. I couldn't visit him, and if he wanted to keep the job, he had to stay there—otherwise he might not be allowed back in.

We had a decent-sized backyard with a deck jutting out from the guest bedroom/GG's room, a couple soccer nets, and a tree swing. But hello? I was thirteen, not seven. Plus, kicking around a soccer ball by myself got old fast. I wandered into the garage, hoping to find something to do. That's when I spotted the box Dad had given me before he'd moved to Paris last fall. He'd said it was stuff I'd kept at his Brooklyn apartment with some other sports equipment he couldn't take on the plane with him.

The first thing I saw was our baseball mitts. Mine was nestled inside Dad's bigger one. Just looking at them made me think about this day last fall. Dad and I were in Prospect Park, and there were tons of people there—none of them wearing masks or face shields or jumping into the bushes to get out of each other's way. Instead, everyone was having picnics and cheering for these little kids playing peewee soccer and stopping to say hello and let their dogs sniff each other. Dad and I were tossing around the ball, nice and easy, not even talking, just enjoying the *thwack* of the ball against our gloves, the sunshine, that fall smell of dried leaves. Afterward, we walked to Peppino's, this pizza place we both like, watched the

Yankees crush the Red Sox on their TV, and polished off an entire extra-large pepperoni.

Remembering that day made my chest tight and tingly. I picked up our gloves and pulled them apart. That's when I noticed what was lying beneath them: the Bow of Light.

Okay, it wasn't the actual Bow of Light, but it was a real bow, and there were some arrows scattered beneath it. The tips were blunt, but they could do more damage than your average suction-cup toy arrow, judging from the warning label on the bow in bright red print: ADULT SUPERVISION REQUIRED.

I dug through the recycling bin for some empty cans to build my own Dark Beast Ganon, or Dark Beast Canon, as I renamed him, because he was made of, well, you know . . . cans. But Mom had been hoarding beans and soup for the end of days like everyone else freaked out by Covid, so there weren't a ton. I had to use empty Ensures—nothing as scary as a monster made of old-people nutrition shakes—and even then, he wasn't exactly a fearsome size. To give Dark Beast Canon a little more height, I pulled the metal café table to the edge of the deck and arranged his can body on top. Then I crouched behind this big azalea bush in the back of the yard with the Bow of Light and pretended to be Link, cheered on by Zelda to fight.

"Go, Link; aim for the glowing points," I said in a high, Zelda-like voice.

Goofy, I know, but it was fun, especially when I leapt out from behind the bush, strung an arrow into the bow, and let it fly. Dark

Beast Canon collapsed with a loud, satisfying clatter as cans rolled across the deck.

Looking back, this was probably what roused GG. But at that moment I wasn't thinking about her at all. I wasn't thinking about anything—Dad, the pandemic, Mom taking away my Switch. I was free of all that, back to being a hero on a quest, the destiny of the kingdom in my hands. I rushed onto the deck, gathered up the cans, and remade the monster. Then I retreated behind the azalea bush and reenacted a long conversation between Zelda and Link. I got myself so fired up that when I finally jumped out from the bush, I shot off an arrow before really looking. At first, this didn't seem like a big deal—maybe I'd dock myself half a heart for bad aim. But as I followed the arrow's path, I realized it was headed past Dark Beast Canon and straight for GG, who stood in the open door.

"GG!" I shouted.

But it was too late. There was a loud *plink*, and the next thing I knew her pants were covered in brown liquid. For a heart-stopping, panicked moment, I thought I'd shot my great-grandma before I remembered blood was red, not brown. That's when I noticed the can at her feet. I hadn't hit GG but the chocolate-flavored Ensure she'd been holding.

GG looked from me to her Ensure-drenched pants and gave a funny, little laugh. This startled me almost as much as having shot at her. She hardly ever laughed.

"I'm sorry, GG. I'm so sorry!" I yelled. "Hold on, I'll get a towel."

Just then, Mom's car pulled into the driveway. The car door

slammed. Footsteps hurried toward me. I tossed the Bow of Light into the bushes. Or at least that's where I was aiming when I popped it up and it landed at Mom's feet.

It took Mom about two seconds to figure out what had happened and immediately send me to my room. I could hear her helping GG into clean clothes and stomping down to the basement to throw her pants in the wash. Then she barged in for A Talk.

"Your great-grandmother's here so we can keep her safe, not use her for target practice!" she said.

Truth be told, I was pretty shaken up by the whole incident myself, but Mom made it sound like I'd lined GG up for execution.

"I'm really sorry," I said. "But I wasn't *trying* to hit her. I didn't even know she was there!"

Mom gave me the stink eye. "Did you *look*, Matthew?"

My inner lawyer was telling me not to answer this, so I just said, "She appeared out of nowhere."

"Right," Mom said. "That great-grandmother of yours is a real ninja."

"It was an accident, okay? I apologized to her right after it happened. She was fine. She even laughed."

If Mom hadn't been so hell-bent on making me feel like the world's biggest jerk, I might have asked her why she thought GG had laughed—it was almost as if being shot at had lifted GG's spirits. But Mom barely seemed to be listening to me.

"She's a hundred years old, Matthew. You could have hit her in the eye or knocked her off-balance!"

"I said I was sorry," I muttered.

Mom didn't seem to hear this, either.

"You shouldn't even have been playing with that bow and arrow," she continued. "I've texted your father. Why he left it—"

"It's not Dad's fault."

"No," she agreed. "It's yours."

"Okay, I'm sorry. I really am. It was a stupid thing to do." I waited a beat to show her I meant it. Then I said, "Can I get my Switch back now?"

"No!"

"But I went outside! And I apologized!"

"I'm sorry, Matthew, but you need a break—a real one."

WHAT?! I was this close to finishing *Zelda*! *Stay calm*, I told myself.

"How long?"

I swear she gave this evil-genius smile. "Two weeks."

I doubled over as if an arrow had hit *me* in the gut.

"Dad would never do that!"

Mom shrugged. "His house, his rules. My house, my rules."

"But I can't even go to his house anymore!" I shouted. "He's on another continent!"

"I'm sorry you're stuck with us, Matthew," Mom said. "But your screen time has been out of control. You need to detox. And since you seem to enjoy digging through other people's boxes, I'd like you to spend some of your newfound time helping GG go through her boxes."

"You mean those boxes in her room?"

"Exactly."

Practically every morning, Mom declared that today was the day she was going to go through the boxes, which GG had kept in storage at the nursing home. But practically every evening, Mom collapsed on the couch at nine thirty, saying she was too exhausted to start.

"It would be a good activity for the two of you," she added.

I tried to imagine what was in them. False teeth. Expired coupons. Ancient underwear. Boy, was I regretting live-action *Zelda* now. I didn't want to sit in that dusty, sour-smelling room and ask GG about her stuff. I wanted to see my friends. I wanted to see my dad. I even wanted to go back to middle school (who'd ever thought I'd say *that*?). But there was nothing I could do.

My panic must have become visible, though, because her face suddenly softened. "Once you've finished helping GG go through her boxes, we can discuss getting your Switch back, okay?"

2

MILA

Kyiv, Ukraine, USSR
1932

I was stampeding down the stairs like an elephant, as Dasha liked to say, when I saw the tip of the envelope beneath the front door.

"Milachka, slow down!" shouted Dasha from the kitchen. "You'll break your neck!"

The world according to Dasha was a dangerous place. She warned me constantly—drafts, cats, splinters, irons, bathtubs. She told tragic stories: a friend who did not tuck away her braids while frying up cutlets and went up in flames; a cousin who scratched a mosquito bite until it grew infected and killed him; a man from her village who laughed so hard at his own joke that he choked to death on a pickle. She had connections to more people who had died freakish deaths than seemed possible. The real risk, I concluded, was knowing Dasha. (I told her this once, but she was not amused.)

The one danger Dasha never had to warn me about was child-birth. My mother died giving birth to me. It had happened so long ago—twelve years—that it hardly bothered me. Papa himself named me Lyudmila (Mila for short), which means "loved by the people," and I was. I had Dasha, who took care of me in a practical way, and Papa, who loved me as much as two parents. Papa was an orphan, but I still had a family—Papa Stalin, the supreme leader of the Soviet Union, who loved all children, and my fellow Young Pioneers, especially my best friend, Katya.

That fall, I'd developed a passion for parties. Everyone in Class Six had parties with both boys and girls, games of charades or lotto, a magician, or at least someone playing the accordion or piano. I was very popular at these parties; Papa would only let me go to the homes of his most loyal and very best comrades, so my presence seemed like a sign that Stalin himself approved of the festivities. But I preferred to think that Papa's position was not the only reason I was the toast of Kyiv—or at least Lypska Street. I was an excellent dancer, too.

Another invitation! This was naturally what I thought of when I saw that white edge of an envelope poking from under the door. It was a Sunday morning, the perfect time to drop it off. I was instantly full of anticipation—Who? What? When? Where? Katya had been talking about having a New Year's party in January, if her father allowed it. She liked Vanya Boyko, whom I had a crush on before I danced with him and he crushed my toes. Or was it from Nina Kravets, who was leader of our Pioneers group? It couldn't be from

Dima Demchak, because he moved away in September after his father was arrested for hiding his family's social origins (his grandfather had been a wealthy landowner!). Dima once gave me a Bumble Bear chocolate—made by the Red October factory, which makes the very best—but Papa said Comrade Demchak was a class enemy and that I should be careful whom I accepted gifts from.

I crouched down and pulled up the envelope—releasing a cold puff of December air—and held it up to find my surname, Lomachenko, scrawled on it. The sloppy handwriting alone should have been a clue that the message inside was not from anyone at School No. 6, but I was blinded to this detail by my own excitement. I tore it open then stood there, puzzled. Nothing was inside. Had the sender forgotten the invitation?

I pulled the flaps of the envelope wider. Slowly, my eyes began to focus on a gray speck inside. I poked it and it skittered onto my finger. I screamed—more out of surprise than actual fear. Dasha raced into the foyer, but Papa was faster. He took one look at the empty envelope then knocked the louse off my hand and crushed it with the heel of his boot. He snatched away the envelope just as two more lice tumbled out of it onto the floor.

"Get them!" he shouted at Dasha.

They leapt around the foyer, stomping ferociously like a pair of Cossack dancers. The sight was so comical that I couldn't help grinning as I cheered them on. At last, a shout of "Got you, traitor!" paired with the *thwack* of Papa's slipper signaled victory. I gave the troupe a hearty round of applause, but they showed no appreciation.

Papa ran to my side and grabbed my hand, studying the spot where the louse had landed.

"No mark," he said, tenderly kissing my hand. "It didn't have time to attach itself."

Then he swung around to face Dasha, his face scarlet.

"Foolish woman!" he roared. "Never let her open mail!"

Dasha winced, as if he had struck her.

"It wasn't Dasha's fault, Papa," I said. "I thought it was for me."

I smiled to show that no harm had been done, but Papa stared at me in silence.

"You are too trusting," he finally said.

"No, Papa, you are too serious. Look, you've frightened poor Dasha."

Dasha's face had gone colorless. Only her greenish-gray eyes swam back and forth like a pair of nervous fish. Papa had that effect on people—no one wanted to displease him. But he wouldn't even look at Dasha. He stared only at me.

"Do you know why those lice were sent to us?"

"A joke?"

Papa glowered at me. "This is not a time for jokes! Lice carry typhus. The enemy was trying to infect us."

My eyes darted down to my hand. Typhus was a horrible disease—Dasha had told me about an epidemic during the war that had killed half her village. First you got a horrible fever, then you started vomiting and ended up covered with spots.

"Are you sure?"

Papa nodded solemnly. "You've seen these people pouring into the city?"

"Kulaks?"

"Yes," Papa said darkly. "Them."

Since early that fall, people from the countryside had been arriving in Kyiv, claiming there was not enough to eat. Papa told me not to believe their lies. They were kulaks, wealthy peasants, who, along with priests, aristocrats, and tsarist sympathizers, were our class enemies. In the Pioneers, we'd learned all about the importance of ridding society of kulaks, who refused to give up their land to join collective farms and hid their grain so they wouldn't have to share it. Papa said they'd rather beg on the street than work together for the common good. The only reason there were food rations at all in the cities was because of the kulaks and their greed and laziness.

"The police caught a band of their children trying to shove an envelope just like this one under Comrade Gavrilok's door. Under interrogation they admitted to pulling lice off the bodies of those sick with typhus and slipping them under Party officials' doors in hopes of infecting us."

"That's evil, Papa!"

Papa's dark blue eyes softened. "Are you surprised? Just because you are a child, Milachka, doesn't mean you can't act for evil . . . or good. Think of poor Pavlik Morozov . . ."

Pavlik Morozov was a thirteen-year-old Pioneer leader who, in September, had denounced his father to the authorities for illegally helping kulaks. A few days later, Pavlik's own family had brutally murdered him. I had thought a lot about poor Pavlik since reading his story in the October issue of *Pioneer Pravda*. There was no doubt in my mind he was a hero for denouncing his father, and I agreed with the rest of my Pioneer group, which even wrote a letter to the judge that his killers should receive no mercy. But I wasn't sure I could do what Pavlik had done. I didn't tell anyone this, of course. I simply reassured myself that Papa would never commit a traitorous act.

"But you still shouldn't be so cross with Dasha," I said. "She didn't know about this kulak scheme."

Dasha bowed her head. "Forgive me, Comrade."

Papa pulled me close, wrapped his arms around me. The buttons of his *stalinka*, the same military-style tunic Papa Stalin himself wore, pressed against me. But I could tell from the position of his chin that he was looking over my head at her.

"You are forgiven, Daria Petrovna. You know my anger comes from love. Mila is my only child, my soul . . . If harm were to come to her—"

"No harm will come to her," Dasha said.

"Papa," I interrupted, pulling away. "This is all unnecessary! I'm fine. Dasha, you are forgiven. Can we have something sweet?"

I had discovered a secret stash of Bumble Bear chocolates earlier that morning in the pantry. Dasha looked searchingly at Papa, who gave a nod. His dark blue eyes crinkled, and I knew Dasha would bring them out along with steaming mugs of tea.

Papa turned to me, the smile to which I was accustomed softening the lines on his face. "What are you so sure of, little fox?"

"That I am about to get a treat, which I deserve."

Papa laughed at my cheekiness. "And I suspect you want a story, too?"

"Absolutely."

Many Sundays, Papa had to work, but, on the ones he didn't, he would light a fire in the fireplace of what in tsarist times had been a fancy parlor and tell me stories as he sipped his tea. When I was small—maybe four or five—Papa told me that he wouldn't fill my head with the kind of stories he'd heard as a child—of princesses and witches, talking animals and fairies. They were lies, he explained, and he wanted to treat me like the intelligent being I was. The world was changing in ways far more wondrous than those made-up tales. He told me about the workers who built the Volkhov hydroelectric plant, with its eighty thousand horsepower turbine, in under five years, and the polar explorers, who braved the brutal conditions of the Arctic for Soviet glory. He told me about the Pioneer, not much older than myself, who helped the Red Army defeat resistors in Tajikistan, and the fastest winch operator in the coal mines in Donbass.

Although I was way too big for it, as soon as the fire was struck, I settled on Papa's lap. Dasha brought the chocolates and tea, and Papa told me about the daring voyage of the A. *Sibiryakov*, a Soviet icebreaker that set off last summer in an attempt to make the first successful single-season crossing of the Arctic Seas. In September, the propeller shaft broke, and the ship drifted for eleven days before the crew improvised sails and coaxed the ship into the Bering Sea and on to its final destination, completing a world record. The returning sailors received many honors from Papa Stalin. Oh, it was a fine tale, and best of all—as my own papa liked to remind me—it was true.

But I couldn't help glancing down now and then at my hand. I could still feel the spot where the louse had landed, the tingle of its weight. The kulak children who had sent it were my enemies, but I still felt hurt by their hatred, as if it had been a simple misunderstanding. I pictured telling them about the A. Sibiryakov, about our glorious future. Never did it occur to me that I was the one who had misunderstood.

3

MATTHEW

Leonia, New Jersey, USA
2020

After twenty-four hours without my Switch, all I wanted to do was flop on the couch, like Link with half a heart. But the very next afternoon, as soon as I finished my school Zooms and lunch, Mom sent me to GG's room to begin my duties.

GG sat propped up in bed. She wore a turban and a purple house-dress and looked like some sort of royal person.

"Hi," I said, trying to sound more excited than I felt. "Mom wants me to help you go through your boxes."

"Not today," she said.

"But Mom wants—"

"No," GG said.

I suddenly wondered if Mom had known GG was going to put up a fight. They knew each other better than your average grandmother/granddaughter; GG had helped take care of Mom after her own mother—GG's daughter—got sick with cancer. You think she would have warned me, though. It wasn't like GG to be so resistant.

"Come on," I said. "The sooner we get through these, the sooner you'll get back to . . ." But then I couldn't think what GG had to get back to. It made me a little sad. "Uh, watching TV."

GG shot a nervous glance at the boxes as if she didn't like the idea of my rooting through her false teeth and ancient underwear any more than I did.

"Which one do you want me to start with?" I asked.

There were five of them lined up against the wall. She pointed reluctantly to a medium-sized one on the end.

As I hauled it over and scissored open the packing tape, I thought about that public television program where people show experts some old knickknack from their attic that then turns out to be worth a bazillion dollars. Mom once told me GG was born in Ukraine during the Russian Revolution. What if she had something like that, maybe some lost treasure of the tsars? (In fourth grade, we had learned that the tsars were the wealthy Russian kings and that the Bolsheviks killed the last one, along with his entire family, during the Russian Revolution.) Imagining becoming instantly rich and famous gave me a little more enthusiasm for the task.

But as I lifted the sides, my fantasies of jewel-covered eggs and golden sabers instantly vanished. Inside the box were a bunch of record albums. I knew what they were because Dad was always talking about vinyl and how it has a better sound. I flipped through GG's records, but they were all boring classical stuff—mostly piano concertos.

"We don't have a way to play these," I said.

Even if I wasn't crazy about her music, I felt sorry breaking this to her. She must have liked these records to save them.

"Maybe Mom could buy a record player?" I said. "Set it up for you here?"

"No need," she said. But I caught her glancing over at the records, just a flick of her eyes.

"I don't think they cost a lot. Mom could order one on Amazon. It's not like she has to go out or anything. I can talk to her—"

"Don't," GG said. Her voice was soft, almost whispery, but firm. "Just want quiet."

I didn't totally believe her, but what could I do? I stacked the records straighter so they would look neatened up in case Mom checked. That's when I noticed some papers and a bronze pin at the bottom of the box. Embossed on the front of the pin was a woman in a knee-length skirt, throwing a bowling ball. WOMEN'S LEAGUE HIGH SERIES was written on the top, and a date—1958. I held it up so GG could see.

"Did you bowl?" I asked.

I couldn't imagine GG even lifting a bowling ball now. But she grinned at me. "Yeah."

By this time, I'd opened the papers. They were score sheets with GG's name, Nadiya Johnson, written at the top, and her team, The

Knockouts. I'm a terrible bowler—my ball always ends up in the gutter unless I roll it from between my legs like a six-year-old—but GG had gotten strikes at least half the time.

"You're really good," I said.

"Was," she corrected.

"Did you start playing as a kid?"

GG laughed at that, and I remembered that she lived in Ukraine. I guess they didn't have bowling there.

"After the war," she said. "Tom moved us. St. Paul."

Tom was my great-grandfather. Most of what I knew about him was that he'd fought in the Second World War at the Battle of the Bulge.

"Did you win tournaments?" I asked.

"Some." But I could tell from those score sheets that she was just being humble. Who knew old GG was practically a pro bowler?

"You should give me some tips," I said. "There're these bowling birthday parties, and I'm always the biggest loser. We could even go . . ."

Then I remembered that we couldn't go anywhere and that no one was having any birthday parties, least of all inside a germy bowling alley with everyone sticking their fingers inside the same ball and sharing deliciously gooey neon cheese nachos from the food bar.

"I mean someday."

I couldn't help it—I let out this big sigh.

"Now," GG said. "Show me."

For a split second, I thought she'd forgotten what was going on out there, too, and wanted me to haul her over to the bowling alley. But then I realized she was waiting for me to show her my form right there in the room. So, I stood up and mimed throwing a ball down an imaginary lane. I felt pretty stupid, but GG didn't laugh or anything.

"Shoulders," she said. "Square 'em."

I did it again, keeping my shoulders facing the imaginary lane.

"Bend your knees," GG said.

She gave a few more suggestions, which I followed. Finally, she made an explosion sound, like I'd hit a strike. It was goofy, but I couldn't help grinning.

"My pin," GG said, waving me over.

I brought it over to her. Her hands shook as she unhooked the back. Then she wedged it into my hoodie.

"Champion!" she said.

"Thanks, GG," I said, pulling it out. "But it's yours."

"Keep it," she said, folding my fingers around it.

"Are you sure?" I asked.

She nodded, so I pinned it back onto my hoodie. "It's really cool, GG. Thanks."

Just touching it with my finger, I could imagine her rolling a strike that handed The Knockouts a tournament victory. It must have made her feel the way defeating a boss in *Zelda* felt for me. When I got my Switch back, maybe I could show her.

"Let's do one more," I said.

I went over to the boxes. Now that I knew she had mad bowling skills, I was hoping for some other interesting discovery about GG—maybe she'd also been an Olympic sprinter or something.

I grabbed one in the middle that looked particularly old, the cardboard sagging in on itself. "How about this one?"

But GG looked frozen, as if someone had cast a spell on her.

"Are you okay?" I asked.

She flickered to life. "Throw it away."

That should have been easy for me—after all, it was one less box to go through. But I was curious. She had saved whatever was in that box a long time. Why toss it now?

"I'll just take a quick look," I said. "In case there's another pin."

I sliced the tape and pulled open the sides. But what I found was the opposite of interesting. It was a pile of yellowed papers, folders, and notebooks. It looked like the kind of mess I cleaned out of my locker at the end of the year. I dug around, checking to see if there was anything beneath it. But all I found, several layers down, was a faded black-and-white photo of two girls with huge eyes standing against a fake woodland backdrop. The photo looked as if it had been taken two hundred years ago, that's how old-fashioned those girls looked, with their sharp cheekbones and frozen, unsmiling expressions. I was glad I'd found it, though. I couldn't believe GG wanted to throw it out. She had probably forgotten it was there.

I brought the photo over to GG's bed and held it up in front of her.

"Who's this?"

GG took the photo and gently touched the face of each girl. She didn't say anything, so I glanced at the back of the photo. That's when I noticed someone had scrawled: *Nadiya and Helen*.

"Hey, GG," I said. "It's you! Who's Helen?"

Her blue-gray eyes became watery. She started blinking fast, but a tear escaped and ran down her cheek. Watching her reminded me of Dad tearing up after I'd lost it and started bawling when he'd told me he'd taken the Paris job. If you ask me, a grown-up crying is way worse than a kid full-out losing it. I didn't know what to say, but I felt I had to say something.

"Are you okay?" I asked, feeling stupid because she obviously wasn't.

She swiped at her eyes, but tears were running down her face. She shoved the photo into my hand. "Put it away."

"But—"

"Do it!"

She sounded frantic, so I put it back in the box.

"Please," she said. "Go."

I just stood there. I was stunned. But I also really wanted to know what had rattled her.

"Was that photo from when you lived in Ukraine?"

GG pointed to the door. She wasn't going to tell me anything. Still, I didn't want to leave, not with her all upset like that. But just then, my *Zelda* ringtone—the theme song for the Lost Woods—chimed. The number started with +33, which meant it was Dad. It was already nighttime in France, and if I didn't take his call, he'd head off to bed and I'd miss him. So I followed GG's orders and took off.

"Hey, Dad," I said, scurrying into my bedroom.

"Mattie! What's up?"

It was a relief to hear his voice, but, at the same time, I felt like someone had a foot on my chest.

"Not much," I said.

Actually, a lot had happened, just over the past hour. That moment with GG and the photo had been really strange. But it also felt kind of personal, so it didn't seem right to run off and blab about it to someone else.

"Sources say you found my bow and arrow," Dad said.

"Sources" was how Dad referred to Mom. He thought it was pretty funny, being a reporter and all. Usually I did, too, but I didn't really want to hear another lecture, especially since GG seemed a lot more upset now than when I'd shot at her with an arrow.

"Mom took my Switch," I said. "And I have to help GG organize her stuff."

"Seems fair as far as punishments for rogue archers go."

He was trying to be funny again, but I wasn't in the mood. I climbed to the top of my bunk bed and flopped down.

"My Switch?! Seriously, Dad! I'm so bored. It sucks here."

"I'm sorry, Mattie. I know it's tough being stuck at home, not seeing friends or going to school."

Or seeing you, I thought. But I didn't want to say it. I was afraid

I'd get all choked up like GG. I suddenly wondered if Helen, whoever she was, had left GG, too.

"Work busy?" I said.

I needed to change the subject. Luckily, Dad was always eager to talk about his job.

"Relentless. I toured one of the city's busiest Covid units yesterday. It was just devastating . . ."

He rambled on about overworked doctors and patients spilling out into the hallways. Despite the horror of it, he sounded proud to be on the front lines.

"Is that safe?" I interrupted, realizing I probably sounded like Mom.

"Absolutely. I had to wear full PPE—I felt like I was in a space suit."

I tried to feel reassured.

"Listen, Mattie, I've been thinking," he continued. "We're living through real history with this pandemic. Like your grandkids are going to ask you about this someday. Have you thought about keeping a journal?"

"Not really."

Typical Dad: Everything was a news story to him. But I didn't want to be a reporter. I just wanted to forget this whole mess was even happening.

"We're still taking our Alps trip, right?" I said.

Before he'd left, Dad had bought me a ticket to Paris for July.

After seeing the city, we were going to spend two weeks hiking in the Alps.

"For sure," Dad said. "I've already blocked off the vacation. But in the meantime, do me a favor. Think a little more about that journal idea. In fact, I'm going to send you one. A nice Moleskine. It's a brand based on the notebooks that famous writers used in Paris. You can write down everything that's happening, how you're feeling."

I was feeling like Dad had forgotten that I hated writing, especially about my feelings. But I didn't tell him that.

I thought Mom would be all interested to hear how it went with GG, but at dinner that night, she didn't even ask. She'd set up trays in the TV room so we could eat there while watching the evening news. This wasn't at all like Mom—she was usually very anti–screen time at meals—but the Covid news was getting crazier, and I guess she wanted to stay on top of it. Everyone was worried about doctors getting sick and people with preexisting conditions—which, judging from the prescription drug ads that ran during the breaks, was most everyone. Bergen County, where we lived, had the highest number of cases of any county in New Jersey. "It's only a matter of time," a health official warned, "before local hospitals run out of beds."

Mom kept sighing and putting down her fork and shaking her head.

"We *cannot* get this," she said.

She glanced toward GG's room. I knew exactly what she was thinking: There was about zero chance that someone as old as GG could survive it.

"Don't worry," I said. "She's safe here."

I wasn't sure anyone was safe anywhere, especially after watching all that scary news, but Mom looked like she needed someone to reassure her.

"She didn't even want to come here," she said, with a flip of her eyes at GG's door.

"What do you mean?" I thought Mom had just told GG she was taking her in and GG had said, *Great, let's get out of here!* It wasn't like Sunset Acres was such a wonderful place—they'd thrown a nice enough party for GG back in January when she'd turned one hundred, but everyone was always shouting because half the people there were deaf, and the halls smelled like pee.

"She said if she got Covid, she got Covid. She'd lived longer than she should. She wanted to die already. She didn't want to burden me."

Mom grabbed her plate, stood up suddenly. "I told her she was crazy if she thought I was just going to leave her there to die."

She stomped off to the kitchen. She seemed angry at GG, but I had a feeling it was more complicated than that. No one likes hearing someone they love say they want to die, even if they are a hundred years old.

I helped Mom load the dishes into the dishwasher without her even having to ask. But she didn't notice. After we were done, she told me she had a headache and needed to lie down in her room. Normally I wouldn't care because it would be the perfect opportunity to play my Switch without her interrupting me. But now, hanging out in the living room all by myself felt kind of depressing.

Mom, at least, had given me back my phone so I messaged Josh—Bored what u doing—but he didn't write back. He was probably having dinner with his family—his parents weren't divorced, and he had a brother and sister, too. He complained about being stuck in the house arguing with them all day long, but the five of them also played FIFA and Monopoly together, and there was one night where the kids got to cook for the adults and make stuff like pancakes for dinner. Then I tried Adam, this other kid I'm pretty good friends with, but he didn't answer, either.

I played Roblox on my phone until the battery died. I was feeling twitchy; all I wanted was my Switch. If I defeated Dark Beast Ganon—and I was *this* close—Zelda would share the last important memory of life in Hyrule before everything went bad and Ganon took over the kingdom. Using what I learned from the past, I could restore safety and order, and return Zelda to her throne.

I'd get back to *Zelda* a whole lot faster if I threw out that box and never mentioned the photo inside to GG again. But then I touched her pin, thought of her looking at that photo and trying not to cry. I had to ask her one more time.

4

HELEN

Brooklyn, New York, USA
1932

Pop sat on one side of the kitchen table, and I sat on the other, glaring at each other like adversaries in a chess match. Except there was no board between us, just a plate of stuffed cabbage.

"Eat it," Pop said in Ukrainian.

I stared at the pale greenish-gray lump sitting in a congealed puddle of orange liquid. Even when it was hot, I hated the taste of those wilted leaves, with their sweaty odor, the mushy rice and ground meat inside them. But it was nearly 9:00 P.M.—over two hours past dinner—and the cabbage roll had grown cold.

"No."

Pop could have convinced me to end our standoff—he could have said *Mama spent all day cooking* or *Just a few bites, dear.* But that wasn't the kind of father Pop was. He slammed down his fist, making the plate clatter.

"Eat!"

"No," I said, this time in English. It was the language of freedom, and I refused to be ordered about.

Pop's face turned red, but he didn't move. No matter how angry he got, he never hit me or Peter. At least I could give him credit for that. But I knew he would sit there all night until I picked up my fork and ate.

I could hear Mom sigh from the bedroom. If it had been up to her, she would have scraped the cabbage roll off my plate and sent me to bed an hour ago. But she wouldn't intervene—she respected Pop's authority.

"You're lucky," she would say to me whenever I complained about him. "Pop has a good job. He provides for us."

I couldn't argue. Fathers all over the country were out of work or worked two or three part-time jobs to support their families, while Pop worked full-time at a printing press. In Red Hook and Gowanus, families lived in tin shacks with no drinking water, while we lived in a two-bedroom apartment in East New York with a radio on which Peter and I listened to *Tarzan of the Apes*. I was grateful for all of this (*Tarzan* especially). Too many times, on my way home from school, I'd passed furniture heaped up on the sidewalk outside an apartment where a family had just been evicted. Pop made sure we could always pay the rent, but I still didn't think that gave him the right to be a dictator.

I crossed my arms over my chest. I could be as stubborn as he was. I was his daughter, after all, his firstborn, with the same widow's peak and blue-gray eyes. But I knew Mom's sigh had been meant for me. *Give in*, it said.

No, I argued.

Mom's cuckoo clock ticked loudly into the silence, counting out the beats of our imaginary conversation.

Please, he's tired. Let him go to bed. Put your pride aside.

What about his pride? Why can't he be the one to give in?

Show him you're trying. Just one bite.

No!

But even as I resisted, tears pooled in my eyes. My bottom was already stiff and half-numb, and the thought of all those hours sitting silently across from him, trying to keep my eyelids open, exhausted me. Even if I made it through the night, Pop would still be sitting there as patiently as a mountain in the morning, the plate of stuffed cabbage waiting between us.

I grabbed my knife and stabbed the gray-green skin of the cold cabbage roll, cutting through a fibrous white vein, until I had a small piece on my fork. Then I jammed it into my mouth and chewed. It tasted gelatinous, and my stomach churned, but I forced myself to swallow. The acidic sauce burned, like anger, in my throat.

"There!" I shouted at Pop in Ukrainian, dropping my fork. "Are you happy?"

He looked sadly at me, and I thought he might come over then, give me a kiss on the head, and send me to bed. How I longed for that dark room, the heavy covers of my bed, the rhythmic sounds of Peter breathing in his sleep.

But instead he said, "Eat it all."

There is no reason to linger on the scene that followed: how the tears ran down my face, how I blindly stabbed at the cabbage roll with my fork. How I jammed it into my mouth and gnashed my teeth against the bitterness filling my mouth, my stomach, my heart. When the plate was empty, when there wasn't a scrap of that horrible cabbage roll left, I ran from the table and into my room, stifling my cries so as not to wake Peter.

Pop must have ordered Mom to leave me be, because she didn't come to smooth my hair or rub my back the way she usually did when I was upset. I huddled in a tight ball under my covers, slammed my fist into my pillow. How I hated him! Someday, I told myself, I would be all grown-up and never have to listen to him again. Already I was twelve and a half—just six more years and I could get a job and never touch another cabbage roll again, just eat 3 Musketeers and Snickers all day.

In the middle of this dark fantasy, I fell asleep and when I woke the gray light of a December morning was streaming through the window. Peter sat on the floor, his tongue hanging out in concentration as he fiddled with the wings of his balsa-wood plane. I wasn't surprised to see him there; he was seven and an early riser.

"What are you doing?" I asked in English. Ever since Peter had started school and learned English—which he'd picked up even faster than I did—we spoke it together, even at home.

"I'm going to fight the Red Baron," he said.

He looked very serious but also very small in his oversized pajamas. I had an urge to swoop down and tickle him, but I knew he'd get cranky about it.

"Be careful," I said. "He's an ace pilot. Dangerous."

He nodded in a disinterested way as if he had no time for my worries. His tough-guy act cracked me up. I was still grinning when Mom opened the door. She was wearing her blue housedress and apron.

"Good morning, children."

Mom was from Belarus and spoke Russian, which was the first language I learned and the one we spoke most commonly as a family. But Peter and I understood and could speak some Ukrainian, too, from Pop and his friends.

"Pop is leaving for work now," she continued. "Say goodbye."

Peter jumped to his feet, airplane in hand, and flew out to Pop. But I didn't move. Now I was supposed to act as if the previous evening had never happened?

My hard stare made perfectly clear that I couldn't forget it because Mom said, "Come now, Lenachka. You must put it behind you."

"No," I said in English. I suddenly wished she'd call me by my English name, Helen, instead of Yelena, my formal name, or my nickname, Lenachka. But she couldn't even pronounce it right since H sounds differently in Russian.

Mom bent down to pick up the dress I had slipped out of last night. I usually didn't leave my clothes crumpled on the floor like

Peter, who was a slobby boy, but she didn't say anything. She just shook it out and hung it over her arm.

"I've made you a special lunch for school today," she said.

I almost said, "Is it cabbage rolls?" But Mom would laugh, and if I made a joke, I'd forfeit my right to be angry.

I sat up in bed. "I don't want to say goodbye," I said, switching to Russian because I wasn't mad at her. "I don't want to talk to him at all."

Mom gave a small nod. She wouldn't force me. Unlike Pop, it wasn't her way.

"You need to start getting ready," she said.

Then she left, closing the door behind her. I could hear Peter, who my parents and their friends called by his Russian nickname, Petya, wishing Pop a good day. I imagined Mom handing Pop his lunch. "*Ya tibya lyublu,*" I heard her say in Russian. *I love you.*

I heard the apartment door close and felt a twinge in my chest. Pop was gone, and I was the one who hadn't said goodbye. It was only after the horrible thing that happened later that day that I was able to identify the feeling that had accompanied that twinge: regret.

5

MATTHEW

The next day, when I went into GG's room, I didn't start grabbing at her boxes right away. Instead, I set up our Sonos, then searched on my phone for one of the composers from her record collection. He had this crazy Russian name, and it took me forever to spell it halfway correctly, but finally his piano concertos appeared. I had no idea which one to choose, so I just selected Piano Concerto Number One and hit PLAY.

This whole time GG had been watching me out of the corner of her eye. She was slumped down in bed. She wasn't wearing her turban, and tufts of yellowish-white hair were sticking up all over the place like she'd been rolling around in bed all night.

A blast of horns filled the room followed by some violins, then a piano with loud, banging chords. It was very dramatic music, kind of angry, not the vibe I was going for. I almost hit PAUSE when I noticed GG. Her eyes were shut tight, and her hands were clasped together, like she was listening with all her might. Just then, the music started to swell and soften, and I heard a high, raspy sound. It took me a moment to realize that it was coming from GG. She was humming along with the music.

We listened to the whole concerto. It went on for a long time, too—over a half hour. I didn't love it, but I could tell GG did. I enjoyed watching her. She was really in the zone, the way I get when I play *Zelda*. She kept humming along, her eyes shut tight. It was only when the piano had finished a mad series of scales and the violins hit the last notes and it was finally over that she opened her eyes and unclenched her hands. Her eyes were all watery again. But she was looking at me this time, not away.

"Please, GG," I said gently. "Tell me about the photo."

She sniffed. The end of her nose looked kind of damp, so I brought her a tissue from this box Mom had left next to her bed. I was reaching out to give it to her when she grabbed my hand. She held it tight, as if she was afraid.

"There were . . . three . . . of us," she sputtered.

At first, I thought maybe I wasn't understanding it right. There were only two girls in the photo.

"What do you mean?" I asked.

"Three girls," she said. "Nadiya."

"Right. You."

She waved her hand impatiently, as if this wasn't a point we needed to keep going over.

"Helen."

"The other girl in the photo."

"Yeah."

I waited for her to tell me the name of the third girl, but she was staring off into space.

"Who was the third?" I finally asked.

No response.

"GG?"

But she'd shut off like a phone when the battery is drained and the whole screen goes black in the middle of a text and no amount of hitting the POWER button will turn it back on.

I wondered if I could find an answer in the box of papers and notebooks. I hadn't really bothered to look at them before. I crouched down next to it, lifted the flaps, and peered inside. Some of the papers were typed, others handwritten. Some were in English. Others were in another language with different letters that I guessed was Ukrainian or Russian, but someone had also translated them into English. I reached in to grab some of them, but just then, GG jerked back to life.

"No!" she said. "Close it!"

She was staring straight at me.

"Sorry, GG," I said. "I just wanted to know about the other girl."

"Forget it," she said. "No other girl."

Then she collapsed against her pillow and turned away. I knew she was lying, but what could I do? I closed the flaps even though I was dying to go through those papers. I asked GG if she wanted to hear more music, but she shook her head. I tried to get her to go through another box, but she wasn't interested in that, either.

Mom was in her bedroom on a work call when I gave up on GG, but she must have heard me, because she called out, "Package for you, Matthew. On the kitchen table."

I was briefly excited. Even though Mom wouldn't let me open packages myself in case they were covered in Covid germs, and I didn't wash my hands as carefully as she did, deliveries had become a pathetic highlight of my day. But then I saw what she'd left for me: a fancy-looking red notebook with an elastic strap. A note from Dad was printed up on an Amazon slip: *Write what's wrong. Love you, Dad.*

I groaned. Very punny. I grabbed a pencil off the table, opened to the first page, and scribbled, *What happened to GG?*

That's what I wanted to think about. Not everything that was wrong with my life.

Who's the third girl? I added.

I underlined this three times.

Then I wrote, *How do I get GG to tell me more?*

But there was no magic in writing down the problem. I shut the notebook, securing it with the elastic strap, and grabbed Dad's note. I was about to crumple it up when I realized who could help me answer that question.

I whipped out my phone and called Dad. He picked up on the fourth ring.

"Hey, Mattie," he said. "Can I call you in a couple hours? I'm finishing up a story."

"I just need a few minutes," I begged. "It's really important."

"Is everything okay?"

He sounded worried. Maybe he thought I'd shot off another arrow.

"It's fine. I've just got a question. How do you get someone to talk who doesn't want to? Like when you're reporting?"

"What's this for?" he asked. "Are you interviewing someone?"

"A school project," I said.

I didn't want to tell him about GG.

"Great question," he said. I could almost see him sitting up taller in his chair, rubbing his hands together like he'd been waiting his whole life for me to ask.

"What I try to remember is that most people really want to tell their stories, even the hard ones. But they're also afraid of being judged or misunderstood. So I try to establish trust, show them I'm going to listen and be fair."

I yanked open the elastic strap, flung open the cover, and scribbled down notes.

Establish trust

Listen

Show ur fair

"How do you do all that?" I asked.

"Sometimes I don't ask them the question I want to know most—at least right away. I let them talk about whatever they want to first, give them space to get comfortable with me. I also try to establish a personal connection. Not so much that I'm trying to be their friend—I have to keep a professional distance because I don't want anyone to feel that they were tricked into talking to me. But I want them to know I'm a real person, with feelings and a heart, who they can entrust their story to."

"So you tell them about yourself?"

"Just a few things. Sometimes I tell them about you. How I have this great son. How I really miss him."

"Stop it," I said. That funny feeling was starting in my chest again.

Dad laughed. "Okay, Mattie, hope that helped."

"It did," I said. "Thanks."

"Hey, gotta run, but before I go, did you get the Moleskine?"

"Yeah," I said. "I haven't written in it yet, though."

I wasn't sure why I lied. Maybe because beneath the lines about GG and listening and trust, I'd scribbled another I couldn't actually say: *Miss you too.*

6
HELEN

Brooklyn, New York, USA
1932

I had just unwrapped the white paper around my lunch when Irene Fitzgerald pointed an accusatory finger at it. "*What* are you eating?"

"A caviar sandwich," I said.

"What's that?"

My favorite lunch was what it was. Just as Mom had promised. She had spread a thick layer of butter onto two slices of rye bread and topped it with a glistening layer of red caviar.

"Bread and . . ." How to explain caviar? "Fish eggs."

Irene wrinkled her freckled nose. "You eat fish eggs? Yuck!"

I wanted to tell Irene she was a real rube. Black caviar was a delicacy and one of the most expensive foods in the world. And even red caviar, which was bigger and much cheaper, tasted salty and sweet, like a summer's day at Coney Island. I glanced at Ruth Spitz, whose parents had a grocery store on Pitkin Avenue and who knew the most about the world outside Brooklyn. But she was Jewish, and I wasn't sure Jews ate caviar, besides which she didn't exactly jump in to defend me. She turned away to talk to her friend Esther, the two of them probably hoping that Irene wouldn't zero in on their lunches next.

"Do they have little fish babies inside?" Irene asked.

"No," I mumbled. "They haven't been made into fish yet."

"Let me see you eat one of them," Irene said.

I shrugged and scooped a single egg onto my finger.

Irene leaned in as if I were one of the freaks from the Coney Island boardwalk. Her friends Margaret and Rita and some of the other girls were watching me as well. I felt my cheeks burn.

"I'm actually not hungry right now," I said, lowering my finger.

"Well, I don't blame you," Irene said. "It's slimy."

I wrapped up my sandwich even though my stomach was rumbling with hunger and my mouth was brimming with saliva. Irene slid her bowl toward me.

"Want some of my soup?"

I stared down at the thick green sludge dotted with a few skin-colored cubes. Unlike Pop, Irene's dad didn't have a regular job, and she had six brothers and sisters, so she ate the cheap school lunch. Today, split pea soup was on the menu.

"No thanks," I said. "I'm just not hungry."

I thought about sneaking away to the bathroom and eating my

sandwich there. But before I could decide whether I really wanted to take the risk of someone finding me, the bell rang. I walked to the garbage and threw my sandwich into it.

Pop's voice roared in my head. *Yelena! How dare you throw away a good lunch?*

My name's Helen! I shouted back. *And no one else eats this stuff!*

Still, my heart lurched at that white paper lump lying next to dirty napkins and apple cores. What had I done? The country was full of hungry people; even here at school there were kids who would stoop to eat fish eggs. Worse, I pictured Mom smiling as she'd spooned the caviar onto the buttered bread and smeared it around, imagining how much I would enjoy it. I almost reached in and grabbed it back. But then I spotted Irene and Rita heading my way, and I left my special lunch, uneaten, in the trash. I couldn't enjoy it, not if I wanted to fit in with everyone else. Didn't my parents get that? Hot tears filled my eyes. Of course they didn't, and they never would. I was alone out here, trying to figure out how to be an American all by myself.

How I managed not to cry I'll never know, but I hardly heard Mrs. Weber droning through the countries of Asia—Manchuria, Siam, French Indochina, Republic of China. There were thirty-six kids in the class, and because I hardly ever spoke, but also never got in trouble, Mrs. Weber had assigned me to the last row. Still, I always followed what Mrs. Weber was saying, even if I was too afraid to raise my hand in case I said something foolish.

Which is why I was so embarrassed when I realized she'd been calling my name.

"Helen, are you awake?" she snapped.

"Yes, Mrs. Weber."

"I have a note that you must go to the principal's office at once."

I had never been called to the principal's office. My breath quickened. A ridiculous thought filled my head. They must have found my sandwich in the garbage. No one was supposed to waste food. They would know at once it was me. Who else ate fish eggs?

"It says to bring your things," Mrs. Weber added.

Were they suspending me? I sprang to my feet, accidentally knocking my geography book to the floor. A few of the boys in my row tittered. I snatched it up and shoved it into my satchel with my other textbooks. Then I scurried out of the classroom into the cool emptiness of the hall. My face burned. What if Pop was there, telling Mr. Smith, the principal, about the stuffed cabbage, Mom crying about the caviar sandwich beside him?

I thought about running right out the door and never coming back. But where would I go? I had to face whatever punishment awaited me. My only consolation was that I could warn Peter so he wouldn't make the same mistake. *Don't let Mom give you a caviar sandwich. The other kids will just laugh, and you'll get embarrassed and throw it away.* At least I could help him fit in and not make a fool of himself.

I hesitated in front of Mr. Smith's door then gathered my courage and pushed it open—

It was just as I feared. Mom was in the waiting area, slumped in a chair, her face ashen. I ran up to her and fell onto my knees.

"I'm sorry, Mama," I said in Russian. "I shouldn't have—"

But she just looked at me blankly.

"Lenachka," she said in a quivering voice. "Pop had a heart attack."

7

MATTHEW

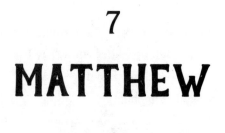

Leonia, New Jersey, USA
2020

The next morning, when I came to GG's room, she was watching the news. I really wanted to turn it off—it was bad enough to sit through all those reports about dying people and funeral homes overwhelmed with bodies every night with Mom—but instead I pulled up a chair and sat there, half watching the TV and half watching GG. Unlike Mom, she didn't sigh every two seconds or secretly blow her nose into her napkin after some particularly sad story. She just looked on, as if there was nothing surprising about the world coming to an end.

"We don't have to do boxes today," I said when the news finally switched to a commercial. "I'm not in the mood anyway."

I don't think GG expected this because she stopped acting like I wasn't there and looked me over. "You okay?"

"Yeah," I said automatically. But then I realized that this was my chance to show her—as Dad had put it—that I was a person with a heart. "No."

GG turned off the TV. I'd felt better talking with the ads running in the background. It seemed too quiet now. She didn't ask me what was wrong, but it was clear from the way she was staring at me that she was waiting for me to say more.

"I miss my friends," I said. "Getting out of this house. Even school."

"Your dad," she added.

It didn't exactly take Sherlock Holmes to figure this out, but I was still surprised. It was a relief not to have to say it myself, just to nod.

"Miss mine, too," she said.

"He must have died a long time ago," I said and then immediately felt stupid because it wasn't like anyone ever stops missing their parents. But GG didn't take offense.

"Long time," she agreed.

"How old were you?" I asked.

GG hesitated. "Younger than you. Not much, though."

I pictured Dad in a French Covid ward, hooked up to a ventilator. My eyes got all watery, but I didn't want to end the conversation when she was finally talking, so I pretended I had something in my eye.

"What happened to him?" I asked.

But GG didn't answer. I wondered if he'd died in some horrible plague, and she didn't want to frighten me. "Your age in that photo," she said.

It took me a moment to understand. "You were my age in the photo?"

"Yes."

"Neat," I said, but I felt even more excited that she'd brought up the photo herself. "Can I see it again?"

I expected her to say no, but she pointed to the old box. "Bring it."

I was still afraid she might change her mind, so I nearly fell over myself racing to that box and pulling out the photo. Looking at it again, I was struck by the sadness in young GG's eyes.

"Had your father already died when the photo was taken?" I asked.

She nodded.

The other girl, Helen, had her hand clasped protectively around GG's.

"Who was she?" I asked.

GG shifted herself to the far side of the bed. She was pretty tiny—I was taller than she was—so she made a lot of space. I thought maybe she wanted me to sit down next to her, but she pointed to the box.

"Take it all out," she said.

I felt a surge of excitement. GG was finally going to tell me more. I dragged over the box then scooped up all the notebooks and papers and placed them next to her. GG slowly arranged them into piles. When she was done, she named them.

"Diaries," she said, pointing to the notebooks.

"Letters," she said, pointing to a pile of envelopes.

"Histories," she said, patting a thick folder.

"Articles," she said, jabbing at another folder.

"Official," she said, slapping a pile of printed documents.

"Okay, got it," I said.

I reached for one of the notebooks, but GG blocked me, faster than I thought she could. Up went a crooked finger, stopping me.

"My way."

She wanted to show me what to read and in what order. That seemed fair enough. She circled her hand over everything.

"My story. Helen's story."

But something still didn't make sense.

"What about the third girl?"

She winced. "Wait," she said.

I couldn't rush her—that was part of the rules, too. I wondered if there were any others.

"Does Mom know this story?" I asked.

She shook her head, put her finger to her lips.

"It's a secret?"

GG nodded. Her voice dropped to a whisper. "A terrible secret. Changed my life."

Even though her room was like a sauna, I shivered. It was obvious that whatever had happened to that third girl was so horrible that it still upset GG nearly a century later.

"I can keep a secret," I said. "I promise. It's not like I see anyone anyway."

I hadn't meant to sound sorry for myself. It was GG I should be sorry for, keeping some terrible, life-changing secret all to herself. But GG reached out and stroked my hand.

"Alone," she said.

I felt a lump in my throat, tried to swallow it down. "Yeah."

GG didn't make me talk about it, though. She just sighed. "The third was Mila."

8

MILA

On the Thursday after Papa saved me from the typhus-infested lice, I had my weekly piano lesson with Anna Mikhailovna. As usual, Dasha met me at school and walked me to the music studio, which was the front room of Anna Mikhailovna's third-floor apartment. Usually I marched ahead of Dasha in protest—I was much too old to be escorted to my lesson like some little kid!—but I still felt badly that Papa had given her such a scolding and matched my pace to hers. It was snowing and the gray sky seemed close overhead as we cut through Mariinsky Park. The trees were exceptionally beautiful. The fresh snow bent every branch, like a ballet mistress adjusting the arms of her troupe into ever more artful poses. I couldn't help myself—I began to dance, leaping into the air, falling back into the snow.

Dasha shot me a glance. "Your scarf has unraveled. Your neck is cold."

I almost told Dasha that it was amazing that she could feel my own neck—I hadn't been aware we were sharing it—but then I remembered my intention to be kind, so I cut short my performance and readjusted my scarf.

"Don't worry, Dasha," I said soothingly. "I won't catch cold. Has there been snow in Obukhiv?"

Obukhiv was the town closest to Dasha's village. She hadn't lived there for years, but she still regularly corresponded with her nieces who did.

"Of course there's been snow," she snapped. "It's winter."

Seeing the mood she was in, I gave up my attempt at conversation. We emerged from the park onto Revolution Street in silence magnified by the falling snow. The breadlines were not as long as usual, but I still felt sorry for those who had to wait on them for their allotted loaf of black bread; Dasha did our shopping at the special distribution center for Party officials. There were fewer rations there, but Papa was still angry that the workers had to suffer. The rations, he explained, were the fault of kulaks, who sabotaged the harvest, and lazy peasants who refused to work for the common good.

Ten minutes later, I knocked on Anna Mikhailovna's door, breathless from the three flights of stairs and sweating beneath my woolen winter layers. I had studied piano with Anna Mikhailovna since I was seven years old—she was my favorite teacher, and I was her favorite student—she never told me that, of course, but a teacher's pet knows! She noticed before anyone else if I was feeling unwell or heavy-hearted—not that I often was—and would quietly alter the lesson to cheer me up. But she was strict and couldn't be easily pushed around or sweet-talked, like Dasha. She had no family other than her mother, Olga Stepanovna, who also lived at the studio. But I liked to think that Anna Mikhailovna thought of me as the kind of child who was clever and worthy enough to be her own.

Standing outside her door, I recognized the familiar melody of a piece I, too, had once played: "Hiking March" from Kabalevsky's "Pioneer Life."

"Come in, Mila!" Anna Mikhailovna shouted over what I felt was a rather plodding performance of it.

I let myself in, leaving the door open for Dasha, who was climbing up behind me at a slower pace. A blond boy of eight or nine shared the bench with Anna Mikhailovna, who sat perfectly straight, her gray-flecked brown hair pulled into a tight bun.

"A march, Volodya, must be played with energy!" she said, giving four brisk claps. "With determination!"

Volodya mercifully thumped the last few notes, then gathered up his books while I peeled off my layers. His mother, who had been sitting in the armchair Anna Mikhailovna positioned across the room for parents and minders, nodded at me.

"Listen to Mila play it," Anna Mikhailovna said and waved me over to the bench.

I plunked myself down and played a rousing version of the

march, which was greeted by applause from Anna Mikhailovna, Volodya's mother, and Volodya after his mother gave him a sharp elbow.

"Just think of May Day," I told Volodya, knowing he marched in the holiday parade with his school just as I did. "That's the rhythm."

Volodya nodded, looking more tired than inspired. His mother stood up, and the two of them bundled into their coats.

By this time, Dasha had joined us, collapsing into the armchair. As usual, Anna Mikhailovna darted into the back room she shared with Olga Stepanovna, who emerged a few minutes later with a cup of tea for Dasha. This was largely ceremonial since Dasha usually only took a few sips before setting it down on the little round side table and falling asleep. She was supposed to watch to make sure that I had practiced sufficiently, and that Anna Mikhailovna was not filling my head with too much "intelligentsia nonsense" from her own pre-Revolutionary days at the conservatory. But we had an unspoken pact: I never told on Dasha, and she gave satisfactory reports about me and Anna Mikhailovna.

After we ran through the practice pieces for that week, Anna Mikhailovna glanced over at Dasha, whose head was tipped back and was gently snoring, then pulled a new piece from her leather file of sheet music.

"It's time you played some Tchaikovsky, Mila," she said. "He composed an entire collection of pieces for young people called *Children's Album*. This one is called 'Baba Yaga.' Surely you must know who she is?"

I did, thanks to Dasha, who had told me about her before Papa had ordered her to stop telling me fairy tales.

"She's a witch who lives in the forest in a house with chicken legs."

Anna Mikhailovna nodded. "That's right. Why don't you try it?"

I played "Baba Yaga" two or three times, working out the challenging technical aspects. It was in a minor key, had lots of eighth notes, and demanded a fast beat, which I was determined to keep up with better than Volodya. I thought I was doing a pretty fine job of it—even hitting all those staccato sharp notes—but when I had finished, Anna Mikhailovna looked dissatisfied.

"Mila, what do you think is happening in this piece?"

I wrinkled my brow to show her I was thinking hard. (Teachers always liked that.) "Baba Yaga is out in the forest, maybe whizzing around in her mortar and pestle. Some children are running away beneath her."

Anna Mikhailovna leaned closer, her voice hushed so as not to wake up Dasha. "Yes, yes! The children are running hard, fast, trying to get away. They are frightened. Terrified."

Anna Mikhailovna's fingers leapt to the keyboard, racing up and down it like a pair of giant spiders. Then she abruptly stopped.

"But when you play, it sounds like a happy May Day march through the woods."

She plonked a few notes, grinning idiotically.

I laughed at her demonstration, but the foolish look on her face made me uncomfortable. Was Anna Mikhailovna suggesting that

May Day—the holiday when we celebrated our great Soviet State and workers—was idiotic? That couldn't be what she meant. Even so, I was glad Dasha appeared fast asleep so she wouldn't report any of this to Papa.

"You just mean I must play it more darkly?" I asked.

"Yes." But she sounded hesitant as if she still wasn't sure I understood. "Mila, tell me. Have you ever been afraid?"

The truth was that I rarely had been. I always felt safe thanks to my own papa and Papa Stalin. But then I felt the ghost of a prickle on my hand, and before I could stop myself, the story of the lice in the envelope came spilling out.

"It was the first time I was really frightened, after Papa told me. But just for a minute."

Anna Mikhailovna didn't say anything, she just stared, as if she had never imagined a person like me. Finally, she sighed.

"If that is the first time you've been truly afraid, you've been very lucky—or very foolish."

Foolish? What did she mean by that?

Just then, Dasha stirred, and we both froze. I didn't want Dasha to hear me talking about the lice, which I knew was still a tender subject. Anna Mikhailovna looked even less eager to have Dasha overhear us. A fluttering snore from Dasha's upturned nose reassured me, however, that she was still asleep. Nevertheless, I decided to remind Anna Mikhailovna of what we both truly believed.

"All children in the Soviet Union are lucky," I said. "Papa Stalin protects us, unlike children in capitalist countries, who are forced to work and cannot play or go to school."

Anna Mikhailovna smiled, but her gaze had shifted back to the sheet music. "Of course."

"I'll try it again and think about the lice," I said.

I played the piece two more times, trying to transpose my fear onto the image of those children running from the witch through the dark forest, their little hearts pounding, branches scratching their cheeks. I tried to let the terror flow into my fingers and onto the keys until I was breathless. But toward the end of my second rendition, Anna Mikhailovna rested her fingers on top of mine. "Perhaps we should stick with more cheerful pieces."

"Wasn't that better?"

But something had come over Anna Mikhailovna. She took back the sheet music, returned it to her leather file. Then she faced me, her voice both stern and gentle at once.

"Someday you will be ready to play that piece. When you are, come to me and I'll help you."

Little did I know, just a few months later, I would take her up on this promise.

9

HELEN

Brooklyn, New York, USA
1932

I lay in bed with the lights off, hoping Mom would think I was asleep. But it was only seven fifteen. "*Buck Rogers* brought to you by Kellogg's!" the radio blared through the bedroom door. Mom had done a good job of not frightening Peter; he was happy to eat the Mary Janes my godmother, Mary, had brought him (her favorite candy because it shared her American name) and listen to an extra show. He didn't understand how serious the situation was. But I did. The doctors weren't sure Pop was going to make it through the night. They'd sent Mom home and promised to call Dr. Polonsky, who lived a few blocks away and had a phone, with any news. All afternoon, friends and neighbors had come by with pots of soup, but the delicious scents that filled the air seemed all wrong. Only Peter had an appetite.

HELEN

I squeezed the cross in my hand until it dug into my palm. *Please, God,* I prayed, *let Pop be all right. I'll never argue with him again. I'll eat everything anyone gives me. I'll wear this cross and never take it off as long as I live.*

Pop had given me the cross for my tenth birthday, but I hadn't worn it except on a few special occasions, like Easter. I'd told him that I was afraid of losing it, and he and Mom seemed to understand—it was solid gold, after all, and Pop had saved up to buy it. But the truth was I hadn't wanted to wear it because it was different from the crosses most kids at school wore—it had two extra crossbeams. I didn't want to explain that it was an Orthodox cross. At school every year, we had to fill out a form with our religion; the choices were Protestant, Catholic, and Jewish. I never knew which one to check. There was no box for Eastern Orthodox. Most Americans had no idea it was its own separate branch of Christianity. It was hard enough that we followed a different calendar and celebrated Christmas on January 7 instead of December 25 like everyone else.

But now I clung to all three of those crossbeams and prayed. I was praying so hard that I didn't even notice that *Buck Rogers* had ended until the bedroom door opened and Peter scurried in. I closed my eyes tight and slowed my breathing, pretending to be asleep.

"Change into your nightclothes," Mom whispered to him in Russian.

"When will Pop be back?" Peter asked, banging open his drawer.

"Shhh!" Mom said. "Soon."

"Will Pop feel better tomorrow?" Peter asked.

"I hope so, darling."

I could hear the rustling sounds of Peter wrestling with his clothes. Then a creak as he climbed into his bed and another deeper one signaling that Mom had perched beside him.

"I miss him," Peter said.

Mom sniffed. She was trying not to cry. "And he misses you."

There was the soft smack of her giving him a kiss.

"I know," Peter said sleepily.

He was a good child. He deserved to be loved. Not like me. Before I could stifle it, a sob escaped my throat.

"Helen," Peter said in English. "Are you okay?"

"She's fine," Mom said, saving me from having to answer. "Lenachka, go to the kitchen. I'll make you some warm milk."

Still clutching my cross, I slipped out of bed, turning away so Peter wouldn't see my tearstained face. A few minutes later, Mom joined me in the kitchen. She didn't say anything, just poured milk into a pot and lit the stove. She wasn't heavy but broad in the hips and shoulders, and it comforted me how she took up so much space.

"Here, Lenachka," she said a moment later, placing a steaming mug of milk in front of me. "Drink, darling."

But her tender words just made me feel worse. Tears streamed down my cheeks.

Mom handed me her handkerchief, which she'd embroidered herself with pink roses.

"He's a strong man, Lenachka. God is watching over him . . ."

I bit my lip and closed my eyes tight, trying to stop the flood of tears.

"I didn't—" My voice cracked. "Say goodbye."

Mom patted my closed fist, the one still holding the cross. "How could you know? How could anyone—"

"No . . ." I said, whimpering. "This morning when he left. He's going to die, and I didn't say goodbye!"

I collapsed onto the table, nearly knocking my head on the mug of milk. I squeezed my eyes, wanting to disappear into the darkness behind them. But Mom was behind me, her arms around me, her voice gentle in my ear.

"Lenachka. He knows you love him."

I jerked upright.

"No, he doesn't!"

I was weeping loudly now.

"Shhh," Mom said. "You'll wake up Petya."

I clapped my hand over my mouth. Everything I did seemed to hurt someone.

She pulled her chair next to mine, stroked my hair.

"You're being too hard on yourself."

I took a breath, dabbed my eyes with her damp handkerchief.

"He just wanted me to eat my stuffed cabbage. And I didn't want to. I made him sit there. He was tired—"

My face burned, but I felt compelled to confess all if it.

"Then at school, I threw out my caviar sandwich because this girl Irene made fun of it. She said it was disgusting. So I threw it out." I gulped down a sob. "And then you came and said Pop had a heart . . . I killed him!"

My shoulders heaved as I tried to stifle a new round of weeping.

A smile played on Mom's lips. "By throwing away a caviar sandwich? It's a terrible waste, yes, but in all my years, I've never heard of anyone dying because their beloved daughter wouldn't eat or threw away a sandwich."

The way Mom put this, it did sound ridiculous, but I wouldn't let myself off so easily.

"I made him angry, and that anger made his heart—"

"You made him sad," Mom corrected. "But he was already sad. Do you know why Pop focuses so much on food?"

"Because of the Depression. Not everyone has it."

"Not just that," Mom said. "Pop got a letter recently from his brother's family in Ukraine. They said they were starving, that they had nothing to eat."

I was so surprised that I stopped crying.

"I thought Pop's brother died a few years ago."

"He did. But his wife and children are still alive and living in the village. They begged your father to send money so they could buy food. He did, but he isn't sure they received it. He wrote to find out, but there are censors, and he doesn't know if the letter made it through."

I pictured Pop sitting across from me at the table. He'd been staring at me, but what if he'd been seeing his brother's family—my aunt and cousins? How selfish I must have looked to him, refusing to eat Mom's cabbage roll, when his own family was starving.

"Why didn't he tell me about this?"

Mom shrugged. "He wanted to protect you. You're still a child."

I was about to protest—I was almost thirteen!—but my behavior the previous evening now seemed terribly childish. I already felt years older than I had that very morning. "Can't we help them?"

Mom sighed heavily. "How much can we do from so far away? Pop already tried. And now . . . we have troubles of our own."

"I feel a hundred times worse!"

Mom put her hand back over mine and looked me straight in the eye.

"You and your brother are what keep Pop from despair. Never forget that. Giving you food and safety, a future here in America, has been the great joy of his life."

I nodded, too overcome to say anything more.

Mom wiped at her eyes, handed me my mug.

"Drink your milk, Lenachka. Then pray for Pop and go to sleep. His fate is in God's hands."

I drank the warm milk and gave Mom a kiss on the cheek. She hugged me tight. "Good night, Lenachka."

I padded back to my bedroom, exhausted, but still, I couldn't sleep. I imagined Pop had felt the same way, up late, thinking about his relatives starving in Ukraine, hoping he could help them with what little extra money he could send. He'd probably felt as powerless to save them as I felt now to save him. I wondered if it had been just as hard for him to swallow down Mom's stuffed cabbage—not because he wasn't hungry or didn't love it, but because every bite filled him with guilt.

I couldn't help Pop, but perhaps there was a way for me to take his burden and try to help his family. Pop kept his correspondence next to his accounting ledger and bills in the desk drawer of the secretary. For the first time in my life, I was grateful for the Russian lessons my parents made me take twice a week. I could read the Cyrillic letters, find my aunt's address. I couldn't send her money, though. I hardly had any—just an emergency nickel for the bus and eight cents I'd been saving for candy. I would have to send her something else.

It would have to be something valuable that she could trade to buy food.

I instantly knew what I would send! I was clutching it in my hand. Pop's cross. But if I just put it inside an envelope with a letter, chances were the Soviet censors would find it and take it. The Soviet government was against religion. I had to hide it, but how?

I twisted the bottom of my nightgown, thinking hard, until my fingers answered for me. Mom had made the nightgown for a taller girl, meaning to let down the hem when I grew. I could open up the hem, hide the cross inside, then sew it back up. I'd send the nightgown as a gift. "Check the hem for size," I'd write my aunt. There was nothing suspicious about that. I decided not to tell Mom—she had enough to worry about, and I was afraid she wouldn't approve. I'd have to make up some excuse when she noticed my nightgown was missing, but she wasn't going to be in a noticing mood for a while anyway.

It was a relief to feel there was something I could do to help Pop.

10
MATTHEW

Leonia, New Jersey, USA
2020

GG closed the folder marked PERSONAL HISTORY, so I had to stop reading.

"Helen's cousins—the ones starving in Ukraine—were you one of them?" I asked.

It made perfect sense. GG had lost her father, just like Helen's cousins had.

GG let out a deep sigh. But before she could say more, there was a knock on the door, and Mom rushed into the room.

"I've got an hour before my next meeting—Jack wants a Covid issue, and we're crashing it—so I've got to give GG her shower now."

I would have tried to hold her off for a few minutes so I could get GG to confirm my theory, but GG's eyes were frantically darting between the pile of papers and me, telegraphing a message I imme-diately understood: *Put them away before Mom sees.*

I scooped up the piles and shoved them back in the box even though Mom wasn't the least bit interested. She was already rush-ing around, gathering towels, laying out a change of clothes for GG after the shower.

"Matthew," she said. "It's a beautiful day. Go outside."

Not again! Hadn't we both learned our lesson about the dangers of the great outdoors?

"But there's nothing to do out there," I said, following her into GG's bathroom.

"Find something," she said, adjusting a metal chair with a gray plastic seat. "Just stay out of the garage."

I guess that was *her* lesson learned.

"What's that for?" I asked, pointing to the metal chair.

"When you're GG's age, you can't exactly stand in the shower."

I hadn't really thought about that before, probably because I'd always stayed out of GG's bathroom.

"I should really be getting her outside, too," Mom muttered as she fiddled with the seat. "There's just no time."

"Maybe I could take her?" I asked.

"That's kind of you, Matthew, but probably not the best idea." Then she turned and shouted out the door. "GG, I'm coming to get you undressed!"

That was my cue to leave. I parked myself on the front stoop, where I figured I could sit in the sun and watch some actual live humans. But it wasn't the most uplifting experience. People out walking with strollers or dogs veered into the middle of the road to avoid getting too close to one another. Almost everyone in a car was delivering groceries or Amazon packages. The only normal sight was my ten-year-old neighbor, Jake, who was riding his bike and asked me if I could join him. But I wasn't sure how Mom would feel about that—what if he got too close and breathed on me and GG got sick?—so I told him I had to do homework.

I figured I could ask GG the cousin question again, but when I went back inside, she was taking a nap, and when she finally woke up, it was time for her lunch and she told me she was too tired to talk.

This got me thinking: When Dad was reporting a story, he always talked to a bunch of people, never just one. If I couldn't talk with GG, maybe it was a good time to find another source. I couldn't interview Helen or this Mila person, but as far as other sources went, I had a pretty good one: Mom knew GG better than anyone else alive. I wouldn't let on about GG's secret, but I could still ask Mom some questions.

But Mom was in meetings all afternoon, and when she finally emerged from her room, she was in a big rush, making GG's dinner, microwaving last night's lasagna for us, then shoveling it down before taking another call from work. It wasn't until that evening, when she came to my room to nag me about the mess and say good night—one of the only parts of my life that the virus hadn't changed—that we had the chance to talk.

"Hey, Mom, did GG ever mention someone named Mila?"

"Do you really have to leave your dirty underwear on top of your retainer?" she said.

"*That's* where it was!" I reached down from my bunk bed, ready to jam my retainer into my mouth, but Mom refused to hand it over.

"At least give it a rinse first."

"You didn't answer my question—"

"What? Oh, Mila. No, that doesn't ring a bell."

"How about a Lyudmila? Someone back in Ukraine?"

Mom shook her head. "GG never liked to talk about her past there. I think it was too painful for her."

"Why? What happened?"

"I don't know."

"Did you ever ask?"

"A few times. But she never wanted to talk about it, so I didn't push. There was enough painful stuff going on . . ."

"You mean with your mom?" I asked.

Mom bent down to pick up a crumpled piece of graph paper, which I identified as my Pre-Algebra homework. I couldn't see her face. "Yeah," she said. "Go wash your retainer."

I took my retainer to the bathroom, splashed a little water on it, then shoved it into my mouth. When I got back, Mom was tossing my dirty socks into the laundry bin.

"How about a cousin named Helen?" I asked.

"Not that I remember."

This surprised me. Perhaps my cousin theory was wrong? Wouldn't GG have told Mom about her own cousin?

"She would have been from Brooklyn," I said.

Mom just shrugged. "I don't know. GG left Brooklyn after she married Grandpa Tom. I don't think she really kept up with people there—just a few Christmas cards and letters. Why? Did you find something from these people?"

"Just a couple of old cards," I lied.

"How are your organizing sessions going?" she asked. But I could tell from the tone of her voice that she was still distracted—either by work or Covid or my mess.

"Good," I said.

Good was my go-to response to *How was school?*—the most annoying question in the history of the world. It hit me, though, that she didn't ask that anymore. I never thought I'd miss it. But I also never thought I'd be home from school for weeks on end without being able to see my friends or my dad. Normally, on a Thursday night like this one, I'd be looking forward to pizza, which was always the Friday school lunch, then hanging out after school in Josh's basement playing Mario Kart, then going to Brooklyn Saturday morning with Dad, maybe stopping at a diner for greasy home fries and eggs on the way.

Mom gave me a kiss, turned off the light. As soon as she left, I grabbed my phone and watched some YouTube videos of the hiking trails in the Alps that Dad was taking me on that summer. They had these fantastic views—one even went by a glacier—and cows from the mountain pastures wandered right onto the trails. At night, Dad had explained that we'd be staying in these hiker huts, which were fancier than they sounded since they served dinner and dessert. I fell asleep imagining Dad in the bunk below, the world back to normal, as he wished me good night.

11

MILA

Kyiv, Ukraine, USSR
1933

Why did I answer the door that March morning?

Katya Gavrilok was supposed to come over. Katya and I had our own club called "Committee of the Motherless Daughters of the Communist Party." She was the General Secretary, because her mom had died more recently, and I was the First Party Secretary, and sometimes we'd line up the statuettes of activists I'd collected from the Lomonosov Porcelain Factory and make them our committee members. Then we'd take minutes and vote on resolutions like "May 15 is the National Holiday of Motherless Daughters" or "Motherless Daughters Should Get Extra Cake." Or we'd work on our letter offering honorary membership to Svetlana Stalina, Papa Stalin's seven-year-old daughter, whose own mother had died in

November. Then Katya would talk about her mom, how she missed the smell of her and wished her father hadn't given away all her clothes after she'd died.

I thought it was Katya at the door. That was my defense. I had no idea she was running late.

Dasha was cooking—on Sundays she made *varenyky*, and already the house smelled deliciously of frying onions. Sometimes she would let me mix the onions with the cooked potato and pinch the little crescent pockets of dough around the mixture. But she never allowed me to drop them into the pot of boiling water or scoop them out when they floated to the top. "Too dangerous!" she would say, handing me the ladled spoon for the cold, safe sour cream. (Never mind that I had helped cook and serve hot meals at Artek, the Pioneer camp I'd attended last summer.)

"It's Katya!" I shouted, and because Dasha had no reason to think otherwise and because the onions were likely just short of golden and might burn if she left them, she let me race down the stairs and throw open the door.

"Hi Ka—" I started to say.

But the name fell away, and I stared in horror at the child standing in her place. Pale eyes peered out of sunken sockets, and a skeletal hand reached out to me.

"Lomachenko?" the creature croaked.

I instinctively drew back even as I recognized the creature was a girl. She was smaller than I, and disturbingly out of proportion—

round in the middle but with sticklike limbs and a large head. An unhealthy whitish down covered her sunken cheeks. Her tights pooled around her spindly legs, and her feet were bundled in rags.

"What do you want?" I said.

"I am Lomachenko!" she said.

This made absolutely no sense. I was Lomachenko. And yet there was something familiar about her, which made her gibberish even more disturbing. She was clearly one of the kulak children. Perhaps they had realized their plan to infect Papa and me with typhus had failed, so they had sent this girl to spread the pestilence in person.

She smiled at me, a sickly grin, and took a step toward me. I came to my wits just in time and slammed the door in her face.

Dasha ran into the foyer, wiping her hands on her apron. "Mila, what's going on?"

I just stood there and pointed to the door.

Dasha ran around me and opened it. I couldn't help looking for the girl, but she wasn't there. I felt a rush of relief. Perhaps I had just dreamed her. Then I heard sniffling and looked down. She had collapsed in a heap.

Dasha's eyes widened.

"My God," she murmured.

Papa would be enraged if he heard Dasha talking religious nonsense—the State had banned religion, which Papa said the tsars had used to fool and manipulate the people—but I couldn't blame her reaction.

The girl saw us and staggered to her feet. "I'm Nadiya Mykolaivna Lomachenko," she said, enunciating each word as if to make certain we understood.

"Who?" Dasha said.

"Nadiya Lomachenko," the girl said. "Lev Stepanovich Lomachenko lives here?"

Dasha nodded.

"He's my uncle."

I looked at Dasha and she at me. This made no sense. Papa had never mentioned having had any brothers or sisters; besides, he was an orphan, he had no family. I waited for Dasha to send the girl packing. But she turned and shouted.

"Lev Stepanovich?!"

Papa was upstairs, working in his bedroom study. Perhaps he didn't hear us or chose not to respond. Since New Year's, he had been consumed with Party affairs. A record number of enemies had infiltrated the Ukrainian Communist Party, and Moscow was concerned. He retreated often to his bedroom study, where he stayed awake half the night reading files from the OGPU or secret police. All this work wasn't good for him—he was short-tempered with Dasha and even with me. We were not supposed to disturb him.

"Fetch Papa," she said to me.

I raced upstairs and burst into his bedroom.

Papa looked up from his desk, his eyebrows bowing toward his nose in displeasure.

"Milachka, you're not supposed to—"

"There's a girl downstairs! She claims you're her uncle!"

Papa just sat there, as still as one of my porcelain statuettes. I wondered if he hadn't really heard me.

"This girl says she's a relative—she looks half-dead," I added.

I had barely finished when he dropped his pen and marched from the room, his face pinched with rage. I could barely keep up with him as he hurtled down the stairs. The girl was now standing in our foyer—Dasha must have let her in.

"How dare you!" Papa shouted, poking his finger angrily in the girl's direction. She was so slight that this gesture seemed powerful enough to knock her down. As it was, she lurched back.

"Please, Lev Stepanovich!" she cried. "I'm your dead brother Mykola's daughter! I'm the last one alive!"

"I have no brother!" Papa roared, his face red and spit flying.

He turned on Dasha. "Who is this filthy kulak? Why did you let her in?"

"She s-said—" Dasha stammered.

"She's lying!" Papa shouted. "Get her out of here!"

He didn't bother waiting for Dasha, though—he lunged at the girl, who shrieked in fear.

Up to this point I had been too confused to do anything. But now I wedged myself between him and Nadiya, who huddled behind me, whimpering.

"Papa!" I said. "Can't we just give her something to eat? Look at her!"

This seemed to give Nadiya courage because she piped up behind me. "Please! I have nowhere to go. I came all the way from Bila Tserkva—"

Papa looked at Nadiya, as if seeing her for the first time, then at me.

"Get her a piece of bread," he muttered to Dasha. After she disappeared into the kitchen, he turned to Nadiya and pointed to the door. "Then out! And tell your kulak parents to stop spreading lies."

He was grumbling now, not shouting. Still, when he snapped, "Mila, upstairs!" I dared not object. By this time, Dasha had emerged from the kitchen with a parcel. From the shape and weight of it, there was clearly more inside than a single piece of bread. Papa's back was turned, so he did not see this, but I did. She handed it to Nadiya, who was crying softly.

"Papa," I said, catching up to him on the landing. "Even if she's lying—"

But before I could finish my plea, he whipped around to face me. "Of course she's lying! I have no family. How can you be so naïve?"

"I'm not naïve!" I said defiantly. "But she's starving—just look at her! She's not lying about that!"

"All the more reason to be suspicious!" Papa hissed. "A desperate enemy is a dangerous one."

"Are you sure she's an enemy—?"

Papa bent close, his breath hot on my face. "Where is your vigilance? Everyone is a possible enemy!"

The front door banged shut. Nadiya was gone.

I jutted out my chin. "Even you?"

Papa's hand flew into the air, and my eyes widened. He had never hit me. Even Dasha had swatted at me in a fit of frustration, but never Papa. The back of his hand stopped inches from my face, trembled there.

Then the strangest thing in the world happened. His eyes filled with tears. As if I had hit him.

"Papa?" I said gently.

But he wouldn't look at me.

"Go to your room."

As I trudged to my room, I tried to console myself. At least, thanks to Dasha, Nadiya had something to eat. And probably Papa was right—that she had parents who had put her up to this act. I told myself this was true, if only so I didn't have to imagine her hopeless and alone.

Ten minutes later, Katya finally arrived. I did not tell her about Nadiya. Instead, we played Committee of the Motherless Daughters of the Communist Party. I let Katya take the lead as usual, but only half listened. We voted for a resolution, "Motherless Daughters Should Stay Up an Extra Half Hour," and then Katya talked about how her mother would let her sit in her parents' bed while she brushed and braided Katya's hair. Now her father didn't even allow her in his room.

"Do you trust him?" I asked.

Katya gave me a funny look, although I wasn't sure if it was because I had stepped out of character as First Party Secretary Lomachenko or because the question was so personal.

"Of course," she said. "He's my father. Don't you trust yours?"

"Absolutely."

The word came instinctively. But the sinking feeling in my stomach made me wonder. I pictured Nadiya trudging through Kyiv in the snow. I had to talk to her again and find out who she truly was.

12

HELEN

Brooklyn, New York, USA
1933

"Page three, right column, 'Roosevelt Yields on Farm Aid Bill.' Margaret, please read."

Margaret Schultz strode to the front of the class, took the newspaper Mrs. Weber handed her, and read, "'Washington, March thirty-first. Slight modification of the administration farm-relief bill was agreed to by President Roosevelt . . .'"

On Friday afternoons, Mrs. Weber brought a copy of the *New York Times* to class and called up her favorites to read articles aloud while the rest of us listened. She did this, she said, to improve our vocabularies and make sure we knew what was going on in the world. I tried to listen, even as the other kids in my row doodled and dozed, because I wanted to become the intelligent type of person who Mrs. Weber said read the *New York Times*.

But the story was filled with words I didn't know—*adjourn*, *commodity*—and soon I was back to my regular worry: What had happened to my cross? Every day, I opened our mailbox, hoping to find a letter from Pop's family thanking me for sending it. I imagined racing up the stairwell to our apartment, handing it to Pop. His face would brighten for the first time in months, and he'd forget all about how he couldn't work, how we'd had to move to a smaller, cheaper apartment, how Mom cleaned houses and office buildings morning till night to support us. He'd read that letter, and all his sadness would wash away and his weakened heart would grow strong. *You saved them, Lenachka!* he would say. *My good, clever girl!*

But it had been three months, and there had been no word from anyone in Ukraine.

"Does anyone want to summarize what Margaret has just read?" Mrs. Weber asked.

I snapped back to class. Ruth's hand was raised, but Mrs. Weber was looking over it to the rest of us. Even though she hardly ever called on me, I quickly peered down at my desk in case she was tempted.

Finally, I heard Mrs. Weber sigh. "Go ahead, Ruth."

"Some extra commodities, peanuts and flax, were added to the president's farm relief bill so more senators would vote for it."

That's what commodities were, I thought, things you'd buy in a store, like the one Ruth's parents ran. Flax, though, I had no idea what that was. I thought about asking Ruth after class, but I didn't want her to think I was an idiot, like Mrs. Weber did. *Helen doesn't have much to say for herself*, she had written on my last report card. *But she has a very nice smile.*

"Thank you," Mrs. Weber said, although she sounded less appreciative of Ruth than disappointed in the rest of us.

I glanced at the clock. Fifteen minutes left. Twenty-five and I would be home, checking the mail. Maybe today would be the day . . . Mrs. Weber called up Joseph, the class math whiz, who took the paper from Margaret. *Listen*, I told myself. But already I could feel my attention drifting.

"Page thirteen, left column," Mrs. Weber said. "Russians Hungry, But Not Starving."

An electric tingle ran through my body. Had I imagined this? Misheard? But no, Joseph was reading now.

"'Moscow, March thirtieth . . . There appears from a British source a big scare story in the American press about famine in the Soviet Union, with "thousands already dead and millions more menaced by death from starvation." Its author is Gareth Jones, who is a former secretary to David Lloyd George and who recently spent three weeks in the Soviet Union and reached the conclusion that the country was "on the verge of a terrific smash" . . .'"

Blood rushed to my face. What was the *New York Times* reporter talking about? Pop's family wasn't just hungry. They had written they were starving, that they had nothing to eat! Maybe, I'd misunderstood what the *New York Times* was saying. I leaned forward, listening with my whole body, trying to make sense of what Joseph was reading.

"'Mr. Jones is a man of a keen and active mind, and he has taken the trouble to learn Russian, which he speaks with considerable fluency, but this writer thought Mr. Jones's judgment was somewhat hasty . . . conditions are bad, but there is no famine.'"

My hand shot up before I could stop it.

"Helen?!" Mrs. Weber said, her voice caught between irritation and surprise.

Joseph stopped midsentence.

Every pair of eyes in that classroom was on me.

"That's not true."

Mrs. Weber smiled at me, but it wasn't a nice smile.

"The *New York Times* is a famous newspaper, Helen. It doesn't print lies."

My face burned. "I'm not saying the author's lying, just that—"

"Reporter," Mrs. Weber interrupted. "An author writes stories. A reporter writes articles. That—as Mr. Walter Duranty points out—is the difference between him and Mr. Jones."

How stupid I sounded, as if I hadn't even understood what Joseph had read! What was I doing anyway? I didn't want to tell everyone about my family, how they sent us a desperate letter, used the very word *starving*. I wanted them to look at me and see Helen, American Helen.

"We're waiting," Mrs. Weber said.

I smiled, trying to hide the tears in my eyes.

Mrs. Weber shook her head. "If you're going to make an argument, children, you need to use facts. You can't base it on stories or rumors. That's the point Mr. Walter Duranty is making in his article. Last year, he won the Pulitzer, which is the top prize for reporting."

Each sentence fell like a hammer's blow, driving me deeper into shame. I tried desperately to hold on to my smile, to keep it plastered on my face, but I felt it stiffen and fade.

Mrs. Weber turned to Joseph, but before she could tell him to keep reading, the bell rang. I leapt out of my seat and raced for the door, plowing into Ruth, who had somehow gotten in my way.

"Sorry," I mumbled and shoved past her into the crowded hall.

"Helen!" she shouted after me. "Wait!"

I swung around, ready to punch her if she blamed me for bumping into her. But she didn't look angry.

"You're right," she said.

I stared at her stupidly.

"About people starving over there. My parents have some Ukrainian customers. They talk."

I wanted to hug her. I wanted to slap her. Instead, I just glared. "Why didn't you say anything?"

Before she could answer, I turned my back on her and marched away.

"Helen!" I heard her call after me, but I didn't stop. It was just like with the caviar. She wouldn't stick out her neck for me.

I sprinted out the door and into the fenced-in play yard next to the school, where Peter was supposed to meet me. It was a beautiful spring day—bright and sunny—and so out of step with my mood that it made me feel worse. Squinting, I scanned the jungle gym, which was crawling with kids, but didn't see Peter. He wasn't on the swings, either. I figured he'd be late, dawdling somewhere on the very afternoon I was desperate to get away. Just then, a flutter of activity in the far corner caught my eye. Two boys were standing over someone, hunched, their arms pumping as they hit him. One of them stepped back and pulled up his sleeves, and that's when I saw that the someone on the ground was Peter.

I ran across that play yard so fast that I probably could have set a world record. In no time at all, I was on those boys, walloping them with my fists, my satchel. They were smaller and younger than me, but I didn't care. It felt good to kick and thrash. Peter was up on his feet almost instantly, snot and tears mixing with the blood from his nose. I felt my knuckles connect with something hard—a bone, a nose, a tooth, I didn't care. One of the boys was blubbering; the other had already run away.

"Get!" I shouted at the crying boy, and he ran.

There was so much noise and action around us that our fight went mostly unnoticed. I pulled Mom's handkerchief from my pocket—the one she'd given me the night Pop had almost died—and handed it to Peter.

"Hold your nose. It'll stop the bleeding. What happened?"

"They bumped into me, but they said I bumped into them."

He took the handkerchief, peering nervously around my back. I knew what he was thinking because I was thinking it, too. Those boys probably had older brothers.

"Let's go," I said.

We walked quickly out of the playground. As we turned off Atlantic Avenue, he pointed to my right hand. "Your knuckle."

It had been stinging, but I hadn't paid it any attention till now. I held it up. A chunk of skin hung from it. I pushed the skin back.

"Probably hit his tooth."

"You don't fight like a girl, that's for sure!" Peter said.

I felt a smile, a genuine smile, play over my lips. "How's your nose?"

Peter pulled the handkerchief away. It was stained with blood that wouldn't be easy to wash out. But his nose had stopped bleeding. I looked the rest of him over. His hair was pasted to his forehead, his jacket was rumpled, but other than his red-rimmed nose, he didn't look too worse for wear.

"Don't tell Pop about this," I said. "If he asks why your nose is red, just tell him you fell on the playground."

Peter nodded and we kept walking, but his expression remained serious.

"Pop's not going to die, is he?"

"He'll be all right," I said, although I really didn't know. "But we have to do what Mom told us and not upset or anger him."

A few minutes later, we entered the dim foyer of our building. Peter ran ahead, up the stairs, while I took out the mail key and opened our box. I reached in, my knuckles still stinging, and felt around for the sharp edges of the envelopes. Then I closed my eyes and tried to will that letter from Russia into being. But when I pulled out the mail and opened my eyes back up again, I saw nothing but bills.

Back in our apartment, Peter was already in the kitchen talking to Mary, who came every afternoon to help with the housekeeping and cooking. Pop sat in his chair, reading *Novoe Russkoe Slovo*, the Russian-language paper, which was printed at the press where he worked.

"Hi, Pop," I said.

He put down the paper and I handed Pop the mail with my left hand. He didn't seem to notice. He just riffled through it with grunts of irritation that I suspected hid his own disappointment.

"How was your day?" he asked.

There was so much I wanted to tell him, so much I wanted to ask: How bad was the famine? Why did Mr. Walter Duranty say there wasn't one? Would we ever hear from our family again? Or were they all dead? But he was still so pale, his brown hair now almost completely gray.

I stuffed all those questions deep down inside and flashed my very nice smile. "Good."

13
HELEN

On Monday morning, I was staring down at my desk, wishing I was anywhere except waiting for Mrs. Weber's class to begin, when a copy of the *New York Evening Post* landed in my lap. I looked up to see Ruth marching past to the front row. There was no time to ask her why she'd given me this paper, but one look at the front page and I didn't need to.

FAMINE GRIPS RUSSIA, MILLIONS DYING, IDLE ON RISE, SAYS BRITON

The paper's date was Wednesday, March 29, two days before the *New York Times* article. This had to be one of the "scare stories" in the American press that Walter Duranty had been referring to!

I tried to catch Ruth's eye, but she stared straight ahead, so I hunched over my lap and read.

> BERLIN, March 29—Russia today is in the grip of a famine which is proving as disastrous as the catastrophe of 1921 when millions died, reported Gareth Jones, Foreign Affairs secretary to former Prime Minister David Lloyd George of Great Britain, who arrived in Berlin this morning en route to London after a long walking tour through the Ukraine and other districts in the Soviet Union.
>
> Mr. Jones, who speaks Russian fluently, is the first foreigner to visit the Russian countryside since the Moscow authorities forbade foreign correspondents to leave the city. His report, which he will deliver to the Royal Institute of International Affairs tomorrow, explains the reason for this prohibition. Famine on a colossal scale, impending death of millions from hunger, murderous terror and the beginnings of serious unemployment in a land that had hitherto prided itself on the fact that every man had a job—this is the summary of Mr. Jones's first-hand observations.

Mrs. Weber's voice interrupted me.

"Helen! Do you hear me? Get out your math book."

I looked up, my face burning, and pulled it out of my satchel. Mrs. Weber started to review long division, but I didn't pay attention. Instead, I finished the article. And even then, Mr. Jones's voice was in my head, repeating over and over again what he had told the *New York Evening Post:* "Everywhere was the cry, 'There is no bread, we are dying.'"

Had Pop seen this story? Did he know how bad things were? I couldn't ask him. It would upset him to talk about this, and Mom had warned me that it was dangerous for his health to upset him. Plus, what could he do? Without his job, we barely had enough money to feed ourselves. If only I could find out if my cross had reached Pop's family. In a situation as bad as Gareth Jones described, it could be the difference between life and death. But there was one thing I was sure of: Mr. Walter Duranty had gotten the story wrong. My face burned for a different reason—not shame, but anger.

As soon as Mrs. Weber dismissed us for lunch, I raced into the hall, newspaper in hand.

"Ruth, wait up!"

I was afraid she might pretend not to hear me, just to get back at me for the way I had run off Friday, but she stopped and let me catch up. Ruth and I were the same size, but she looked older with her fashionable bob of auburn curls and serious expression.

I pointed to the article. "How did you find this?"

She shrugged. "I went to the library and looked through last week's papers. It was actually easy. I started with the New York papers first, and there it was."

It occurred to me that she hadn't just found the article, she'd also broken library rules to bring it to me. I'd been to the Arlington Avenue library plenty of times—before his heart attack, it had been one of Pop's favorite places to take Peter and me on Saturday mornings while Mom did the shopping. The newspapers there were just for reading—you weren't allowed to take them home. If you broke a library rule, you could lose your card. I still remembered the day I had gotten my own card—how Pop told me I could take out any book in the whole place, learn about any subject in the entire world. Ruth had risked losing this for me.

"Thank you," I said. "And I'm sorry I lost my temper."

Ruth looked me straight in the eye. Her intense stare made me want to look away. But I felt I owed it to her to accept her scolding. Only it wasn't me she scolded.

"You were right," she said. "I was a coward. I should have spoken up."

I wanted to throw my arms around Ruth, hug her, but instead I just murmured, "I didn't say you were a coward."

"You meant it, though."

Ruth grinned. I realized how rarely I'd seen her smile. It made her eyes soften and showed off her dimples. She was really very pretty, as well as smart. I felt a pang of envy before I remembered that she wasn't lording it over me but trying to make up for her own mistake.

"Well, I don't think you're a coward now."

"Good," Ruth said. "Let's go get lunch."

Together.

She didn't say it, but I knew that's what she meant.

"Okay."

As we walked side by side to the lunchroom, Ruth cocked her head at the paper. "Did you read it?"

"Every word."

"Did you notice that it said Moscow doesn't allow foreign reporters outside of the capital?"

I nodded. "Mr. Jones was the first foreigner to visit the countryside—"

"So what's Walter Duranty basing his reporting on, then?" Ruth asked. She gave a snort before answering her own question. "What the Soviet government is telling him. He's not even questioning the official story. Instead, he's attacking the one man who's actually been outside Moscow."

My hands drew into fists, stretching the skin of my still-sore knuckles. But there was no way to fight Mr. Walter Duranty. I couldn't knock him down in the schoolyard like Peter's bullies.

"We could show this article to Mrs. Weber," I said. "Or you could. She'll trust you."

"Ha!" Ruth said. "She'd still just say that Duranty's been reporting longer than Jones—"

She was right. "And he has that big prize—" I added.

"Forget Mrs. Weber anyway," Ruth said. "You should write the editor of the *New York Times*. Tell them Duranty's got it wrong."

We had just entered the lunchroom. I stopped, turned to her.

"Me?! Why would the editor of the *New York Times* listen to me?"

Ruth looked at me thoughtfully.

"Lomachenko," she said. "That's a Ukrainian name, right?"

I nodded.

"That's how you heard there was a famine—from your family?"

"Yes. So?"

"You must know other Ukrainians. Ask them what they've heard from their families; write it down. Send *that* to the *New York Times*."

There were so many reasons I wanted to tell Ruth she was crazy. I was just a kid. No one listened to me, not even my own teacher; why would some important editor at the *New York Times*? I was a girl; were there even women reporters? Almost all the stories were written by men. Not to mention that I couldn't even read all the big words in the paper or express myself intelligently. But most ridiculous of all was Ruth's belief that the world would listen to people like Pop and Mom and their friends and family. Nobody wanted to know us, to hear our stories. The best we could hope for was to blend in. I couldn't explain all that to Ruth, though. I just focused on the obvious problem.

"But those are just people's stories."

"Isn't that what reporting is? Telling people's stories?"

"I'm nowhere near where the famine is. I'm thousands of miles away—"

"So is Walter Duranty. He's in Moscow." Ruth pointed to the newspaper in my hands. "Look, did you see the article right below the famine one about the Reich Jews asking for an end to protests against them? I have family in Germany. Hitler, the new chancellor, hates Jews—his government just arranged a boycott of Jewish stores. Some of the papers say he shouldn't be taken seriously, that he's a clown, but my uncle wrote us that my cousin was beat up by his supporters, so we do."

Her brow creased with worry, but her voice remained defiant. "People's stories matter."

I shook my head. "No one will listen to me."

Ruth shrugged. "I did."

"No one else will."

"Why not try?" Ruth asked. "There's no harm in it."

"My father's sick. I'm not supposed to talk about things that might upset him. And even if I were to talk to his friends, if it got back to him that I was asking around—"

But as I rambled on, I knew I was making excuses. The truth was, I was afraid—and not just of Pop finding out. This was like raising my hand and saying who I was not just in front of the class, but the entire world.

"Well, it's up to you," Ruth said. "But just think about it this way. Even if you don't send those stories to the *Times*, by writing them down, you're saving the real history. You wouldn't want Walter Duranty to be the one everyone believes in a hundred years, that no one was starving, and everything was fine."

A hundred years. As I followed Ruth to a lunch table, I thought about that. Pop would be long gone by then. I would be, too. I didn't like the idea of his sadness not mattering, of his family not mattering. It was bad enough to have my cross disappear into nothingness, helping no one. And like Ruth said, I didn't have to send off the stories to the *New York Times*. I could just collect them.

"Maybe I'll ask a few people," I said.

"You should," Ruth said, sitting down across from me. "See what they tell you."

I nodded, even though my chest felt tight when I imagined asking people to tell me the kinds of family stories my own father wouldn't even tell me.

Ruth waved, and I turned to see Esther heading toward us with her own brown bag lunch.

"Don't tell anyone else about this," I said.

"I won't," Ruth said. "But will you tell me how it goes?" Then she gave me another rare Ruth smile. "We can meet up at the library."

"Sure," I said. I liked the idea of talking to Ruth again.

14
MATTHEW

Leonia, New Jersey, USA
2020

It wasn't just GG and Helen. All three of them were cousins. That's what GG had meant when she'd said there were three of them: three Lomachenkos. This was a family story, which meant it was my story, too. Helen and Mila were my great-great-aunts, though I still found it weird that Mom had never heard of either of them.

Later that afternoon, I dragged the Moleskine notebook and my laptop up to my bunk bed. Then I drew a family tree. Ukrainians seem to like giving people as many names as possible for maximum confusion, so I listed them by first name only to help me keep everyone straight. I didn't know Pop's real name, so I became this crazy internet sleuth and googled some key words: "Lomachenko," "1930s," "Brooklyn." I finally turned up some records from the 1930 US census, which the government uses to count the population, that listed Helen's whole family. I even figured out the name of the girls' grandfather after a little more googling turned up how in Ukraine everyone's middle name is based on their father's name. A "patronymic," in case you want to be all fancy about it. Here's what it looked like when I was done:

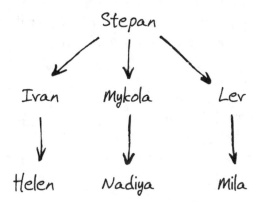

THE LOMACHENKO FAMILY

Stepan

Ivan   Mykola   Lev

Helen   Nadiya   Mila

But the greatest surprise of all was discovering that GG had almost starved to death in this famine. I wanted to know more so I googled "Ukrainian famine 1933." Then I took some notes in the notebook on what I found. Turns out the famine was such a big deal that it has a special name—the Holodomor, which in Ukrainian means "death by hunger." I was surprised that I'd never heard of it before GG's story because the famine killed nearly four million men, women, and children. I saw a few photos of victims who looked the way Mila had described GG—big heads on wobbly bodies with sunken eyes. But a lot of photos were blocked by this kid protection software Mom put on my laptop, so I knew they were even worse.

What Helen had discovered was right, too: The Soviet government, led by Mila's beloved "Papa" Stalin, had denied to the rest of the world that the famine was taking place. But clearly some people knew what was happening—Ukrainian immigrants, like Pop, whose families wrote them letters, that British guy who'd left Moscow to see for himself. There were even a couple of other journalists who'd gotten wind of it. My favorite was Rhea Clyman, this Canadian lady with only one leg (she'd lost the other in a streetcar accident) who in the early days of the famine sneaked into Ukraine and reported what she saw until the Soviets found out and threw her out of the country. I wrote a list of every single one of these fearless reporters. Why had it taken so long for the rest of the world to believe them?

I called Dad in Paris. He answered on the fifth ring.

"Hey, kiddo."

He sounded out of breath. Back in normal times I would have just assumed he'd run for his phone, but all I could think was what if he was coming down with Covid?

"You okay?"

"Totally fine," Dad said. "Just back from grabbing some takeout, took the stairs, part of my daily workout."

I felt my own breath return to normal. "You just got dinner? It's almost ten o'clock there."

"Yeah. Busy day. I'm still waiting for a read-back from an editor in New York. What's up?"

Part of me just wanted to say *nothing*. I could tell he wanted to get to his food or wait for his edit or whatever. But he was supposed to be here for me, too.

"Did you know there was this big famine in Ukraine when GG was a kid? I started reading about it. Millions of people died, but most of the world didn't know it was happening because the Soviets denied it. There was this one big-deal American reporter who just reported what the Soviets wanted him to, that no one was starving."

"Walter Duranty," Dad said. "A lot of us reporters know about him—a cautionary tale. He worked for the *New York Times*."

"Right! That guy! But here's my question. A few other reporters were saying it was true. Why didn't people believe them?"

Dad sighed. "I get comments every day from readers who think I'm making up stuff or lying. I mean, think of all the people today who don't believe in climate change, who think it's fake news."

"But isn't that just today?"

"It's worse now in some ways, but there's always been pressure on reporters to tell certain stories and not others. It's even harder when you're a journalist reporting on a government that doesn't believe in a free press. Those few reporters reporting the truth about the famine had to be really brave. History proved them right, but it took time and enough people speaking up and saying, 'Yeah, that *is* what happened. That *is* the truth.'"

I wondered if Helen had been one of them.

"My read-back just came in," Dad said. "Sorry, Mattie, I need to go."

"It's okay," I said.

"I can call you back in a little bit?"

"Nah, it's okay. I can't wait for this summer, though, when we'll finally be in the same time zone."

"Right," Dad said.

Was there hesitation in his voice, or was he just distracted, maybe even already looking at his edit?

"Love you," he added.

"Me too."

I pushed my doubts away. It was easy enough because I kept thinking of GG, alone and starving, her own family refusing to help her. But Mila must have found her. That much I knew.

15

MILA

Kyiv, Ukraine, USSR
1933

Over breakfast, I casually asked Dasha where she thought Nadiya had gone. Papa was already at work—he had left early, kissing me goodbye as if nothing had happened—but he must have ordered her not to talk about Nadiya, because she just shrugged.

"Who knows? Finish your breakfast."

I wasn't discouraged. Not at all. If anything, Dasha's silence made me more determined. I took a map of Kyiv from Papa's office and approached the matter methodically. Lypky, where I lived, was mostly government buildings and homes; anyone wandering the neighborhood aimlessly was likely to attract the attention of the police. But less than a ten-minute walk downhill was Khreschatyk, the busy main thoroughfare of Kyiv.

Normally, on Mondays, after classes were over, Katya and I

led a Class One section of Little Octobrists, the rank before Pioneers. We read them books like *May Day*, in which children gather round a table piled high with cakes to share stories about May Day celebrations around the country, or we guided them in simple exercises and chants to teach them that all Octobrists must keep themselves healthy and strong. But that afternoon, I told Nina Kravets I was feeling ill and asked her to take over for me and help Katya. She readily agreed, and just after 2:00 P.M., I left School No. 6 by myself and headed down to Khreschatyk.

It was a sunny afternoon in late March, with the temperature finally above freezing, and Radyanska, the main square, was filled with all types, from workers to saleswomen, Party officials to beggars. As I looped around, dodging the tram and circling the monument to Karl Marx at its center, I saw the usual street children, but none who looked like Nadiya. I finally approached a group of raggedy boys begging across from Party headquarters. Papa was always warning me to stay away from these children, who he said were hooligans and thieves, but I needed the kind of information only they could provide.

"Excuse me, Comrades," I said politely.

The boys looked at me in wonderment. They had dirty faces and were nearly as thin as Nadiya.

"I am looking for a girl who came from the countryside and is now living on the street."

The boys tittered disdainfully.

"What?" I demanded.

"That's half of Kyiv," said the oldest, who was missing several teeth.

Don't exaggerate, I wanted to say, but instead, I pushed away my irritation and described Nadiya as best I could. What I remembered most was that she looked half-starved, though I feared this hardly seemed like a distinguishing feature to boys like these.

"Probably got taken away by the police," said the same boy.

"Where would they take her?" I asked.

"The Collector. Or, depending on how starving she is, under Besarabsky."

The other boys laughed grimly, but I didn't follow. I had no idea what the Collector was. Besarabsky was the indoor marketplace at the end of Khreschatyk. "What do you mean *under* it?"

"They got a big freezer and no food these days," the boy explained. "So that's where they put all the people who die of hunger."

I rolled my eyes. "You're making that up."

The boy looked squarely at me, his dirty face serious. "Am not."

Papa would be furious to hear such lies. There were no dead bodies stacked up under Besarabsky market! These street children had dangerous ideas and ghoulish imaginations.

"What's that other place you said—the Collector? Is it a children's home?"

"Supposed to be a shelter, like where they clean us up and sort us out," said the boy. "But it's more of a prison."

I raised my eyebrows at this dramatic talk.

"Where is it?"

"Near the Golden Gate."

I dug into my coat pocket, which was bulging with chocolates, and pulled out a Bumble Bear, which I gave him in exchange. He snatched it up almost as fast as the other boys gathered round me.

"Where'd you get chocolate?" one asked.

"Oh, can't you see, she's got influence," another said.

The toothless boy unwrapped his reward and shoved it into his mouth. The others watched, their nostrils wide and lips quivering. They were such a pitiful sight that I doled out one to each of them even though it left me only a few in reserve. I was half-frightened they might follow and rob me of the rest, so I hurried off with the excuse that I had to catch a tram. But when I looked back, they were standing in the same spot, chewing those chocolates as if under a spell.

Fifteen minutes later, I jumped off the tram near the ruins of the Golden Gate, the medieval gateway to Kyiv. I had never gone this far by myself, but I felt perfectly safe. A loudspeaker mounted at the corner boomed out messages praising Papa Stalin and the socialist fatherland. Like Khreschatyk, there were plenty of people on the street, most of them standing in breadlines.

I approached a young woman, all cheekbones and eyes, waiting at the end of one.

"Comrade," I asked. "Where is the Collector for homeless children?"

The woman stared, and I was self-conscious of how well-dressed and -fed I looked, hardly in need of such a place.

"I am looking for my cousin," I added.

It felt daring to say the word out loud, and I imagined she might challenge me: *You don't have a cousin!* But that was Papa's voice. The woman simply accepted my claim and gave me directions to a building a few blocks away.

"Or," she said, "follow the trucks. The police round up the children inside them, and there is often one idling in front to take them away."

"Away where?"

The woman just gave me a strange look. "I hope you find your cousin."

I ran the rest of the way, a sense of uneasiness nipping at my ankles: What if Nadiya was already gone, hauled off to some orphanage far away?

I turned the last corner, breathless, and found myself staring at a large building, half sandstone and half brick, four stories high. An army-green truck was parked in front of it, just as the woman had said it would be. But, to my relief, there were no children inside, about to be taken away.

I turned my attention to the factory-like building. It was ugly and uninviting but not half as much as the face of the guard who stood by the front door. I couldn't help remembering what the toothless boy had said about the place being more of a prison. But I wasn't going to let a sour face stop me—I boldly walked right up to him.

"Comrade," I said. "I am looking for a friend. May I go in?"

I had decided not to say *cousin* in case he asked me my name. But the guard didn't even bother to look at me, never mind ask me my name or who I was looking for.

"No one is allowed."

"Why not?" I asked.

For the first time, he truly looked at me, from tip to toe.

"This is not a place for you."

I could see what I was up against. I dug into my coat pocket and held out my last three Bumble Bears.

"I just want to know if she's here. Can you check for me?"

The guard stared at the chocolates wolfishly. His tongue darted up to lick his lips. He looked left and right, across the street, to make sure no one was watching.

"What is your friend's name?"

"Nadiya Lomachenko."

It was the only name I knew for her. I didn't know if it was her real one.

The guard unlocked the door and disappeared inside. I waited impatiently. What would I do if she was there? Maybe I could convince the guard to bring her out or at least pass on a message. But I was out of chocolates.

A minute later, the door opened.

"No Lomachenko," the guard said.

"Are you sure? She may have just arrived today—"

"I told you, she's not here."

He held out his palm, and I reluctantly dropped the chocolates into it. He shoved them into his coat pocket.

"Now move along," he said, waving me away. "Someone's coming."

I scurried across the street just as the door behind him opened and a man ran over to the truck. He unlocked the back door and swung it open then stood there, waiting. I quickly positioned myself behind a streetlamp to see if some actual children might emerge from this place. Perhaps the guard had lied or gotten the facts wrong and Nadiya would be among them.

But when the doors finally burst open, there were no children, just the hunched figures of four men holding the corners of a sagging tarpaulin. Whatever was weighing it down was lumpen and covered by a dirty sheet. The men staggered along toward the truck. As they turned to steer it toward the open door, an impossibly thin arm slid out from beneath the sheet and dangled over the side.

I felt my blood run cold, as if I were becoming one of those dead children. For that's who was under that filthy sheet; judging from their shapes, half a dozen at least. I turned away, started running, but I couldn't escape what I had seen. My mind leapt and bucked like a frightened horse—imagining their bodies, open eyes and frozen mouths, imagining thousands like them—a whole city of the dead—in the freezer under Besarabsky market. My terror followed me all the way back to the Golden Gate, where I stood shaking as I waited for the tram, the loudspeaker on the corner blaring about the wonderful life children led in our socialist paradise.

I was so shaken that I missed my stop and had to backtrack by foot to Lypska Street. I had stopped seeing what was in front of me.

I navigated purely by instinct, like a cat trying to get back to its former home. I wanted to be there, to be safe, to have Dasha fret over me and Papa put his arms around me and tell me about record-breaking explorers and heroic workers and feats of engineering. But I knew I could never unsee that thin, limp arm. It pulled at me, pulled at my heart.

I was a half block from home when I spotted her. In my disoriented state, I thought I was imagining the sight: a skeletal waif bundled in rags peering at my door from across the street. I blinked twice to see if she would disappear, but she just stood there. Then she hung her head and staggered away.

I took off at a run. She limped faster.

"Nadiya!" I cried.

She spun around, her enormous eyes blinking fearfully.

"What do you want?"

The wind could still blow her away, but the fierce look in her eyes was new—and familiar.

"Are you really my cousin?" I asked.

"I don't lie," she said through gritted teeth.

I wanted to tell her that Papa didn't lie, either. But she wobbled, and her spindly arms shot up to regain her balance. This could have been part of her act, but it made me abandon my interrogation.

"Where's the bag of food Dasha gave you?"

"It was stolen while I slept. Can you give me more?"

Her voice cracked, and I knew she was telling the truth about that. Whoever she was—kulak or cousin—I just wanted to help her.

"Yes, but you can't stay on the streets. You'll starve to death or the police will catch you . . ."

Her eyes flashed with challenge. "Tell me, then, where else can I go?"

I wanted to say, *Home with me*. But I couldn't. Papa would throw her back out, and Dasha might give her a few scraps, but she'd never dare cross Papa and help her more than that. I couldn't bring her to Katya or any of my other friends in the Pioneers. They would suspect she was a kulak or some other class enemy and report the whole episode to Papa. Where could I take her? In all my life, I had never felt so helpless. A sheen of cold sweat broke onto my temple. If Nadiya walked away, I knew I'd never see her again or find out who she really was. I pictured her being carried out of the Collector under a sheet.

I grabbed her bony hand, pulled her weightless body toward the only person I could think of who might help.

"Come with me!" I said.

Then I ran, my heart pounding, as if Baba Yaga herself were chasing us.

16
MILA

Kyiv, Ukraine, USSR
1933

*B*ang, bang, bang!

I pounded on Anna Mikhailovna's door, trying to be heard over the bright and happy notes of Kabalevsky's "A Game in PE Class." As soon as I'd taken her hand, the fight and fury had gone out of Nadiya. She'd sagged against me, silent as a mouse. The wobbling hadn't been an act. She'd collapsed a few blocks from the music studio, and I had half dragged, half carried her the rest of the way. I tried not to think about the possibility that Anna Mikhailovna would send her away, too. Dasha expected me home within the hour. What would I do?

Just then the music stopped, and I heard footsteps. The door swung open, and Anna Mikhailovna stood in front of me, her brow furrowed.

"Mila?"

The words tumbled out in a great rush. "This is my cousin, Nadiya. She's come all the way from the country. Papa won't take her in. She needs help!"

Anna Mikhailovna looked from Nadiya to me then back to Nadiya.

"Sonya, from the top!" she called through the open door.

"Come," she said, then she whisked us past a girl with pigtails busily thumping on the piano to the back room. I had never been there before—it was her private living space—but at that moment, I hardly noticed the details, just that her mother, Olga Stepanovna, rushed over to help support Nadiya. She was a little old lady, hardly taller than myself, but to have someone else care made me unspeakably grateful.

"Do what you can for her, Mama," Anna Mikhailovna said quietly before turning to me. "The lesson ends in ten minutes, then I have a break. We can talk just the two of us."

Then she left.

On opposite sides of the room, beneath the eaves of a sloping roof, were a pair of narrow beds. Olga Stepanovna and I helped Nadiya to the closer of the two. The old woman covered Nadiya with a blanket and tottered off to switch on an electric burner on a table in the corner, placing a kettle atop it. Nadiya had already closed her eyes, but she opened them feebly when Olga Stepanovna returned with a cup of tea and a heel of bread. Olga Stepanovna dipped the bread into the tea to soften it.

"They're falling over in the streets," she muttered.

She said nothing to me, so focused was she on Nadiya, but I didn't mind. I was too busy thinking about my talk with Anna Mikhailovna and how to conduct it quickly so I could get home in time. It was already nearly four thirty, and Dasha would raise the alarm if I wasn't home by five.

It was a relief when Sonya stopped playing and Anna Mikhailovna returned.

"Come, Mila. Let's talk."

I rushed out into the studio room, barely waiting for her to close the door behind us.

"You can take Nadiya, can't you?" I pleaded. "She can stay here with you?"

Anna Mikhailovna turned to face me.

"Mila, do you realize what you're asking?"

I felt a chill in my veins at this question, which was really an answer. But I had prepared for doubts. I marshaled my arguments.

"I know she's another mouth to feed, but I can bring you extra food . . ."

Anna Mikhailovna waved her hand in irritation.

"It's not feeding her, it's her being here at all! No one in Kyiv is allowed to take in people from the countryside, even their closest relatives. Your father must have told you this . . ."

I shook my head. I was beginning to realize that there were a lot of things Papa hadn't told me.

"Well, then, now you know. To live in Kyiv, you must have a passport that says you're a resident of Kyiv. The authorities cordoned off the city a few months ago to prevent starving villagers from pouring in—it's a wonder your Nadiya even made it through."

Starving villagers? She meant kulaks. But I let this slide. I sat down heavily on the piano bench. "Surely children don't require this passport?"

"No," Anna Mikhailovna admitted. "But a child can still be a class enemy, especially one from the countryside. What if a neighbor or even one of my students notices she's living here and reports us?"

Then Papa could help, I thought automatically. But this wasn't true. Papa hadn't helped Nadiya—even after I'd begged him to. It would be foolish to promise Anna Mikhailovna his protection.

Anna Mikhailovna seemed to read my mind, gave a little snort. "Your father was wise to distance himself from Nadiya, especially if she shares his blood. Think of Pavlik Morozov, the martyr of the Revolution. What is the lesson of this hideous fable? Even family must be sacrificed for the Great Soviet . . ."

Anna Mikhailovna stopped suddenly, her eyes catching mine. Her face paled.

"Never mind all that," she murmured. "Never mind."

This went much further than the "intelligentsia nonsense" Papa had worried about. To call the story of Pavlik Morozov a fable, and in such an angry tone . . . Anna Mikhailovna was talking like the enemy. But what cut me even deeper than what she said was the realization that she had stopped because she was afraid—afraid of me!

"Anna Mikhailovna," I said, my voice quivering. "I would never tell on you."

She nodded, but the fear was still in her eyes. She didn't trust me, didn't trust that I wouldn't tell Papa. No wonder I didn't know what was really happening. How many people had silenced themselves when I came into a room? How many people had I frightened simply by being Papa's daughter? I was a monster without even knowing it.

It was all too much. I burst into tears. I tried to stifle them, but my shoulders shook, and I covered my face in my hands.

"Papa won't even help Nadiya," I said between sobs. "Why would I tell him what you said? Why would I—"

"Hush, I believe you," Anna Mikhailovna said gently. I heard her footsteps, felt her hand stroke my head. "You're a good girl, Mila. Your eyes have been opened today, that's all."

I only cried harder. Then I felt the weight of her body sink onto the piano bench next to me, and she began to play. It was a piece I'd never heard before. It was slow and somber, filled with minor chords, and yet not sad.

"What is this?" I managed to ask through my tears.

"Tchaikovsky's *Children's Album*," she said quietly. "It's called 'In Church.'"

It was religious music, music that wasn't supposed to be played anymore. But how could I close my ears to something so beautiful? The steady procession of chords, the way the notes crescendoed, rising up, like when your spirits start to lift after feeling down. My shoulders stopped heaving, and my breathing slowed. As the last chord gently faded, I took a deep breath, wiped the tears from my face.

"Better?" Anna Mikhailovna said.

I nodded, and something of the old me came back. I looked my teacher straight in the eye. I had only one argument left, but it was my strongest.

"Without you, she'll die."

Anna Mikhailovna looked away, sighed. But before she could answer, the back door opened, and Olga Stepanovna shuffled through.

"She's fallen asleep," she said.

"Did she eat anything?" Anna Mikhailovna asked.

"A bit of bread soaked in tea. But that's enough. It's dangerous to feed the starving too much at once. Their stomachs aren't used to it. Perhaps after your five-o'clock lesson—"

"What time is it?" I interrupted.

"It's nearly five now—" Olga Stepanovna said.

I leapt to my feet. "I need to go! Anna Mikhailovna, what will you do? Must I take her?"

But before she could answer, Olga Stepanovna interrupted, "Take her? The child is barely alive!"

"We can't keep her," Anna Mikhailovna said. "It's too dangerous."

"Puh!" said the old lady. "Living is dangerous."

The two women looked at each other, but neither spoke. Though it wasn't my usual nature, I kept quiet, too. No argument seemed as powerful as their silence. Still, it was torturous to wait, knowing precious seconds were ticking by.

A knock on the door startled us all, followed by a boy's voice. "It's Kolya!"

"Coming!" Anna Mikhailovna shouted. Then she turned to me.

"She can stay tonight. Tomorrow we'll decide what to do."

"Thank you!" I said and dashed out the door. There was no way I wouldn't be late. My only hope was that I could make it home before Dasha left to find me at school.

17

MILA

I stumbled into the foyer at five fifteen, panting and covered in sweat.

"Dasha?!"

"In the kitchen," she called back.

I collapsed against the door. She hadn't left. I caught my breath, hung up my coat, and smoothed my hair, then wandered into the kitchen as if nothing was amiss.

"What are you cooking?" I asked, though I knew the answer from the soup pot on the stove and Dasha's fingers. They were stained bloodred, like a murderer's, from peeling beets.

"Borscht," she said.

I waited for her to ask why I was late, but she was chopping potatoes and didn't even look up. She seemed distracted by the task in front of her. How lucky I was that she had decided to make borscht today!

"The Octobrists were a handful," I said, plopping myself down in a chair.

"Oh?" she said.

"Yes," I continued. "Vanya yanked Yulka's braids, so Katya and I had the class form a disciplinary committee to vote on his punishment. He's really very naughty."

This was all true, if not true today. Still, my heart fluttered like a trapped bird. I was ready for her to ask if Vanya was the reason why I was late, but she just kept chopping potatoes and throwing them into a bowl of salted water.

"Did you have a good day?" I asked.

Dasha shrugged. "I managed."

"I love borscht," I said.

"Many people do."

Dasha was in a mood; was it because of my lateness?

"Is everything okay, Dasha? I can help—"

She put down her knife and looked up at me. "In my village, we used to make borscht together—my mother and sisters—a big pot of it. It tastes different, Mila, when you make it all alone."

"I can help—"

"No. You might cut yourself or get burned."

She picked up her knife and went back to her chopping. But this time, I didn't think, *Silly Dasha, always so overprotective.* Instead, I wondered if she worried about my getting hurt because she feared Papa might punish her.

"I'm sorry," I said though I couldn't say for what.

I started toward the door, then turned back to her. "Even though I can't help, I love you, Dasha."

Dasha's knife froze. She blinked hard, her voice thick with emotion. "I love you too, Milachka."

Relief coursed through me. I ran up and gave her a kiss on the cheek.

"Never kiss someone holding a knife," Dasha grumbled, but she accepted my peck. "You'll get cut."

Was this another of Dasha's country superstitions? There were so many of them: Never shake hands over a threshold or you'll have bad luck; never sit on the cold ground or you won't have children; never whistle indoors or you'll lose money. I didn't know, and, in any case, I didn't ask. I had just remembered the other lie I needed to tell.

"I'm going to be late again tomorrow. Katya and I were chosen for a special May Day preparation committee that's meeting after school."

"I'm sure Papa will be happy to hear that," Dasha said.

She was right, of course; Papa would be delighted by such news. But what if he mentioned it to Katya's father, who asked Katya about it?

"Don't tell him, Dasha! It's a surprise."

"A surprise, eh? Well that's nice. I won't say anything then to anyone. It'll be our secret."

For a second, I had the impression she was talking about something more than the May Day committee. Was it possible she knew about Nadiya? But she gave no sign—no knowing wink or smile. Her expression as she chopped was blank. She must have felt my stare, because she looked up.

"Go on," she said. "Surely you have schoolwork to do?"

That evening, Papa called me over for a story. He seemed in a rare good mood, humming a patriotic song under his breath. But instead of snuggling into his lap, I settled across from his armchair on the couch.

"What's this?" he asked. "Not Papa's little girl anymore?"

I couldn't tell him the real reason I was upset. "I'm getting a bit old to sit on your lap."

Papa nodded as if he understood, but a little sigh escaped him. "I suppose you have to grow up someday."

"I'll be thirteen this fall," I said coolly.

"Thirteen on November thirteenth!" Papa said, his blue eyes crinkling. "No longer a child. May I sit next to you at least?"

"Of course."

Papa stood up then sat down next to me on the couch. "I will sit here very formally," he said. "We will be like two grown-ups. Very serious."

But then he winked at me and I couldn't help smiling. He pulled me toward him and kissed me on the top of the head.

"Oh, Milachka, I'll love you forever. You're my sunshine."

"Papa," I blurted out, "are there dead bodies under Besarabsky market?"

He pulled away, his face darkened.

"Who told you that?"

"A boy at school," I lied. "He said that's where they take the bodies of people who've starved—"

"Nonsense!" Papa said. "We may be hungry here in the city, but no one is starving except for suicidal kulaks who refuse to work and take to the road. And there's room enough for them in the cemeteries. No one is under Besarabsky market."

See, I told myself, *that boy was lying*. The dead children under the sheet were kulak children whose uncaring parents had sent them to the city to beg and torment us. Nadiya was one of them, not the long-lost cousin she claimed to be. Anna Mikhailovna was just embittered by her intelligentsia sympathies. Everything was as it was, as I'd understood it to be.

Papa drew me into the warm crook of his shoulder. I relaxed against him, comforted by the familiar smell of his *stalinka*.

"Is that what you were all upset about, little fox?" he murmured. "Never mind those kulak lies. How about a true story? I have just the one! Have you heard of *Maxim Gorky*?"

"The famous writer?"

"No!" Papa beamed. "The airplane!"

Papa launched into the tale of how Papa Stalin had just commissioned a new airplane from Andrei Tupolev, the top aircraft designer at the Central Aerohydrodynamic Institute in Moscow. Named in honor of our greatest writer, the *Maxim Gorky* was going to be the largest airplane in the world, with a sixty-three-meter wingspan and eight engines. Inside the main cabin, there would be a propaganda factory with a printing press, a photo lab, a radio set, and even a library. An entire factory of eight hundred workers had been given the honor of building the new airplane. For its inaugural flight, Papa said, forty of the nation's most productive farmers and factory workers would be chosen as passengers. But everyone would get to enjoy this miraculous achievement of Soviet aviation: There were plans to beam Communist slogans onto the clouds using the onboard projector.

Papa had a dreamy look in his eyes, as if he were already flying high above the earth on the *Maxim Gorky*. I tried to go there with him, but then I remembered the Collector, and the dead child's arm yanked me back to the ground. I suddenly wished that Nadiya had never shown up at my door. I missed feeling that Papa and I were united in a great struggle. Doubt was a much lonelier place.

18
MATTHEW

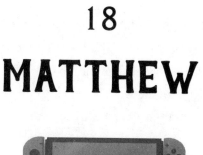

Later that afternoon, I googled the *Maxim Gorky*. I figured Mila's dad had exaggerated, but it turned out that everything he'd claimed about this crazy plane with its onboard propaganda operation was true. What he couldn't know, because it didn't happen until two years later, in 1935, was what happened to the *Maxim Gorky* on an exhibition flight over Moscow. Farmers and workers were not actually invited on board as special guests, but the families of the plane's builders were. The farmers and workers ended up being the lucky ones though; the *Maxim Gorky* collided with a fighter plane flying loops around it to demonstrate its size. It crashed over the city, killing everyone on board as well as nine people on the ground.

Reading about the fate of the *Maxim Gorky* added to the sense of dread I already felt about Mila. At least GG had somehow managed to survive. I wrote down what GG had told me in the notebook, adding what I'd learned about the *Maxim Gorky*.

I was finishing up when Mom barged into my room. I could tell she was annoyed from the way she marched over to my bed.

"Did you do your math problem set last week?" she asked.

I immediately closed the notebook.

"Of course I did."

"I just checked, and you have a zero for a late assignment."

"What?" Then it hit me. "Oh, shoot! I forgot to upload it."

"This is the third time now! You're supposed to check, make sure all your homework is in."

"Sorry," I said. "I'll do it now."

I hopped off the bed, surveying my room for the problem set. Mom, sensing I had no idea where I'd put it, circled me like a blood-thirsty shark. "This should be your responsibility, Matthew, not mine! I have enough on my plate."

"Sorry," I said again and made a dive for a pile of papers on my desk that I hoped—but inwardly doubted—included the missing problem set.

Mom looked at her phone, groaned. "I was going to take GG out for a walk. Too late now. Listen, Matthew, I'm going to give her dinner, then I've got to finish editing this piece. We'll do frozen pizza later, but you need to find that homework and upload it by then or I will seriously hold on to that Switch for the rest of your life."

I should have kept my mouth shut, but she'd brought my Switch back into it, and those were fighting words.

"I said I'd do it! You know, some kids don't even log on. Their parents don't care! They let them play video games all day."

I didn't actually know this for a fact, but my friends were always claiming kids like this existed. Anyway, it was a big mistake. Mom turned around, hands on her hips.

"Well, you're not those kids and I'm not those parents. I don't care if it's the apocalypse out there, you're going to your classes and you're getting your homework done and uploaded, preferably without my needing to remind you every two seconds on top of everything else I have to do!"

With this, she stalked out of my room, muttering more complaints—no doubt about me—under her breath. Before I could stop myself, I grabbed the notebook, opened it to a blank page, and scribbled: *I hate Mom!!! I want to live with Dad!*

It felt good for about two seconds, but then I remembered I still needed to find the stupid problem set, I had no idea when I was going get to my Switch back, and I couldn't even see Dad until the summer. At least I had GG's story, but like everything else in my life, it was a mess. Somehow GG had made it to Brooklyn and Helen, who wanted to help her, but then GG hadn't even kept in touch with Helen. What had happened between them? My hunch was that it involved Mila, but I wasn't sure how.

Zelda can make you feel confused, too, sometimes. It's an open-ended game, which means it's easy to get stuck wandering aimlessly around Hyrule. You can end up on a side quest and wander off in the wrong direction. It's important to keep a sense of your main objective.

In GG's case, my main objective was finding out what had happened, not just to Mila but to her. The one thing I knew for sure was that she had survived the famine and made it to her family in America.

"Tell me more about Helen," I said to GG the next day. "How did she find you?"

I figured this, at least, was the happier part of the story. But her face crumpled.

"Too late."

19
HELEN

Brooklyn, New York, USA
1933

That evening, when Mom came home from her cleaning jobs, she was lugging four large bolts of cloth. She put them down next to the secretary and gave me a hug. Peter was already asleep, and Mary had left—Mom's hours were getting later as she took on more offices, which could only be cleaned after they closed for the day.

"What are those for?" I asked her in Russian.

"I'm helping Mr. Grushko, the tailor," she said.

I wasn't fooled by her cheery tone or the word *helping*, and neither was Pop. Mom was taking a second job. Pop looked up from the biography of Abraham Lincoln he had asked me to get him from the library and grunted.

"When?"

"I'll do it in between cleanings," Mom said. "It's easy work, sitting in a chair."

Pop shook his head but didn't say anything.

"It's beautiful cloth, isn't it?" Mom said, as if the quality of the cloth made it okay that she was going to work herself to death. I didn't say anything, either. I had seen Pop open too many bills. I had eaten too many meatless meals. I had felt my toes pinched inside shoes that had grown far too small and watched Peter's pant cuffs rise higher above his ankles as he grew. I was afraid we'd have to move yet again. When I walked past furniture on the street from another eviction, I imagined our own lying there.

"Can I help?" I asked. I knew how to sew, not as well as Mom, but enough to hem and darn.

Mom kissed my forehead. "You're a good girl, Lenachka. But Mr. Grushko is paying for my tiny, straight stitches. Your job right now is to go to school and take care of your brother."

She didn't say Pop, too, but only because he was listening.

"Can I at least get you dinner?" I asked. "Mary left some—"

"I'm not that hungry," Mom said. "I'll help myself in a bit. You should be getting to bed."

Mary always left dinner for Mom, but Mom rarely ate more than half of it. Sometimes she saved the entire meal, leaving me a note to pack it for Peter and me to have at school. I glanced at Pop, certain he felt the same terrible guilt that I did, but he was staring down at his book.

A few minutes later, Mom tiptoed into the bedroom to pull

Peter's blankets up around him and give him a kiss. Then she came to my bedside.

"*Spakoynoy nochee*," she said in Russian, which meant *good*—or really, *calm*—*night*. But I didn't feel calm.

"Mom," I whispered, pulling her close, "you can't do everything yourself. Can't we ask for help?"

Mom sighed. "Lenachka, so many people have helped us already—the Abramoviches, the Jewish family that owns the printing press, gave Pop an extra month of wages; the church helped pay the rent for the first month after his heart attack. Mr. Oleynik has paid all our utility bills. The Rudenkos bought you and Petya Christmas gifts. Mr. Tarasenko, the baker, still hasn't asked us to pay for a single loaf of bread. And Mary—"

Mom's voice caught in the dark.

"We can never pay back all these wonderful people. How could I ask them for more?"

I knew people had helped us after Pop had gotten sick, but I hadn't quite realized how many or how much. Tears stung my eyes.

Mom squeezed my arm. "Pop will get better, Lenachka. But we need to keep his spirits up. You and I can do that. We don't talk about this. We're strong. We're going to be strong for Pop, yes?"

"Yes," I whispered.

Mom gave me another kiss, then I heard the mattress creak, and she left to spend the night like some fairy-tale mother, sewing to keep us fed. I wiped my eyes, took a deep breath, and that's when it hit me. I could thank people and ask them for their own stories at the same time! I decided to start that very weekend. I tried to think how a real reporter would prepare for an interview. I'd need a notebook to write down what people said. I settled on an old accounting ledger of Pop's—it seemed more serious than my school notebooks. Reporters asked questions, too, so I prepared some in my head.

I decided to start with Mr. Oleynik, Pop's closest friend and Peter's godfather. Mr. Oleynik was from a poor Ukrainian family but had become an engineer, and everyone thought he was *kulturni*, meaning cultured and smart. He had no family of his own in America and had always been kind to us, even before Pop's heart attack, once taking Peter to the Museum of Natural History and me to a traveling performance of the Ballets Russes. I fell asleep remembering *Swan Lake*, and the beautiful ballerina's feathered white tutu.

But I felt far less calm the following Saturday afternoon, when I knocked on the door of the Bobrovs' apartment. Mr. Oleynik lived with them as their boarder, and Mrs. Bobrov cooked all his meals. She answered the door and gave me a smothering hug.

"Lenachka!" she said in Russian. "What are you doing here? How's your father?"

"Good," I said. "Is Mr. Oleynik in?"

"*Jhah-nee!*" she shouted. I stifled a giggle. Mrs. Bobrov preferred to call Mr. Oleynik by the American first name Johnny, like the *Tarzan* actor Johnny Weissmuller. She always pronounced it in a way that made Peter and me laugh.

Mr. Oleynik padded out, wearing his suit—I'd never seen him in anything else—and slippers. He was the same age as Pop but looked younger and less gray, especially now.

"Lena, I've been thinking about you all," he said in Ukrainian. "How's Pop? How's Mom and Petya?"

"They're fine. I was wondering if I could talk to you about something."

"Of course," he said, then, turning to Mrs. Bobrov, he switched to Russian. "Can we sit in the living room, Anna?"

"Go ahead! I'm hanging the wash. You want some tea?" She didn't wait for us to answer but hurried off to the kitchen.

I followed Mr. Oleynik into the small living room, which was covered in crocheted doilies, Orthodox saints, and a studio portrait of Mrs. Bobrov's two sons and their children. Snake plants hung across from a birdcage.

"How's Caruso?" I asked.

Mr. Oleynik whistled, and the little yellow canary inside twittered back.

"He declares himself well."

It was their favorite trick, and it made me smile.

Mrs. Bobrov returned with a tray of tea and hard candies.

"Thank you," I said and picked a lemon one for me and an orange one to give to Peter later.

"If you're here long enough, I'll give you some borscht, too," she said, then disappeared back into the kitchen. I could hear her shouting out the window to the neighbors as she hung out her wash.

"Tell me, Lenachka," Mr. Oleynik said. "What's on your mind?"

I nervously twisted the crinkly edge of my candy. But the words of gratitude came easily.

"I wanted to say thank you. Mom told me how you paid our bills after Pop's heart attack."

"That's kind of you, Lenachka. But hardly necessary. Your pop is as close to family as I have here. He would do the same for me."

I seized my opportunity. "You still have family in Ukraine, though, right?"

"Yes, my sisters."

I took a deep breath. "I heard there's a famine there, a really bad one. I'm actually, um, collecting stories about it. Have you heard anything about this from your family?"

I waited for him to challenge me—*Collecting stories for what? Why should I tell you about these things? You're just a child.* But he leaned in eagerly.

"Absolutely, Lenachka, it's true. My sister Yustina wrote me that her family was starving. They had nothing to eat but a few potatoes. She begged me to send money."

I quickly wrote all of this down.

"Can you tell me anything else she told you?"

"I can read you her letter," Mr. Oleynik said.

"I'd like that."

He left the room and returned a few moments later with an envelope and a package. He showed me the envelope first, which was from Ukraine, USSR (the Union of Soviet Socialist Republics). I wondered what details a real reporter would gather. His sister's full name and her town seemed important to show that Yustina was a real person, so I copied them down. Then Mr. Oleynik read the letter inside—"'We are perishing from hunger . . . already many people in our village have died. Please, I beg you, help us as much as you can—'"

Mr. Oleynik's voice wavered, and he halted at times to collect himself. In addition to his sister's plea, I wrote down this description because the letter's impact on Mr. Oleynik seemed important, too.

"The Soviet government has a system where you send it money and it gives your family food through a special shop," he explained. "It's why the Soviet censors let these letters through. The government wants our currency. It's worth more than their rubles."

"So they must know people are starving."

"Undoubtedly! But they also like to pretend nothing of the sort is happening, especially when it doesn't benefit them."

He tucked away the letter then showed me the package, which was addressed to his sister. Stamped on the front was RETURN TO SENDER. "I tried to send Yustina some canned food myself, and look what the censors wrote on it." He flipped over the package and pointed to a sentence in Russian scrawled across the back: *We do not have any hungry people.*

I took out my notebook and pen. "May I write that down?"

"Yes, of course, write it down, but it's just an official's lies."

I thought of my own package, wondered if it would be returned the same way. But so many months had passed, it was more likely gone for good, my cross lost or stolen with it.

"I'm not allowed to talk to Pop about any of this," I said when I was done writing. "It's too upsetting."

"It's wise for you not to," Mr. Oleynik said. "I don't even have a weakened heart, and talking about the suffering in the old country breaks mine."

I closed my notebook and gave him a hug, even though I was sure this wasn't what a real reporter would do.

"Thank you, Lenachka," he whispered, hugging me back.

"Do you know anyone else I could talk to whose families are starving?"

"Oh, certainly." He named a few families from church, then some friends of his and Pop's from the Russian Brotherhood Organization—the men's club they belonged to. I added their names to the list already in my notebook.

"All of us wish we could bring our families here. But it's much harder now than it used to be. The Soviets let only a few people out, and this country lets so few people in. It's not like it used to be. Your poor pop was trying everything to get them—"

"He was trying to bring his brother's family *here*?"

This was new information.

"Yes, before he got sick, of course. He hired an immigration lawyer, some Polish fellow on the Lower East Side."

There was so much about Pop's cares and worries I hadn't known.

"We haven't received a letter from them in a long time," I said.

Mr. Oleynik nodded sympathetically. "Like many of us. Some letters make it through, some don't."

Perhaps Pop's family had received the cross and sent a letter to tell us, but it hadn't made it through? There was still hope. And Pop and I weren't alone. Others were worried, too. Others felt just as powerless.

"Thank you," I said to Mr. Oleynik. "And please don't tell Pop we talked about this."

"No need to worry. When I see him, we talk about lighter things, like the Depression." He laughed and shook his head. "What a world. You'll be telling your grandchildren about it someday."

"I certainly will," I said.

Or the notebook would. But it was hard to think of waiting that long to tell the truth.

20
MILA

Kyiv, Ukraine, USSR
1933

The next day, as soon as school ended, I hurried over to the studio, arriving between lessons as Anna Mikhailovna had asked. She swiftly led me to the back room. I was delighted to see Nadiya, propped up in a chair next to Olga Stepanovna, who was reading to her from a book of fairy tales. Her face was still gaunt, her cheeks still covered by whitish down, but her skin wasn't so deathly pale, and most important of all, the fear in her eyes was gone.

"You look much better!" I said.

I was overstating the case. But I wanted the women to feel the night she'd spent with them had made a difference.

"I feel better," Nadiya said, with a smile at Olga Stepanovna.

Olga Stepanovna beamed back at her.

"Mama has fallen head over heels for her," Anna Mikhailovna said.

I searched her face, hoping this meant Nadiya could stay.

"No need to stare at me like that," Anna Mikhailovna said. "We won't turn her out on the street. She can stay until we figure out a better solution."

Last night, in Papa's arms, I had convinced myself she was just a kulak's daughter. But I could never have convinced myself not to care if she'd ended up dying on the street. Relief flooded through me. I ran to Anna Mikhailovna and threw my arms around her, nearly toppling her over.

"Mila!" she complained, but I could tell from the way she let me embrace her that she wasn't truly angry.

"Thank you!" I said, then ran to hug Olga Stepanovna. "And thank you, too!"

"But, Mila," Anna Mikhailovna said, in her sternest tone. "You cannot tell anyone she's here. Not your father, not Dasha. Not even your closest friend. No one!"

I stood as erect as I could and looked directly at Anna Mikhailovna. I felt as if I were taking the Pioneer oath all over again: *I, Lyudmila Lvovna Lomachenko, solemnly promise: to love and cherish my motherland passionately, to live as the great Lenin bade us, as the Communist Party teaches us, and as required by the laws of the Young Pioneers of the Soviet Union.* Except that this was an oath to do the exact opposite: to protect not my motherland, but a single one of her daughters.

"No one," I repeated firmly. "I promise."

"Where does Dasha think you are now?" Anna Mikhailovna asked.

"On a May Day committee, at school."

Anna Mikhailovna frowned. "Don't tell lies that can be easily disproven."

"She won't check," I said. "School is a safe place—she doesn't worry when I'm there."

But then I thought of Katya. What if Dasha said something to her about the May Day committee we were on? I couldn't risk Katya telling Dasha that she had no idea what Dasha was talking about. I would have to find a way to explain my lie to Katya.

"What time did you tell Dasha you'd be back?" Anna Mikhailovna asked.

"Not till five. It would be suspicious if I returned early. Can I at least stay till your next break? Talk to Nadiya a bit? We've barely had a chance to talk."

Nadiya looked at me uncertainly. But the others didn't seem to notice.

"If Mila sits with her, I could go to the Torgsin," Olga Stepanovna said.

"What's that?" I asked.

The others looked at me in surprise.

"They're the stores where people can trade foreign money and gold for food," Anna Mikhailovna explained.

"It's how I made it to you," Nadiya added. "I traded at the Torgsin in Bila Tserkva for food. I wouldn't have had the strength to make it here otherwise."

Anna Mikhailovna shook her head. "It's shameful how people have been forced to live."

A loud knock startled us, even Anna Mikhailovna though she was the first to regain her composure. "That's my four o'clock, Grisha," she said at the same moment that a boy's high voice called through the door, "Anna Mikhailovna, are you there?"

Olga Stepanovna rose stiffly and fetched her string shopping bag from a hook on the door, then opened a velvet-lined box and took out a pair of dangly opal-and-gold earrings.

"Coming!" Anna Mikhailovna hollered. Then she turned to us and added softly, "Wait till Grisha starts playing, girls, and only talk quietly."

We both nodded, watching Olga Stepanovna tuck the earrings into her pocket. Although I wanted Nadiya to be fed, I couldn't help feeling a twinge of sadness over the thought of Olga Stepanovna trading them away.

As soon as the two women left, I sat down in Olga Stepanovna's abandoned seat, enjoying its lingering warmth. I heard Anna Mikhailovna's voice on the other side of the door in concert with a boy's, then the scrape of the piano bench against the floor. Nadiya and I stared at each other, but in keeping with Anna Mikhailovna's instructions, we didn't speak. It occurred to me that I didn't know her at all. I had no idea if she was chatty or quiet, if she liked to dance or tell jokes or preferred animals to people. I knew nothing about her, really, except that she'd nearly starved to death.

Finally, Gretchaninoff's "In the Village" began to play, more jaunty than romantic like it should have been.

"I'm glad they're letting you stay," I said.

"Anna Mikhailovna and her mother are good people, very kind," Nadiya said. "Thank you."

"It was nothing," I said.

"It was much more than nothing. Another night on the street, and I would have died. I was starving. All alone. You saved my life, Mila."

But the tears welling in her eyes had the effect of making me feel embarrassed, as if I hadn't done enough. I handed her my handkerchief.

"Well, you're safe now," I said. "And even if you're not my cousin, I won't tell Anna Mikhailovna."

She looked up fast. The angry flash in her eyes was more real than her gratitude.

"I told you the truth. Our fathers were brothers. How could you doubt it? We look alike even."

It seemed preposterous to think I looked anything like her. She was a skeleton of a girl. But there was something about those eyes— and that flash of temper. Papa couldn't do that, though—turn away his own flesh and blood. I understood why she had lied, but I wasn't going to let her make a fool of me.

"Can I ask you about our family, then?"

She narrowed her eyes, as if accepting a challenge. "What do you want to know?"

"When did your father die?" I asked.

"Two years ago."

"What happened? Was he sick?"

She shook her head.

"What happened to him, then?"

Nadiya's thin face hardened. "He was arrested. Nine months later, we received an anonymous letter that he'd died in Siberia. We never learned how."

Papa's brother, arrested? No, this couldn't be our family. But I kept the doubt off my face.

"What did he do?"

"He was a farmer—"

"No, I mean to get arrested—"

"He didn't *do* anything. He inherited a bit of land from our grandfather. He resisted joining the collective farm."

Papa had been right: Nadiya's family were kulaks. But instead of feeling reassured that they had nothing to do with us, I had a chilling thought: What if Papa had known this because Nadiya's kulak family *was* his family? This would mean that Papa was a kulak, too. But Papa hated kulaks. He couldn't be one of them.

"You're certain my father, Lev Lomachenko, is part of your family, that he's not some other Lomachenko?"

She looked straight at me. Her voice didn't waver. "Absolutely."

"Had you ever met him before the other day?"

"How could I? He ran off before I was born to join the Revolution. He didn't have much to do with our family after that."

There, I told myself. She'd never even met Papa. Anyone could make up such a tale. But why, then, did she seem so sure? She didn't seem that good of an actress. And it still troubled me how Papa's reaction to her had been so extreme. Anna Mikhailovna's words echoed in my head: *Your father was wise to distance himself from Nadiya, especially if she shares his blood.*

"I didn't mean to cause trouble for your father," she said, as if reading my thoughts. "But I had nowhere to go, no one left."

"What happened to your mother?"

"She died . . . after—"

"What?"

She blinked back tears. "What do you think happened?"

"She died," I said gently. "But how?"

Her eyes blazed. "What kind of fool are you? She starved to death! Everyone in the countryside is dying—we're being starved to death!"

Her certainty frightened me, and I found myself speaking with Papa's voice. "The kulaks are in revolt—"

"Kulaks?" Nadiya hissed. She looked wild-eyed, flushed, almost feverish. "It's not kulaks who are starving us! It's the Soviet government, the Communists—"

"What are you talking about?" I demanded.

She slumped down, stared silently at her lap. Was she suspicious, afraid I would turn her in for this kind of talk, or simply exhausted? Either way, I wanted to end the conversation, too.

"Never mind," I said. "We can talk about it when you're stronger. We have plenty of time."

21

MATTHEW

Leonia, New Jersey, USA
2020

GG's arm flew into the air. "So foolish!"

"You mean for Mila to think they had time?" I asked.

But GG didn't answer. She stared off into the distance, right through me. I didn't ask again. By this time, I knew that when she turned off like this, she was done.

Instead, I went back to my room and googled "causes, Ukrainian famine." Most of the sites I read agreed with GG, not Mila: It was the government that had starved the people of Ukraine to weaken their resistance to Soviet rule. No wonder Stalin hadn't wanted the world to know what was happening in Ukraine. But what really stunned me was how few people even inside the Soviet Union seemed to know what Stalin was doing. Like Mila, they believed what Stalin told them, that there was no famine and that the only hungry people were their kulak enemies.

I called up Dad, but just got his voicemail. It was almost four, which meant it was almost ten in Paris. He didn't usually go to bed that early. He was probably just working on a story. But I couldn't help worrying: What if he wasn't feeling well? It had been a week since he'd toured that Covid ward, and the TV news had reported you could get sick up to ten days after exposure.

I spent the next hour telling myself not to worry. Dad had promised me he'd call every day, but the truth was he was sometimes too busy, so he'd call me the next morning.

This was one of those times. I was barely awake the next morning when *Zelda*'s Lost Woods theme began playing on my phone.

"Hey, Mattie! Sorry I missed you last night. How are you?"

"Okay," I said, scanning his voice for any hoarseness or congestion, relieved when I didn't hear any.

"Well, that's good. An *okay* is like an *excellent* these days. I was tied up with a late-breaking story. What's going on there?"

I was lying in my bed, trying to remember how many periods of online school I'd have to suffer through that morning. But that's not what I wanted to discuss.

"You know how we were talking about the famine in Ukraine the other day?"

"Sure. Walter Duranty and all that. I love that you're interested."

"I was reading about how Stalin lied, not just to journalists from other countries but to his own people. He pretended everything was going great, that there was no famine. People—especially in other parts of the country—believed him. It's crazy!"

"Sure is," Dad said. "But look what's happening now. At least ten thousand people have died of Covid in New York City, but there are still a lot of Americans who think Covid is a myth or some government conspiracy to take away their freedom. It's the same thing we talked about before—the danger of people getting information from unreliable or biased sources."

I hadn't thought about it, but Dad had a good point. I'd heard on the news about Covid deniers and people upset about masks and stay-at-home orders. "They probably just haven't had Covid really hit where they live yet," I said. "They won't be able to deny it when their family and friends get sick."

"Maybe," Dad said. "But disinformation can be really powerful, especially when it gives people a shared enemy to blame for their problems and a sense of pride and belonging."

Like Mila. Face-to-face with GG, an actual victim, she still denied the truth.

"Does that make sense?" Dad asked, interrupting my thoughts.

"Yeah, it does. So how do you change people's minds?"

Dad gave a sad laugh. "That's pretty tough, especially these days. Not enough people take the time to discern what's based on facts and careful reporting and what's not. There's also so much shouting and villainizing. It makes it hard for anyone to admit when they're wrong. They just get defensive."

"I can believe that," I said, thinking again of Mila. "Especially if you've only had one way of looking at the world."

"That's why it's good to get out of your bubble," Dad agreed. "The truth can look very different. It's also why authoritarian regimes like the Soviet Union didn't let their citizens travel—they didn't want multiple viewpoints and debate."

I sighed. "I'm stuck in a bubble now. I can't even get out of this house."

"We're all stuck. But it's not forever, Matthew."

I don't usually sell out one parent to the other, but it was just so easy talking to Dad. "Mom's so strict. She yells at me about everything."

I thought Dad might say something like, *She used to yell at me, too,* but he didn't.

"She's dealing with a lot. I feel badly I can't help her—at least with you."

"Me? She doesn't need help with me!" Not only had he not taken my side, but he'd made me sound like some needy three-year-old.

"Of course," Dad said quickly. "I forget you're an official teenager now. No trouble there."

"Hah-hah," I said sarcastically. "But I'm easy, really. Just give me a Switch. You'll see this summer."

Dad laughed. "I believe you. But try not to be too hard on Mom, okay?"

"Maybe if she's not so hard on me—"

"Mattie—"

"Okay, fine," I harrumphed.

"Now that's the voice of positivity!"

I couldn't help smiling.

"I gotta run, kiddo. Love you."

"Love you too."

But the second I hung up, I felt he'd rushed off the call. Maybe some message from his editor had come in. I had a bunch of texts myself from Josh.

> Got your switch back?

> Our assistant rabbi has covid

> I heard school might be closed until end of year

I tried to reassure myself that even before the pandemic, Josh was full of crazy rumors—he claimed that there was a body hidden beneath the school parking lot speed bump and that Parker Harris, this annoying, shrieky girl in our homeroom, had swallowed a whistle when she was little. But life had become so unimaginably crazy since Covid—I mean, ten thousand dead New Yorkers? School closed down for weeks?—that I couldn't discount this as just another wild Josh rumor. It got me thinking: If school was still closed in June, would camps and beaches stay closed, too? Would trips be canceled?

No way. I'd get to Paris, see Dad; Covid had to burn out by then.

22

HELEN

"Did you put on your cross?" Mom said.

We were walking together down Glenmore Avenue to the midnight Easter mass. Mom's best shawl, the black wool one with scarlet roses and tassels, was draped around her shoulders—she would use it to cover her head when we entered the church. Pop had taken advantage of Peter's dawdling to walk at a slower pace behind us.

"I forgot."

Mom sighed. "I should have reminded you."

I hated to lie, especially since it made her blame herself. These days, every imperfection—Peter's messy hair or my too-short sleeves—seemed to prove to Mom that she couldn't care for us as carefully as she had before. I wished I could tell her that our family had received it, that it had made a difference, but there was still no response. At least the service was by candlelight. My missing cross would be less noticeable in the dim light.

Mom glanced back, checking to see how far away Pop was. Then she lowered her voice. "I ran into Mrs. Zelenko yesterday."

Mrs. Zelenko was always playing Russian love songs on the record player and liked to gossip, especially about other families we knew.

"Oh?" I said, waiting to find out what bit of gossip Mom had learned.

"She told me you came over to talk to Mr. Zelenko about his relatives in Ukraine last weekend. That you were asking a lot of questions—how they were living, whether they had food—then writing it in a notebook."

This was not the gossip I'd hoped for. I couldn't even deny it. Mr. Zelenko was one of the men from the Russian Brotherhood Organization that Mr. Oleynik had told me to talk to. He had been gruff at first, but by the end of our interview had ended up wiping away tears. I wished Mrs. Zelenko hadn't told Mom. She looked concerned.

"I'm collecting stories about the famine," I said.

"Lenachka . . ." Mom hesitated, as if trying to find the right words. "I wish I hadn't told you. You shouldn't talk to people about it—you'll just upset them."

"I'm not upsetting them," I protested. "Anyway, they're already upset."

"Exactly, so you shouldn't risk stirring up trouble for them."

"How would I get them in trouble?"

"It can happen" was all she said.

I didn't understand. But then I remembered her once telling me that back where she came from, it was easy to get in trouble with the government, especially if you expressed your opinion or complained. Even here in America, Mom was always nervous and eager to please around anyone in a position of authority, even Mrs. Weber.

Mom glanced behind her then added, "Besides, think of Pop. He hasn't heard what you've been doing, thank God. Think how it would upset him."

"But he's been worried about his own family there."

"The less he thinks about them, the better," Mom said. "There's nothing to be done. We need to help him regain his strength, Lenachka, not upset him."

Pop's health was a point I could never argue with.

"I won't talk to anyone else," I said.

I could honestly agree to this because Mr. Zelenko had been the last person on my list. I now had nine of our neighbors' and friends' stories recorded in Pop's accounting ledger. Ruth and I were going to meet up next weekend at the library so I could show her. She was right: The stories were powerful. I still didn't plan on sending them to the *New York Times*, but there had been moments when I'd felt tempted. They certainly challenged Mr. Walter Duranty's so-called reporting that no one was starving.

Normally Easter mass was my favorite. During our usual Sunday-morning services, I grew tired of standing (our church is a traditional Orthodox church: no benches at all and only a handful of chairs, which are for the old or sick). But at Easter mass, the standing didn't feel as hard because we each got candles, even the children. We also got to stay up late because it was held at night. In the darkness, the rhythmic chanting of the priest and the floral smell of incense made me feel as if I were in a peaceful dream.

But this Easter, my thoughts kept returning to what Mom had said. Had I been troubling people and making them sad? I hated to think so. Was it better to put those stories away and hope that someday God lets the truth come to light? As the deep bass of the priest's voice rattled through me, I tried to listen for an answer. All I could hear was the lack of one. This was what the church taught: Life was full of suffering but also moments of beauty like this one. It was a mystery we'd never understand.

Faster than I'd ever remembered, the bells thundered overhead. It was midnight. We lit our candles, one to the next, until the church was aglow. Then the priest led us out the door to circle the church three times. The night air felt fresh and cool. I watched Pop, a rare, peaceful expression reflected on his face. I didn't want to disturb it.

After the third turn, the procession stopped, and we blew out our candles. The air was fragrant with waxy smoke, like after a birthday. Then everyone kissed and exchanged the traditional Easter greeting:

"Christ has risen."

"Indeed, he has risen!"

Over and over again, we repeated this to family and friends, embraced them. Brooklyn slept around us, dark and foreign, but there were no strangers here. At home, we'd break the fast with *kulich*, the special Easter cake Mom baked in coffee tins, and *paskha*, a sweet, creamy spread that tasted like cheesecake without the crust. In the morning, we'd meet with our friends to play the egg-cracking game, where we'd smash our dyed Easter eggs together to see whose was strongest.

Love suddenly coursed through me for all of them—Pop and Mom, Mary, Mr. Oleynik, even Mrs. Zelenko, whom I spotted laughing and kissing ahead of us, Mr. Zelenko standing sternly at her side. I didn't want to accept that their suffering was just life and that there was nothing to be done about it. I wanted to make their lives better. But I couldn't do that if I remained silent and afraid and just stuck their stories in a drawer. I had to speak up and send them to the *New York Times*. Mom wouldn't like it, but to change the world maybe you had to upset people, even the ones you loved. In any case, my mind was made up: Stories were powerful, but even more powerful was the act of sharing them. I would write that letter to the editor.

23

HELEN

Brooklyn, New York, USA
1933

"Let's see it," Ruth said.

I opened Pop's old ledger to the page where I had tucked in the letter. I pulled it out slowly, scanning my own writing. Along with my nice smile, Mrs. Weber had said I had nice handwriting—she'd even told Pop that I could be a secretary. Pop had been insulted—he didn't want me ever to have to work. But that was before his heart attack, before Mom had taken not just one, but two jobs, to support us. I wondered whether now he might see the value of my having a skill.

I had written the letter as neatly as I could in the hopes it would make my words seem smarter. But I worried that my pretty cursive was as empty as my smile.

I reluctantly slid the letter over to Ruth. She sat catty-corner to me at one of the long wooden tables in the Arlington Avenue library. She wore a coral-colored dress with a belt and white buttons. "You look nice," I said.

"I came straight from synagogue. I have to go every Saturday, but I'd much rather be here. I'm really glad you decided to write this letter, Helen."

"I don't know," I said, "it's not very good."

"Who cares?" Ruth said. "The important thing is you did it."

She plucked the letter away, started reading it aloud.

"'To the editor of the *New York Times*.'"

I looked around, expecting someone to hush her. But it was a sunny afternoon in late April, and there weren't many people in the library.

"'I read Mr. Walter Duranty's story in the March thirty-first, 1933, edition of the paper and I think it is not accurate.'"

Ruth stopped reading, grabbed my pencil, and began scratching away at my letter.

"What's wrong?" I asked.

Ruth looked up. "You don't need to say, 'I think.' You sound unsure of yourself."

I knew she was trying to help, but the criticism stung.

"I was just trying to be polite."

"Well, don't. They're the ones who got it wrong."

She started writing. I read over her shoulder.

"'To the editor: I read Walter Duranty's March thirty-first, 1933, story about the famine in the Soviet Union and must report that it is not accurate.'"

"Report?" I said. "I'm not a reporter—I mean a real one."

"Sure you are," Ruth said. "You interviewed, what, eight people?"

"Nine," I murmured.

Ruth smiled. "You're more of a reporter than Duranty."

"I'm thirteen years old."

"He doesn't know that!" Ruth turned back to my letter, kept reading.

"'My family and friends have told me that many people are not just hungry but starving. They know this because they receive letters from their families.'"

Ruth's brow furrowed. "You need to be more direct about it. And tell him who you are."

"What do you mean?"

Ruth jotted in the margin of my letter, then read: "'My relatives in Ukraine are starving and have sent us desperate letters begging for food.'

"Then something like: 'We are not the only ones who are receiving these terrible reports. Many of our neighbors and friends have also heard from starving family members. I have gathered their stories to show you that Mr. Duranty was misinformed. There is clearly a famine.'

"How does that sound? Hey—what's wrong?"

I had slumped down in my chair, head in hands. "I can't do this."

"You're doing it," Ruth said. "This is all stuff you've said to me."

I shook my head, imagined how Mrs. Weber would judge my letter. "I can't write—"

"You can't *fight*," Ruth corrected. "That's all I'm doing. I'm making your words fight a little more."

I suddenly felt exhausted.

"I don't want to fight."

Ruth gave a snort. "I saw you pummel two boys in the playground that day you almost pummeled me."

My cheeks burned. I hadn't realized she'd seen me.

"That was different. They were beating up my brother."

Ruth raised an eyebrow. "Was it?"

"I didn't think about it. I just hit. It's not like writing a letter to the most important newspaper in the world and telling them they're wrong."

"What is the *New York Times* going to do? Hit you back?"

"Make me feel stupid," I mumbled.

"How? You're not stupid. This letter's not stupid."

"You don't understand," I said. "You're smart. You don't know what it's like to feel—"

"Stupid? Maybe not. But I know what it's like to feel I'll never fit in. I'm a Jew. I can't stay at certain hotels down south—they refuse to accept 'Hebrews'—or live in certain neighborhoods or join certain clubs. The best universities take only a few Jewish students. Even here in Brooklyn, some kids from the street once spit on me and called me a bad name. But am I less of an American because of what they think? No. I have a right to defend myself and my people, and so do you."

"I'm sorry you're treated that way. It's not right. But I don't like upsetting anyone or making a fuss."

I could hear Mom's voice in my own.

Ruth shrugged. "Give up, then. Pretend you're not who you are. It's easy enough with those blue eyes and fair hair of yours—you could be anything: English, German, Swedish."

This was true. I could fit in like Ruth never could. But fitting in was also hiding, and I knew what she'd think of me if I made such a choice: that I was a coward.

"Look," she continued, "you did all the work: You collected all these people's stories. You wrote a good letter—I just edited it, that's all."

She stood up and handed me the marked-up page. "I have to get home for lunch. But don't beat yourself up, okay?"

"Thanks," I said, but I knew I sounded as half-hearted as my letter.

After she left, I stared at all my crossed-out words and Ruth's own words written above them. Looking at all those changes made me feel bad about myself and angry at her at the same time; I was clearly a lousy writer, but Ruth was such a smarty-pants. Why was she helping me anyway? Maybe she just wanted to see me make a fool of myself. Maybe she was jealous that she couldn't fit in as easily as I could.

But at the exact same time I was having these thoughts I knew they were unfair. I was the one who had asked for her help. Ruth never seemed to take pleasure in anyone's struggles—she never laughed, like Irene sometimes did, when Frankie Terzini stumbled over his reading. She was proud of who she was; she wouldn't hide that even if she could. And I had to admit, her version of the letter *was* more powerful than mine.

I thought about what Ruth had said. I didn't want to run away from who I was—from Pop and Mom, or their families, or the country they had left behind. I loved them. I wanted to fight for them. But I also wanted to fit in. Was there a way to fit in as an American and be myself? Ruth seemed to believe there was, but that I had to fight for it.

Fight for it, I told myself.

I took a deep breath and copied the letter onto a clean sheet of paper, replacing her words with my own but trying to keep the spirit of Ruth's changes—the same sense of fight. This act of rewriting soothed me and, as I made my changes, Ruth's letter once again became mine. I reread my own words, marveling at how grown-up and confident I sounded, then signed my name with a flourish: *Helen Lomachenko.*

I went straight to the post office and handed the envelope with my letter and the nine accounts over to the postal clerk. As his eyes scanned the address—*New York Times*, 229 West 43rd Street, New York, NY—and he stamped it, I stood up straighter. I was no longer the girl who just sat quietly in the back of the room. I was the girl who spoke up. But would it matter? Would the *New York Times* answer me back?

24

MILA

Kyiv, Ukraine, USSR
1933

Papa kept his desk locked, but I knew where he hid the extra key. I knew all the hiding places in our house because I'd spent many hours searching it for chocolates. Papa and Dasha were forced to become ever more creative in their hiding spots, but I always found them. There was no stopping me, especially when I was determined.

The more I'd thought about it, the more farfetched Nadiya's story had seemed. Papa, the son of kulaks? I didn't doubt Nadiya had suffered—she had clearly starved, and I was glad to have saved her from death on the street. But I would have liked her much more if she'd admitted that the whole story of our being cousins was a lie. I was determined now to prove her wrong—all I had to do was find proof: a document from the orphanage or showing Papa was born in Kyiv, where he claimed. I imagined Nadiya finally admitting the truth—that her own kulak parents had made up this fiction, not to mention her ravings about murderous Party doings in the countryside. Though perhaps she truly believed this herself, and I would have to set her straight.

Dasha was doing laundry downstairs—it kept her busy for hours, and she always chased me away, since it involved boiling water and hot irons. I quietly opened the door to Papa's room and tiptoed inside.

Papa didn't like me poking around his room when he wasn't home, but that had never stopped me. Sometimes I came to look at Mama's photo on his bureau; she had a direct stare that Papa said reminded him of my own. Her eyes seemed to follow me now as I crept across the room to his desk and unlocked the desk roller. Lying inside were official reports from the Soviet politburo in Moscow. I was sure they were Top Secret and Very Important, but they interested me less than the drawers where Papa kept his personal correspondence.

One by one, I slid them out and skimmed the letters and documents inside. They were either from other Party officials or Papa's comrades from the Revolution, and none of the documents related to the orphanage or Papa's childhood. The only personal items I discovered were a lock of ash-colored hair—presumably Mama's—and a medal Papa had been awarded after the Revolution for his service, the Order of the Red Banner, which he wore every May Day.

I went through each drawer a second time to be certain I hadn't missed anything. By the time I reached the last, my disappointment had turned to frustration. I yanked the drawer a little too hard. It flew out completely, and that's when I saw that what I had assumed was the back of the drawer was actually a slat. Behind this slat was a second, secret compartment. There was nothing inside. I slid the drawer back, then pulled out the next one. It didn't have a secret compartment. But two drawers up, I found another that did, and this time, there was something wedged inside it.

I pulled it out. It was a tiny square of paper that had been folded over and over to make it as small as possible. Papa rarely talked about his life in the orphanage. His family had been poor, his mother had given him up. Life there couldn't have been easy. But here, perhaps, was some painful memento. Perhaps a document with his parents' names.

I unfolded the square, revealing a single page of paper. I could see right away that this wasn't a document, but a letter. The paper was creased but not yellowed. One side was covered in jagged handwriting.

Dear Lev Stepanovich, it began.

Forgive me for writing, but our situation is desperate. My late husband, your brother Mykola, left us this address.

My first thought was that Nadiya had planted this letter. But how could she have done such a thing? Dasha could have been in on it! But how would they have known I'd go searching through Papa's desk or find the secret compartment? None of this made the least bit of sense; I was like a drowning person, grasping at the rising water, horrified it couldn't hold me up.

I tried to read on, but the words blurred. I felt dizzy. Then I heard the front door open. There was only one person besides Dasha and me who had a key.

I folded up the letter as fast as I could, shoved it into the secret compartment, then slid the drawer back into the desk.

Papa's voice echoed up the stairs.

"Little fox! I'm home."

I frantically surveyed the desk, trying to remember if the papers were arranged the same way I'd found them. I could only hope he wouldn't notice anything out of place. I pulled down the roller. I could hear his footsteps on the stairs. I tried to get the key into the lock, but it wouldn't go in. My hands were shaking. I gave it a frantic shove and in it went. I turned it then yanked it out and scrambled to the bed.

Papa opened the door. His eyebrow twitched, but before he could express any displeasure with my being there, I pointed to Mama's photo.

"We look alike, don't we?"

I smiled up at him, my voice pleasant. It was all an act. Inside my stomach was turning, as if I'd eaten something bad.

Papa's face softened.

"Very much. Although you're even more of a beauty."

And you're a liar, I thought. But I didn't dare confront him. I didn't want him to suspect I'd spoken to Nadiya or helped her. Besides, he'd just deny it, make up some excuse. I heard my voice, calm and from a distance, as if someone else were speaking.

"You're home early," I said.

Papa unbuttoned the top of his *stalinka*. "For once I could escape! And you know where I went? Straight to the store to buy something special for my favorite girl."

I hadn't noticed until now his bulging pocket. He reached inside it and pulled out a bag of Bumble Bears.

Sweetness, cloying sweetness. I looked at them with disgust. But I took them. He would be suspicious if I didn't.

"Thank you, Papa," I said. "I'm going to share them."

Papa looked pleased. I wasn't always so generous. "I'm sure Katya would enjoy that," he said.

But I wasn't thinking of Katya.

"How about a story?" Papa said. "I'll have Dasha bring us tea."

This was too much. I couldn't bear one of his stories, not now. He would make up a world much simpler and happier than the one that existed. It was he who told fairy tales.

"I still have schoolwork, Papa."

"Ah yes, of course, that's very important. Go, smart girl."

I forced a final smile then slipped back to my room, clutching the bag of Bumble Bears in my sweaty fist. I dropped them on my dressing table and sank into the chair in front of it. Then I stared at myself in the large oval mirror.

I looked the same as I had that morning, when I'd brushed my hair for school, but I was now someone else: Papa's family were kulaks, which meant he was a kulak, and I was the child of a kulak. Papa had been right to tell me to trust no one. I remembered how he had nearly hit me when I'd said, *Even you?* Now I realized how close I had been to the truth. The enemy wasn't outside us, but within: *We* were the enemy.

But what was I supposed to do now? Turn in Papa like Dima Demchak's father for concealing his corrupt origins? Hate myself for being the child of a class enemy? I could do neither. All I wanted to do was run straight over to Anna Mikhailovna's and see Nadiya. But there was no way to do that now, with Dasha and Papa home, and I couldn't keep pretending to be sick at Octobrists—my fellow Pioneers would get suspicious, and word would leak out to Dasha. It was time to figure out a better story, one that "couldn't be easily disproven," as Anna Mikhailovna had warned. There was no other way—I would have to involve Katya.

25
MILA

Kyiv, Ukraine, USSR
1933

I stood up, tightened my red Pioneer scarf, and addressed my audience.

"I hereby announce an important agenda item for the Committee of the Motherless Daughters of the Communist Party."

Katya erupted into rousing applause on behalf of herself and the two dozen activist statuettes we had lined up on my desk behind her.

"First Party Secretary, please continue!" she said.

"Thank you, Comrade General Secretary." I waited a beat, as if for the imaginary audience to settle down. "The item in question is a piano recital."

"A piano recital?" she said, looking confused.

I gave her a hard stare to remind her to keep in character.

"As Motherless Daughters, one of our duties is to bring happiness to our wifeless fathers. To that end, I am preparing a surprise recital for Comrade Lomachenko."

Katya clapped. "Bravo!"

I held up a hand. "Our objective is not so easily attained. While Comrade Mikhailovna has agreed to provide extra instruction to help prepare for the recital, one Daria Petrovna Lisko—also known as Dasha—has proven unreliable when it comes to keeping the secrets of Motherless Daughters."

"Traitorous behavior!" pronounced Katya, or rather the General Secretary.

"She is not a traitor," I said. "Simply careless. But for security reasons, the practice sessions for the recital will be held in secret. Daria Petrovna Lisko has been told that the First and General Secretaries will be attending a school May Day committee meeting at that time."

Katya's brow wrinkled. "Wait, did you really tell Dasha we're on a school May Day committee so you could go to secret practices?"

I debated whether to scold her again for falling out of character. But it was important that she understood her role in keeping up this illusion.

"Yes," I said. "This way she won't inform on me to Papa, and I can surprise her, too."

Katya's eyes narrowed. "That day you said you were sick and couldn't help with the Octobrists, were you really with your piano teacher?"

I waggled my eyebrows playfully and grinned. But Katya didn't smile back.

"You shouldn't keep secrets. Pioneers tell each other everything—"

"This isn't a real secret. I just want to surprise Papa with a new song. And I'm telling you now."

Katya pouted. "I don't like lying."

What would she think if I told her all the lies our parents and teachers had told us? It was so tempting to tell her everything I had discovered—about the famine, the Collector, the lifeless arm. But I couldn't tell her Papa was hiding his origins—it was too danger-ous a secret. Anna Mikhailovna's warning about Nadiya—*Don't tell anyone . . . not even your closest friend*—made me guard the truth inside. Anna Mikhailovna likely wouldn't even approve of my tell-ing Katya I was taking extra lessons without Papa's permission. But so long as Katya backed up my story, that we were preparing a sur-prise recital for him, there was little danger. I had to keep seeing Nadiya, and I needed Katya to keep Dasha off my trail.

I sat down beside Katya on my bed. "You're right," I said. "I should have told you. And I don't like lying, either. But isn't there such a thing as lying for good? I'm lying to help someone."

Every word was true. Only Katya didn't know that the someone I was trying to help wasn't Papa.

"I guess so," she said.

"Likely Dasha won't even ask you about it. If she does, you need only to say that yes, we are on a committee. Which is true! The

Committee of the Motherless Daughters of the Communist Party. We must stick together, Comrade."

I threw my arm around her shoulders.

Katya sighed, but she didn't remove my arm.

"Next time tell me before you launch such a scheme," she said. "I *am* General Secretary, which is a rank above you."

I bowed my head. "Your authority is supreme."

Katya grinned. "Might I join you, Comrade, for one of your practices? I could weigh in on the ideological content of your selections—"

"No!"

I hadn't meant to respond so fiercely. Katya looked at me strangely.

I forced a laugh. "I don't want to ruin the surprise. You will also be one of my honored guests at the recital."

Katya's face softened. I knew she'd like the idea of being included. She was always left with Varvara, the housekeeper, even when her father wasn't working.

"But you must keep it a secret, please, until then."

Katya sighed deeply. "Okay. But I wish I could do something to make my papa happy. I can't play piano well like you—"

I was so relieved that she had agreed to help me that I sprang off the bed and clapped my hands together. "You can do something else. Let's think of it!"

After careful discussion, we decided that Katya should write a poem to Comrade Gavrilok and recite it for him. I set up Katya with paper and pen, and she made a fine start of it, titling her work "An Ode to Papa."

But then she just sat there frozen, pen in hand.

"I don't know what to say."

The truth was there was little to praise about Comrade Gavrilok. He was a cold fish—even Papa thought so. It was Katya's mother who had been quick with a laugh, who had always been kind.

"Compare him to the sun, which helps you grow."

Katya jotted this down, looked up at me. "What else?"

"Cars, airplanes—things with speed and purpose!"

"You are so good at this," Katya said enviously.

I smiled at her. But it didn't feel like a compliment. I was my own father's daughter, a master of lies.

26
MATTHEW

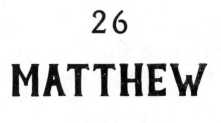

Leonia, New Jersey, USA
2020

"That was a bad idea," I said. "Anna Mikhailovna warned her not to trust anyone, even her best friend."

I expected GG to agree with me, but she just shrugged.

"I feel sorry for Mila. I mean, not as sorry as I do for you. But Mila's whole life was based on a lie."

"She was a fool," GG said.

I was surprised by the coldness in her voice.

"Aren't you being a little hard on her?" I asked. "She did help you."

But she just sighed. "No more today."

I started packing up the diaries and papers, one eye on GG. She was slumped down as if the story had deflated her. I imagined her sitting there after I left, maybe turning on the TV and watching more depressing news. It was barely even three, the sun was shining outside, but Mom was busy again with her Covid stories—I could almost guarantee that she wouldn't emerge until five, when she'd stumble out of her bedroom glassy-eyed and panicked over GG's dinner or the groceries or my homework.

"GG," I said. "Let's take a walk."

She looked back over at me.

"No. Too hard."

But there'd been a beat, a tiny pause that made me think she didn't really mean it.

"Come on, GG, it's a really nice day." I pulled her walker out of the corner, then held out my arm. "And I'll help you. We don't have to go far."

GG studied my arm as if deciding whether it was reliable. Finally, she nodded and grabbed on. She hoisted herself up, and I helped her to the walker.

"Wait," I said. "Let me get something first."

I ran back to the foyer, where Mom kept extra masks, and returned with one for me and one for her. Then I opened the door onto the back deck and helped GG put her mask on. I'd have to help her down a couple of stairs, but I didn't want to risk bringing her out the front in case Mom heard us. She hadn't been wild about me taking GG for a walk. But Helen hadn't listened to her mom, either.

We moved so slowly—GG pushing her walker inch by inch—that it took us ages just to reach the front sidewalk. I finally understood why Mom felt she never had enough time to take out GG—it was more of an expedition than something you did during a quick ten-minute break.

I stayed right next to her, calling out potentially dangerous cracks in the sidewalk, keeping a protective watch for bikes, joggers, delivery people, and kids walking dogs. I wasn't sure how fast I could move her out of the way if someone got too close or a dog jumped at her—I was worried that a Chihuahua could have knocked her down. But GG didn't seem concerned, and after a while, when the only person we saw was a jogger who crossed the street to avoid us, I started to relax.

GG stopped periodically to look up at the sky or point at a neighbor's tulips. I hadn't paid much attention to the sky and flowers before. The few times Mom had dragged me out she'd kept zigzagging all over the street to avoid other people and snapping at me to keep up with her. It seemed kind of miraculous that spring was still happening, as if it hadn't gotten the memo that Covid had canceled everything. New leaves were unfurling on the trees and there were some bushes beginning to bloom with purple flowers. GG steered me over to one of them and pulled down her mask.

"You should probably keep that up," I said.

But she ignored me, stuck her face into the bush. "Smell," she commanded.

I took a quick look around—no one was there—and pulled down my mask. I didn't even have to plunge my head into the bush like she had. The blooming flowers had a powerfully sweet smell.

GG watched me with a rare smile.

"Lilac. Anna loved lilac."

For a moment, I thought she was talking about Anna Mikhailovna before I realized she was referring to her daughter, Mom's mom. A piece clicked together.

"Did you name her after Anna Mikhailovna?" I asked.

GG nodded.

"Because she saved you," I said. "Did Grandma Anna know the story, know who she was named after?"

"No."

"Why not? You didn't want her to know about the famine?"

Just then, a shout interrupted us.

"Matthew!"

I could have sworn GG looked relieved, but all I felt was the opposite emotion. Mom was running up the street toward us. I'd never seen her move so fast. She covered our block-long trek in about five seconds.

"*What* are you doing?" she panted, pulling up in front of us.

I quickly cycled through my options—defiant, innocent, sassy—and decided to go with innocent.

"I'm taking GG for a walk."

Her eyes bugged out at me. "Matthew, what are you thinking? I told you not to take her out. You're not even wearing your masks!"

I pawed at my face, realized I'd forgotten to pull my mask back up; even more important, GG's was still dangling from her ear.

"We just had them down for a second!"

But I knew I was toast. Mom's face was red. I braced myself for whatever was about to come out of her mouth.

Just then, GG grabbed Mom's arm and pointed to the bush. "Smell!"

"GG," Mom said. Her voice quivered, but she didn't full-out lose it like I'd been expecting. "I don't have time."

I should have kept my mouth shut—GG had defused the Mom bomb—but I saw the perfect opportunity to defend myself.

"I know! That's why I was trying to help."

"Well, it wouldn't help if she got Covid, would it?" Mom snapped. "Or fell and broke her hip! You can't just make decisions like this without consulting me!"

"My idea," GG said.

Mom looked from GG to me, let out an exasperated sigh. I could tell she wasn't buying it—GG was no master of lies like Mila—but the fight went out of her.

"Go home and unload the dishwasher, Matthew. *That* would be helpful."

I shot a grateful glance at GG. Then I got out of there before Mom could work herself back up. I had forgotten how fast I could move when I wasn't with GG, but all that speed didn't make me feel better. Mom was always treating me like I couldn't do anything right. Sometimes I felt like it wasn't just Covid that was ruining her life—that it was me, too. I couldn't wait to get to Paris and Dad. Summer couldn't come soon enough.

I had the dishwasher unloaded long before the two of them made it back. I lay on my bunk bed with the notebook writing up the day's developments. But what I kept getting stuck on was how GG had named her own daughter after someone whose existence she refused to tell her about. You'd think she'd want her family to know about the people who'd saved her. Was what had happened to her in the famine just too hard to talk about? Or had she kept silent because of what had happened to Mila?

27
MILA

Kyiv, Ukraine, USSR
1933

The next day, I told Katya I had a practice session and Dasha that I had a May Day committee meeting and went after school to see Nadiya. Anna Mikhailovna met me at the door.

"Where does Dasha think you are?" she asked.

"Here," I said. "I told her you'd requested I work on duets with a few of the other students. She has errands to run, so we made a deal that I would meet her out front in an hour. She doesn't like climbing the stairs."

It frightened me how easily the lies came—Dasha's distaste for the stairs was the only crumb of truth. I especially didn't like lying to Anna Mikhailovna, but I knew she wouldn't approve of my involving Katya. As it was, she considered my story with the same hard look she wore when listening for mistakes.

"I suppose you could work with a few of them," she finally said.

"But let Dasha bring it up herself," I said quickly. "No need to make a big show of it." I couldn't have Dasha thinking I was at school on the May Day committee *and* practicing duets at Anna Mikhailovna's.

Anna Mikhailovna's eyes narrowed. Did she sense my lie? If so, she didn't say. "Very well."

"Can I go see Nadiya now?"

I was eager to slip past her down the hall, but she blocked my way.

"Wait"—she lowered her voice—"about Nadiya."

Fear coursed through me. "Is something wrong?"

"No . . . Yes. She's getting back her physical strength. But I don't think you understand how much she's suffered. You've had such a privileged life, Mila. She's lost everything and everyone. You can't force her to see the world as you do—"

"But I don't see the world that way anymore," I interrupted. "I'm changing."

Anna Mikhailovna smiled. "I know you are, Mila. A kind heart makes change possible. Just try to remember that Nadiya's not a tool of your awakening but a human being whose soul has been injured."

"I understand," I said, and I did. "Today, I just want to give her some chocolate."

Anna Mikhailovna reached out, stroked my hair. In all the years, she'd been my teacher, she'd never caressed me like this, almost like a mother. "Go ahead, Milachka."

Nadiya chewed her Bumble Bear with her eyes closed. It reminded me of the way some people listen to music, one sense overcome by the other. There was no danger of entering into this state of bliss with Anna Mikhailovna's current student, Vera, banging away. But at least the racket gave us cover to talk.

"You have a sweet tooth, like me," I said.

Nadiya nodded with a satisfied "Mmmm."

This pleased me, and not just because we were alike, as cousins should be. I was resolved to follow Anna Mikhailovna's counsel and show her only kindness.

"You can have the whole bag," I said.

She opened her eyes, studied me. I let myself see it now, how they were the same shape and color as my own.

"I couldn't do that," she said. "I'd get sick. Besides, I want to share them with Anna Mikhailovna and Olga Stepanovna."

How generous she was! What a darling! But the more I loved her, the angrier I was at Papa. He had made me believe I was alone in the world, save for him. To think I had a cousin all this time, one around my own age!

"I never even asked, how old are you?"

"Thirteen," she said.

"Just turned it?"

"In January."

"I'll be thirteen in November," I said. "I figured you were younger, but I'm just taller."

"It's hard to grow when you have nothing to eat."

Her rebuke stung. I hadn't meant to insult her or raise the subject of the famine.

"That'll change now," I said, trying to make up for my thoughtless remark. "Olga Stepanovna is buying milk at the Torgsin, and I'm going to bring you Bumble Bears every time I visit. We'll fatten you up!"

Nadiya smiled, but her eyes were knowing and sad, like she was years older than me, not just a few months.

"What?" I said.

"I don't know how long I'll be staying."

"What do you mean? Has Anna Mikhailovna said anything?"

Nadiya shook her head. "I know she's made inquiries. I heard her tell Olga Stepanovna. They won't send me to an orphanage, but there are no other options."

An image of the Collector and the dead child's arm flashed in my head. "Of course they won't send you to an orphanage! Olga Stepanovna treats you like her own granddaughter; Anna Mikhailovna adores you. They'll keep you here."

Nadiya's voice dropped to a whisper. "I don't want to get them in trouble."

My stomach tightened at the thought, but I pushed it away.

"Nonsense! Everyone is careful. They won't get in trouble."

"I've written our relatives in America to let them know what's happened. Perhaps they can take me."

I nearly fell off my seat. "What?! We have family in America?"

Nadiya nodded. "Our fathers' eldest brother immigrated there before the War."

First we were kulaks, now Papa had family in America . . . What next?! I half expected to find out that Papa had fought against the Revolution instead of for it.

"You can't go to America," I said. "We'd never see each other again! Besides, could they even come take you? Anna Mikhailovna is happy to keep you—I know her, I can tell. Enough of this talk. I only wish I had known about you sooner. Two of us only children, we could have been like sisters! I would have liked that."

I waited for her to say she would have liked having me as a sister, too. But she didn't even smile. Instead, she pointed across the room to a pack of cards on the bed. "Do you know Trust/Don't Trust? Would you like to play?"

"Sure," I said. I reminded myself of what Anna Mikhailovna had told me, how Nadiya's soul was injured. I shouldn't have mentioned her old life. But it was still hard not to take the rejection personally.

Trust/Don't Trust was a popular game. Dasha and I played it often. The deck was split between players, and the first player put up to three cards facedown and named their rank—for example, queen, king, ace. Then the second player had to say whether she believed this or not. If the first player was found to be lying, she had to take back her cards. If she was telling the truth, the second player had to take the cards and put down the same rank. The loser was the player left holding the most cards. I almost always beat Dasha, who was a poor liar.

We moved to the bed, and I set up the cards. I wanted to reassure her that all would be well, but the game distracted me. I had expected to win easily. I had even wondered if I should throw the game to lift Nadiya's spirits and make up for my blunders. But early on, she called several of my bluffs, and the ones I called on her were wrong.

"Why are you so good at this?" I demanded as my cards piled up. I kept my voice playful, but I didn't like losing.

"You have an open face," she said.

"Not at all! Most people can't beat me."

"Maybe I sense your feelings because we're cousins."

A tingle of joy replaced my irritation. Maybe she didn't want us to be like sisters, but she still felt our connection. "That must be it," I said.

She beat me, but after this I didn't mind as much.

By the time we'd finished our game, the piano lesson had ended. I could hear Anna Mikhailovna closing the door behind noisy Vera.

"Do you play piano?" I asked.

"No. Our family didn't have one. Besides, I'm not musical."

"Would you like to hear me play?"

I wanted to impress her. I admit that. She had been so much better at Trust/Don't Trust.

"Of course."

She let me take her hand and lead her into the studio. Anna Mikhailovna was putting sheet music back into her leather file.

"Might I play for Nadiya, before I go?" I asked her. "Just for a few minutes, a quick piece?"

Anna Mikhailovna's gaze fell on our hands, clutched together. "Of course," she said with a smile.

I waited until Nadiya had settled beside me on the bench. Then I started to play, not Kabalevsky or any of the bold Soviet marches, but a new Tchaikovsky piece that Anna Mikhailovna had given me. It was called "Sweet Dreams," and it was the next song in *Children's Album* after "Baba Yaga." It was a gentle waltz in C major, meant to soothe the listener after the frantic minor chords of "Baba Yaga."

I could feel Nadiya's thin body leaning against mine as I played. This time, I was the one who closed my eyes, letting the melody run through my fingers. Anna Mikhailovna fell silent, I couldn't even hear the rustle of the sheet music she'd been putting away.

I played the last few bars, slowly and gently. Then I opened my eyes and turned to Nadiya, expecting a smile and applause. But her eyes brimmed with tears.

"What have I done? I've upset you!"

She shook her head, denying what I could plainly see. "It's just . . . very beautiful. Who wrote it?"

"Tchaikovsky," I said.

"You played it well," Anna Mikhailovna said. "With true feeling."

This was high praise, but I was still sorry. "I should go."

Nadiya wiped her eyes, stood up. "I'll come with you to the door."

I retrieved my coat. In the hall, out of earshot of Anna Mikhailovna, Nadiya pulled me close.

"What changed your mind?" she whispered.

I shook my head, not comprehending.

"You found something," she said. "Something that made you believe me."

We were no longer playing a game, but she could still see my hand. There was no point in pretending.

"A letter from your mother to my father."

"He kept it?"

I'd been so angry at Papa that I hadn't even considered the strangeness of this. He could easily have burned or destroyed the letter. Why *had* he kept it?

"Some part of him must care," I said.

I wanted to believe this. But it also made sense, especially when I thought of Papa's extreme reaction to Nadiya showing up at our door: What if all that anger was really guilt?

Nadiya's eyes flashed. "Then it's even worse he did nothing."

But this, too, was right. To know you were doing the wrong thing and to do it anyway . . . I looked down, ashamed for him, ashamed of myself.

"I'm sorry I didn't believe you," I said.

Nadiya waved away my apology. "You helped me, even before you believed me. You're a good person, Mila. One I'm glad to know."

With this, she kissed my cheek. It was at that moment I swore I would protect her till my dying day.

28

MATTHEW

"Wait a second," I said. "Helen's mom said that her aunt and *cousins* had nothing to eat. That means you couldn't have been an only child!"

GG winced, said nothing.

She's lost everything and everyone.

Anna Mikhailovna's words took on a new meaning.

No wonder GG had called Mila a fool. She had just assumed.

"How many of you were there?" I asked.

GG opened the folder titled HELEN'S ORAL HISTORY and thumbed through the pages. Then she handed a section to me.

29

HELEN

Brooklyn, New York, USA
1933

*D*ear Miss Lomachenko, *you have ably shown up the errors of* Mr. Duranty's *reporting. Have you ever considered a career in newspapers?*

Dear Miss Lomachenko, we have decided to take away Mr. Duranty's big prize and give it to another reporter who has brought the truth to light: you.

"Helen!"

Peter elbowed me in the side.

I snapped back to reality; we were walking home from school. It was a warm Friday afternoon in early May, and East New York was a busy hive of kids and families, babies squalling from prams, the El rattling over Pitkin Avenue. I smiled at my dreams of glory. But it felt good to have them.

"What?" I said to Peter.

"I said, I'll race you home."

Peter just wanted to run and play. Life was simpler for him. A few months ago, I might have envied him. He knew nothing about the famine or our family's desperate situation or Walter Duranty. But now I felt the same impulse I imagined Pop had felt for me: to keep his life that way, to protect him from all that fear and sadness.

"Go!" I said.

I took off running.

"Wait, I wasn't ready—!"

I could hear his footsteps behind me. My unbuttoned cardigan blew open, and my satchel bounced against my back. I darted around old ladies, ignoring their annoyed glances. The wind was in my hair, and I was certain it looked a mess. But I didn't care. I slowed down to make sure Peter made it safely across the intersection then raced ahead to beat him up the steps of our stoop. Laughing, I flung open the door to our foyer.

Peter barreled into me from behind. We were both panting.

"I won," I said.

"You didn't give me a chance! You started before I was ready!"

I tickled him until he fell down.

"Stop! Stop!" he gasped between giggles.

I hauled him to his feet, gave him a gentle shove toward the stairs. "Go on, I've got to check the mail."

"You're always checking the mail," he said. "I bet you get love letters!"

I made as if to grab him, and he shot up the stairs singing, "Helen's got a sweetheart" and making kissing noises.

"And you've got a sweetheart, too!" I yelled after him. "Mrs. Zelenko! I heard her tell Mom how handsome you are."

Peter gave a shriek of horror. Mrs. Zelenko was at least forty and as stout as a *kulich*, the round Easter cake.

"Shhh!" I said. But I couldn't help laughing.

The foyer seemed particularly dark after the bright sunlight, but I navigated automatically to our mailbox and shoved in the key. It had been two weeks since I'd sent off my letter to the *New York Times*. Even though I knew the editor might not write back at all, I still had hope.

I reached in and pulled out three envelopes. The first two were addressed to Pop. But the third . . .

It was addressed to me.

But it wasn't from the *New York Times*. The stamps were from the Soviet Union, and the name on the envelope was my Russian name: Yelena Lomachenko. It had been forwarded from our old address.

My breath quickened. This could mean only one thing: The cross! My aunt had received it! She was writing to thank me!

Just then, I noticed the return address: Kyiv.

Why was she writing from Kyiv? I had sent my cross to Pop's village, Bila Tserkva. I tore open the envelope and pulled out a one-page letter. The handwriting was different from my aunt Nastya's. I slowly translated the words.

"No," I whispered. "No, no, no."

30

HELEN

Brooklyn, New York, USA
1933

"You can't tell Pop!" Mom said. "Please, Lenachka, I'm begging you—"

Mom clasped my hands, her voice just above a whisper even though the door to my room was closed. Pop was napping in his armchair, and Peter had gone to play outside. The thimble on her index finger pressed into my palm—in her rush to follow me, she had forgotten to take it off.

"But we have to get Nadiya," I said. "We have to bring her here—"

Mom shook her head. "It's not possible—"

"Yes, it is! Pop was trying. He went to see a lawyer to try to bring them all. Mr. Oleynik told me so!"

"But nothing came of that, did it?" Mom asked, her eyes boring into mine. "Besides, what money do we have to pay a lawyer now?"

"We'll figure something out—"

"No! You can't tell Pop any of this. It'll kill him, Lena. Not even about the cross. If he notices, tell him I made you give it to me. I'll tell him I sold it to pay the bills. You shouldn't have lied to me."

"But Nadiya? What about Nadiya?" I demanded.

Mom let go of my hands, looked down at her own calloused ones. "We've done what we can for her."

"How can we not tell him what happened? It's his family!"

Mom's face hardened. "What good would it do to tell him this terrible news now? There's nothing to be done."

Mom sat down heavily on Peter's bed.

"You don't know what life is like where Pop and I come from, how you can't change it, how so many things are just . . . fate."

Soodba. I had known the Russian word for *fate* for as long as I could remember because Mom and her friends used it so often. When something awful happened to someone, it was *soodba.* You couldn't fight it. You just had to accept it. But people in America weren't like that—they didn't accept the way things were; they tried to change them. I was an American.

"No!" I said. "We can't just abandon her."

My voice was rising.

"Shh!" Mom said.

"It's not what Pop would want!" I yelled.

Mom leapt to her feet. A flush of color rose up her neck. "Only you know what's best for him, eh?! You, who upset him right before . . ."

The stricken look on her face immediately told me she wanted to take it back, but it was too late. I knew where she'd been going.

"So that's what you really think—that it's my fault Pop had his heart attack! You thought it all along, even when you told me it wasn't!"

My own chest ached with the hurt of it. She had lied to me that night in the kitchen.

"No . . . that's not what I meant . . . it's just . . ." Mom put her hand over her temples, winced. "Why do you have to be so difficult?"

"I'm trying to do what's right!" I screamed.

I ran past her, flung open the door, and nearly barreled straight into Pop. He must have heard me coming, though, because he grabbed my shoulders before I could fully knock into him. We stared at each other for a second, then he drew me into his chest and held me tight.

I couldn't stop my tears, even if I'd wanted to.

"I'm sorry I made you have a heart attack!" I said in between big gulps and sobs. "And I'm sorry about your family in Ukraine—"

"Quiet, quiet," Pop said, his voice gentle. "You didn't make me have a heart attack. Mom is just exhausted. The poor woman works constantly."

Through the open door, I could hear Mom weeping.

Pop straightened up, looked me squarely in the eye.

"What is this letter? What have you heard?"

I hesitated, glanced back toward the bedroom.

"Go on, Lenachka," Pop said. "Tell me."

"It's from Nadiya, your brother's daughter." I pulled the letter from my pocket and handed it to Pop.

"Sit down, Vanya, sit down," Mama called to him from the bedroom.

But Pop didn't sit down. He stood and silently read Nadiya's letter. I watched his blue-gray eyes dart left and right, his shoulders slump. I edged toward him, afraid he might collapse. Mom quietly emerged from the bedroom and took up position beside him, clearly fearing the same. His hand finally fell to his side, the letter still clasped inside. But it wasn't her he turned to. It was me.

"You sent them your cross."

I tensed, awaiting his anger, but his voice was soft, wistful almost. I nodded.

He touched my cheek. "Smart girl."

The moment I had so long dreamed of had finally come. But I felt no satisfaction from Pop's praise.

"I didn't save them, Pop. Aunt Nastya, the boys—" My voice cracked. I imagined Peter starving. That sweet little laugh.

Pop took my chin in his hand. "Nadiya," he said. "You saved her."

"She's not safe. She says she's in Kyiv, with kind people but in a temporary situation. We need to get her out."

Pop marched into his bedroom and closed the door.

For a few minutes, neither of us spoke. Finally, Mom shot me a pained look then rushed over and knocked softly. "Vanya, it's me. May I come in?"

"Wait!" ordered Pop from the other side of the door.

I sank onto the couch, feeling Pop's grief as if it were my own. Perhaps Mom was right. Perhaps I should have protected him. It was too late now. If he was sprawled on the bed, clutching his chest, it was my fault—no matter what Pop had said.

Just then, the bedroom door opened, and Pop stepped out dressed in his best suit, the one he wore to church.

"Where are you going?" Mom asked.

He strode across the living room to the coatrack and grabbed his hat. "To Manhattan."

Mom looked at him as if he was mad. But I broke into a grin.

"You're going to the lawyer!"

"Right now?" Mom asked.

It was clear from her tone that she didn't like the idea of Pop going all the way to Manhattan.

"Why not?" Pop said.

Mom hesitated; Pop heard the same worry in her pause that I did.

"I'll be fine," he said. "I'll take Lenachka with me."

I sprang to my feet. "I'm ready!"

Mom looked from me to Pop, shook her head. "We don't have the money—"

"I'll worry about that," Pop said. "Come, Lenachka."

I scrambled for my shoes. Maybe it was just the suit and his freshly combed hair, but Pop didn't look weak anymore. He certainly didn't sound it. Pop and I were a team. If there was a way to save Nadiya, we would find it.

31

MILA

Kyiv, Ukraine, USSR
1933

"It's beautiful, isn't it?" I said.

Nadiya and I stood hand in hand on the viewing platform of the bell tower, gazing out over the green roofs and golden domes of Pechersk Lavra. There was no spot that made me prouder of my native city than this one. The medieval monastery overlooked the Dnieper, the great river that ran through Kyiv. It was a sunny April afternoon, less than a week before May Day, and its gold-domed cathedrals glowed radiantly against the deep blue water below.

"Like a fairy tale come to life," Nadiya agreed.

A brisk wind blew her fair hair around her face—it was fuller now and resembled my own. Over the past month, she'd even grown. We looked more alike. "Two boots of a pair," Olga Stepanovna called us.

"I'm glad Anna Mikhailovna let us come," I said.

After nearly a month in the women's care, Nadiya was strong enough to see a bit of the city. We'd argued that the day was too glorious to spend locked up inside. Anna Mikhailovna had resisted our pleas for an adventure, but Olga Stepanovna had taken our side: "The child could use some fresh air, some color in her cheeks."

Anna Mikhailovna had finally relented but made us promise not to go to Mariinsky Park or Lypky, but somewhere farther, where there was little chance of my running into Dasha or Papa or anyone from school. That's when it'd hit me: We could take the tram to Pechersk Lavra, climb the bell tower.

"Do you want to go down and take a quick look at the museums?" I asked.

After it closed the monastery, the Party had designated Pechersk Lavra a historic site and turned the various buildings into cultural museums. But Nadiya made no reply. She just leaned against the stone parapet. I wondered if she was tired—there was no need to go to the museums, too; the view itself was enough. But before I could say that, she leaned in close.

"What do you think happened to the monks?"

According to one of the exhibits at the museum, monks had lived in the caves beneath the monastery for nearly a thousand years until 1929. But I'd never concerned myself with this question.

"Perhaps they have real work now," I said. "On a collective farm or in a factory."

"More likely they were shot."

I looked around, but there was no one to overhear her. There were only a few people on the other side of the parapet, and the wind swallowed our voices. Still, I found myself repeating what I'd been taught.

"The church enslaved people with religion, made the peasants accept suffering as their lot."

Nadiya rolled her eyes. "And now the peasants don't suffer?"

I knew what Papa would say to this. As angry as I still was with him, his voice was always easy to hear inside my head. *The only ones who suffered were kulaks who deserved their suffering. They were capitalists, trying to exploit the poor and revive the old regime.* But it was preposterous to accuse Nadiya of any of this.

"Are you religious, then?" I asked. "You believe in God?"

I was certain she did, like Dasha, who kept an icon hidden in her room. But her answer surprised me.

"There's no God. I've seen proof of that."

Nadiya looked out over the golden domes and the river. Over my past visits, I hadn't pushed her to talk about what had happened back in her village. Instead, we'd read Anna Mikhailovna's fairy-tale books and gorged ourselves on Bumble Bears. We'd muffled our laughter at Dima, Anna Mikhailovna's most hopeless and tone-deaf student, or played Trust/Don't Trust. I figured she'd tell me her story when she was ready. But maybe I was the one who hadn't been ready to hear it.

"Please tell me what happened to you," I said.

Nadiya swung around to face me. "I already did! The whole countryside is dying, Mila! The Communists are starving everyone!"

This time I didn't argue. "How?" I asked.

Nadiya hesitated. Her face was pinched with anguish.

"Tell me," I pressed.

Nadiya took a deep breath, as if to steel herself.

"I told you how the authorities arrested Papa. After that, they came back and threatened to arrest Mama. They said she was a kulak, too, unless she agreed to give up our land and join the collective farm. What could she do? She was all alone with three children to feed—"

A sickening feeling came over me.

"Wait, you have siblings?"

Nadiya stared out over the Dnieper. Her voice trembled. "Mykola and Antin, my little brothers."

"I didn't realize—"

I had just assumed she was an only child, like I was. How careless I had been, how unthinking! I wanted to ask what had happened to them, but at the same time I didn't.

Nadiya didn't give me a chance. She forged ahead with her story.

"They dragged off our horse, wagon, and plow, and Mama went to work on the collective farm—"

"The right decision," I said, hoping praise could make up for my terrible error. "The State takes care of those who work—"

Nadiya gave a snort. "We were taken care of, all right!"

"The collective feeds honest workers," I insisted. I wasn't even sure why I was defending the Party, because I had lost faith in it myself. But I felt almost frantic about it.

Nadiya glared at me. "Would you stop acting like you know everything, Mila! All you know are your father's lies."

My face burned. *You're the one lying, trying to sabotage the future,* I thought. But this was Papa's voice, a liar's voice. I pushed it away. "I'm sorry. I'm listening."

"Good! Because this is what the State gave her. A single bowl of soup and a slice of bread each day. All four of us had to share it. You try surviving on that!"

We'd always had an entire loaf of bread each day. I often ate two bowls of Dasha's borscht all by myself in a single sitting.

"Luckily, we had our vegetable garden," she continued, "and we still had Zorka, our cow. But people in our village, especially those who couldn't work at the collective or had large families and no way to add to what little the collective gave them, were beginning to starve. Our neighbor, a kind old man who used to give us plums from his tree, collapsed and died in the street. The Hurenko children, who my brothers used to play with, went around the village begging for food, their bellies swelled up—"

"The Party saw this?" I interrupted. "They didn't help?"

"Mila, you still don't get it! The Party set up watchtowers with armed guards to protect the wheat fields. They had orders to shoot anyone who tried to take even a stalk! When it was time for the harvest, they brought workers from the city to load every last kernel onto carts. Then they drove all our grain to the railway station and sent it away."

I felt desperate even imagining this situation.

"Surely they left you something?"

Nadiya gave a hard laugh. "Not only did they leave us nothing, they kept taking! One night, a group of Party activists barged into our house. They complained that our village hadn't given enough grain to the State, that we must be hiding it. They tore through the house like madmen looking for any bit of food as 'proof.' The boys and I were terrified. We were afraid they were going to arrest Mama, that we'd never see her again, like Papa. We huddled around her while they pulled up the floorboards, even searched up the chimney. One of them had a long metal pole that he jabbed into Zorka's haystack looking for hidden bread."

"Are you sure these men were from the Party?" I asked. "That they weren't just thieves?"

"They were both," Nadiya snapped. "Friends in the next village reported the same—tugboat brigades, they called them, barging in with long metal poles, searching for bread."

Maybe these were simply local Party leaders who had gone too far. But why, then, had no one stopped them?

"Did you know any of them?"

"They were strangers, sent from the cities," Nadiya said. "The first time, they found nothing and left us alone, but the second time—"

Her eyes filled with tears.

"What did they do?" I asked in alarm.

"Again they found nothing—Mama was smart enough to bury what food we had in a ditch behind the house. But they said she needed to pay a tax to make up for the missing grain. When they told her how much, Mama gasped. 'I'm a widow,' she said. 'I don't have that kind of money!'

"'We'll take the cow, then,' the man with the long metal pole said.

"'You can't take her!' Mama protested. 'We'll starve!'

"But the men ignored her, marched toward the barn.

"I ran ahead of them to Zorka, threw my arms around her neck. I was the one who milked her every day. I talked to her like a friend. She looked at me with her big brown eyes. She knew we were both doomed.

"After they took Zorka, Mama did everything she could to save us. We dug up rotten potatoes and made them into pancakes and soup. We peeled bark off the trees and boiled it into a paste. We foraged for mushrooms and made bread out of acorns. We caught frogs, mice. But it wasn't enough. We grew thinner, our stomachs bloated. Mykola was nine, Antin five, but they began to resemble little old men, their faces wrinkled."

Their father had been a kulak. He had refused to join the

collective farm. I heard Papa's voice, smoothing it over, trying to make the horror justifiable. But he couldn't, especially now that I knew that *they* were really *us*.

Nadiya's voice dropped to a whisper, her eyes found mine.

"You would have loved them, Mila. Antin had hair like a duck's. It stood straight up. He was always getting into trouble. He loved cherries—he would climb our cherry tree, come in for dinner with his shirt stained with juice. Mykola was quiet. He could watch ants marching for hours. He measured the water of a melting icicle one winter to know how much was inside it. He loved to sled. Winter used to be a lovely time in our village. Ivanko, our neighbor, had a hill; we'd sled down it . . ."

Nadiya fell quiet. I wondered if she was imagining sledding with her brothers. I could almost imagine it myself: Antin's shouts of delight, Mykola's head turned up to watch the snowflakes swirling out of a gray sky, the three of them intertwined on a single sled and streaming down Ivanko's hill, rosy-cheeked, bits of snow sticking to their pale hair. Then I imagined her knowing that this would never happen again.

"Oh, Nadiya," I said softly.

She took a deep breath, shook her head, then grasped the railing, as if to steady herself.

"This past winter, everything was different. People stayed inside, away from one another, hiding what little food they had. The village was absolutely silent. Usually, even in wintertime, you'd hear a dog barking or the clop of horses' hooves. But people had eaten all the cats and dogs and horses, and even the birds."

I couldn't help recoiling at the thought of people eating their pets.

Nadiya's eyes flashed. "You can stand there and make a face, but if you had been there, you would have done it, too. We were starving!"

"Forgive me," I murmured, but I couldn't shake off my horror.

"Mama thought about leaving, taking us to Kyiv or north to Russia, where people said there was no famine. But it was impossible to buy train tickets, and the new system of passports made it illegal to leave. Mama traded her wedding ring for some bread at the Torgsin shop in Bila Tserkva, walking ten miles each way through the snow. But we quickly devoured the loaves she brought home, and she had nothing else to trade.

"We were so hungry, Mila! We had no energy to play, to work, to do anything, even cry. Just lie there in a stupor and think about food. Mama and I ate less, gave the boys more, but it still wasn't enough. They were younger, weaker—"

Nadiya began to sob. I rushed to embrace her.

"A-Antin died first," she choked out. "He always slept next to me. February ninth, I woke up . . . He was already cold. I screamed. But what could Mama do? She closed his eyes, made the cross over him. Mykola was too tired to cry. The next evening, he died in Mama's arms."

By this time, I was crying, too. These boys, Antin and Mykola, were my cousins, my flesh and blood. And Papa had done nothing but turn his back on them.

"I'm sorry," I whispered. "I'm sorry."

"For what? The State starved our family, murdered them!" Nadiya said. "What could you have done, even as a child of privilege? Nothing!"

But Papa was the State. And I had been eating chocolates while my cousins starved. I had a sudden crazy urge to run off to Bila Tserkva with all the food I could carry. But I'd be stopped, maybe even arrested. Nadiya was right—there was nothing I could do. Or almost nothing.

"Someday, will you show me their graves?" I whispered.

"That's the thing—" Nadiya's voice broke. "We couldn't even bury them properly! No one had the strength to dig graves, so we buried them in a common one. Mama wasn't right after that. She hardly ate, giving me what scraps we had left. 'Lomachenko,' she said one night with a bitter laugh. 'Even our name means *scrap*.'"

Nadiya's eyes met mine. "You know that, don't you? *Lom* is a scrap."

"I'd never thought about it," I said.

I'd never thought about any of this.

"One night, she told me about your father, how she'd written him in the fall, begging for help, but she hadn't heard back."

This was the letter I'd found in Papa's desk. But I didn't say it.

"She also showed me letters from Papa's older brother in America. He was kind, sent us some money for food through the Torgsin last fall, even spoke of wanting to bring us to America. But then he, too, fell silent. She made sure I had his address, though.

"I knew why she was telling me all this. Before the famine, an orphan would never have been left alone; a relative or neighbor would take them in. But now everyone was desperate for their own survival.

"One morning, she didn't get up, just lay on the oven, where we made our beds in winter. It was barely warm. We had no firewood—we were burning bits of furniture and thatch from the roof.

"'Mama, please,' I begged her. 'Get up.'

"'Nadiyka,' she said, her voice hoarse. She directed me to her wedding chest, had me pull out a nightgown.

"'It arrived after the boys . . .' Her voice drifted off, she still couldn't talk about their deaths. 'It's from your cousin in America, Yelena. Pull open the hem.'

"I did as she instructed. Inside was a small gold cross.

"'Why didn't you show me sooner?' I exclaimed. 'I could take this to the Torgsin! Get us bread. I'll leave today!'

"'No!' Her voice became sharp, stronger than I'd heard it in days. 'Take it to the Torgsin after I die. Then go to Kyiv. Find your uncle; beg him for help. Once he sees you, he won't turn you away.'

"'You're not going to die!' I insisted. 'We can go to Kyiv together.'

"'I don't have the strength,' she said. 'You'll have a better chance without me.'

"By this time, we were both crying. I rested my head on her bony chest. Her cold fingers touched my hair. 'My good, clever girl,' she murmured."

Tears ran down my face as I pictured this. I no longer even felt pride in my own actions. I was just the latest in a line of saviors, from my American cousin, who'd figured out a clever way to send help, to my aunt, who'd given her own life.

"When did she die?" I asked.

"Two nights later. The burial brigade tossed her onto a cart of bodies and laid her in the same common grave as the boys. I was too numb and hungry to cry, but I remembered her instructions. I left early the next morning, bundled in every last garment we owned between us. The path to the main road was empty. There were no footprints in the snow, no animal tracks. Smoke drifted out of only a few chimneys. Only Mama's dying wish kept me moving. When I reached the road, I walked the ten miles to Bila Tserkva without stopping. I was afraid that if I rested, I would lose the will to continue and freeze, joining the other snow-covered lumps along the road.

"In Bila Tserkva, policemen were turning back people at a checkpoint. But I slipped past them and made it to the Torgsin shop. There I was able to trade the cross for some bread and salt pork. I ate enough to give me strength then headed to the train station. It was a madhouse there, people trying—and failing—to buy tickets north; mothers with shriveled babies begging, skeletal old people trying to trade their embroidery for food. I managed to sneak onto a train headed for Kyiv and hide beneath the benches. But a few miles outside of the city, the police boarded, and I had to hop off. I figured I could walk the rest of the way, but the road into Kyiv had been blocked off. Luckily, several villagers making the same journey knew a bypass through the forest and agreed to help me after I shared the bread I had left. This is how I reached you . . ."

Nadiya fell silent. I knew I should say something to her, some words of comfort, but what? The horror of her story overwhelmed me. I could only think of Papa's role and her mother's misplaced faith that he would help her.

"My father's a liar and a coward! He and Stalin and the whole Party!"

"Shh!" Nadiya said.

A couple were drifting toward our section of the viewing platform.

I could feel the color rising up my face. "Sorry," I whispered. My throat felt tight; a storm of tears gathered in my eyes. I was sorry for my carelessness but also for so much more: for believing everything Papa and my teachers had told me; for never questioning them; for failing to imagine the lives of others beyond my own. Only Anna Mikhailovna had ever told me the truth.

Did Nadiya understand my guilt? Could she forgive me my ignorance? All I know is that after studying my face, she took my hand.

We walked back down the winding stairs and past the bone-white churches, toward the gate leading back to the modern city. Before we left Pechersk Lavra, Nadiya turned to me, her voice softer than the whispering wind.

"Now you understand why I can't speak about it ever again."

32

MATTHEW

Leonia, New Jersey, USA
2020

And yet she did.

Eighty-seven years later, she told me.

GG's face was all twisted up like she might start wailing at any moment. I knew I had to say something—she had lost not only her dad, but her mom and little brothers—all within a few years and in horrible ways—but I had no idea what. *Sorry you lost everyone who mattered to you? Hope you find peace, but we both know you never will?* It was pretty much the worst story I've ever heard, but I had to say something.

"GG, I had no idea what you've lived through. I'm so, so sorry."

It came out right—at least I thought it did. I leaned in to embrace her. But she stiffened and threw up her hand, as if to defend herself. I took the cue and backed off. Maybe the hug was too much.

"No more!" she said. "Get out!"

Back in my room, I told myself that she just needed some space. Remembering her family and telling someone what had happened to them after all these years was clearly upsetting; maybe she wanted to cry without me there. But I still worried I'd messed up somehow, said the wrong thing. Also, now that I knew that Helen's cross had reached GG and helped save her life, it made even less sense why she hadn't kept in touch with Helen.

I texted Dad. Can you call

But he didn't answer.

I grabbed the notebook, took notes on what GG had told Mila.

Trudged through snow alone

Whole family dead

I stopped to make sure my phone wasn't on mute, that my ringer was at full volume. I hoped Dad wasn't touring another Covid ward. Just then a text came through, but it was from Josh.

So bored

Covid sucks

Rain sucks

What r u up 2

I was tempted to write that what also sucked was having your whole family die in a preventable famine, but instead I just wrote, nothing.

> We might walk by your house tomorrow after dinner

Just a couple months earlier, if anyone had told me that I'd be wildly excited to shout across the lawn to my best friend for a few minutes, I would have thought they were crazy. But this now seemed like the social highlight of my entire week. I quickly checked the weather. The rain was supposed to stop by tomorrow afternoon.

> Ill come out

> Text me

I felt a little more cheerful after that. Dad was probably just busy with a story. Anyway, I didn't need him to tell me what to do. I'd check in on GG, make sure she was all right. Then I'd get her mind off her family. I even came up with the perfect plan for how.

After a quick stop in the kitchen, I knocked on GG's door. She didn't answer, but I pushed it open anyway, just a crack.

"GG, it's me. I'm sorry if I upset you. Here, this is for you—"

I stuck my arm through the door and held out a bag of mini Snickers, Milky Ways, and 3 Musketeers. The old Halloween candy wasn't technically mine to give. Mom had stuffed it in the back of the pantry, but I occasionally stole a piece. I knew GG liked chocolate, even if she hadn't grown up with an endless supply of Bumble Bears like Mila.

"Come in," GG said.

She was lying in bed, the journals and papers still scattered around her. As she watched me carry over the bag of chocolate, her eyes brightened, and she hauled herself upright. I arranged one of each bar in my palm then presented them to her. Just as I expected, she pointed to the 3 Musketeers, so I opened it for her. Then I took a Snickers.

"Don't tell Mom," I said.

GG nodded.

We ate silently after that—well not exactly silently, since GG's dentures made this clicking noise. I just ignored it, though. There were enough kids back in school with dental devices that made them chew all gross or who'd get food stuck in their braces. Funny how I could even get nostalgic about the cafeteria and its orthodontic orchestra.

We wordlessly agreed to eat a second piece each.

"Okay if I keep the rest in your room?" I asked.

GG knew exactly what I was up to. "Hide 'em."

She pointed to one of her drawers. Inside were the winter sweaters she wore all year round. I tucked the bag under an itchy-looking lime-green sweater.

"Don't eat them all without me," I said.

GG grinned. My plan had worked. I had cheered her up. But we didn't need to go back to the story. Not today.

"I'll put these away now," I said.

I started collecting the notebooks and papers. I didn't just dump them in the box, the way I used to. I was more careful with them now. I even made sure they were arranged in their proper piles. That's when I noticed a yellowed photocopy in the "Letters" pile addressed to Miss Helen Lomachenko. At the bottom of the letter was the sender's name.

I couldn't help myself: I held it out to GG.

"They wrote her back!"

33

HELEN

Brooklyn, New York, USA
1933

I slid the envelope across the table to Ruth. It was a Monday afternoon, and we were sitting at one of the café tables in the back of Spitz's, her parents' grocery store, drinking vanilla egg creams that Ruth had made herself at the soda fountain. She helped out at the store after school, and I'd taken to stopping by, sometimes with Peter, sometimes just by myself, for a chat or an egg cream or help with my homework. But today wasn't just an idle visit. I'd returned home from school to find a crisp white letter addressed to me.

Ruth immediately turned it over. "You didn't open it yet?"

I shrugged. "I feel like it's for both of us. I wanted to wait for you."

Ruth smiled and slid it back to me. The more I'd gotten to know her, the more I realized she wasn't such a hard smile after all. Ruth was like a Tootsie Pop—she had a hard shell, but she was soft inside.

"Well, I'm here now," she said. "Open it."

I took a sip of my egg cream, stared at the return address, *The New York Times*, engraved in the top left corner. It had been over .a month since I'd sent my letter to the editor. I'd almost given up hope of ever hearing back. I took a deep breath and wedged my nail under the sealed flap of the envelope. Ripping it open, I reached inside and pulled out a single sheet of typed paper.

"Read it out loud," Ruth said.

Dear Miss Lomachenko,

Thank you for your letter and fine efforts as a citizen journalist. The personal stories you have collected are undoubtedly moving. However, your accounts of famine are secondhand; there is not a single interview with an actual famine survivor. In keeping with our journalistic standards, we continue to stand by the reporting of our correspondent, Mr. Walter Duranty, who has covered the Soviet Union for many years with accuracy and expertise.

Sincerely,
Edwin Leland James, Managing Editor
The New York Times

I threw the letter down, my face burning. "It's Duranty's accounts that there's *no* famine that are secondhand!" I practically shouted.

A smile played on Ruth's face.

"What?" I demanded.

"You're angry."

"Of course I'm angry! Aren't you?"

"Terribly! But I thought you'd feel like you'd made a fool of yourself or regret sending the letter."

Ruth was right. The old me would have felt that way. But I didn't now.

"I just want to run down to the *New York Times* office and tell that editor he's wrong!"

I looked at Ruth, hoping she might say this was a fine idea and she would even come with me. I imagined the two of us storming into Edwin Leland James's office together, demanding his newspaper print the truth.

But all Ruth said was, "I understand how you feel."

"What if I write him another letter?"

"And say what?" Ruth said. "That he's wrong? You're not going to convince him, not without those eyewitness accounts. And you can't exactly hop a boat to Ukraine and interview people there, so you need to find survivors here. But are there any?"

She looked doubtful, and I wondered if she was trying to tell me that it was time to give up. But I was Pop's daughter—as stubborn and determined as he was. The evening after we'd spoken to the lawyer, Mr. Kaminski, Pop had announced he was going back to work. When Mom had started to argue, he'd raised a hand in the air. "Absolutely, no discussion!"

Mom had shot me a look, as if this was all my fault, but I had just shrugged. There was no stopping Pop, even if I'd wanted to. We needed more money if we were going to pay Mr. Kaminski to help us bring Nadiya to Brooklyn . . .

Nadiya! I sucked in my breath.

"We're trying to bring my cousin here. She lived through the famine, lost her whole family. She'd be the perfect eyewitness!"

Ruth's eyes flashed with excitement. "She'd fit the bill, all right. But it's not easy getting people into the country—"

"I know. My father's lawyer, Mr. Kaminski, said it was extremely difficult. The Soviet Union rarely lets people leave, and the immigration laws here make it very difficult for immigrants from Eastern Europe to enter. But he also said it's not impossible. Both Nadiya's parents are dead, plus she's a girl."

"What does that have to do with it?" Ruth demanded.

"Mr. Kaminski says the Soviets are worried about another war," I explained. "They want boys for the army."

"And girls are useless when it comes to fighting," Ruth said with a dismissive flick of her eye.

I smiled. "Not girls like us."

"Exactly," Ruth said. "So what's the plan?"

Wasn't Ruth supposed to tell *me* the plan? But she was waiting expectantly, as if I was the one in charge.

"We just need to get Nadiya here." But I knew this wasn't much of a plan. "In the meantime, we need to keep looking for other survivors. There must be a few who've made it out. Will you ask your parents to ask their Ukrainian customers if they know of anyone?"

Ruth nodded. "I'll ask around."

Her instant agreement made my confidence grow.

"Maybe we can look in the papers, too? See if there are any stories about recent arrivals, famine survivors. I can read the Russian and Ukrainian language ones—"

"I'll read the Yiddish ones."

"We make a swell team," I said.

Ruth smiled.

"What?" I said.

"*You* make a swell leader."

A leader. No one had ever used this word to describe me. But maybe, just maybe, I could be one.

34

MATTHEW

Leonia, New Jersey, USA
2020

It wasn't until after online school the next day that *Zelda*'s Lost
Woods alerted me to a video call from Dad. I didn't answer right
away, just so he knew that he wasn't the only one who had things to
do. But I didn't want him to give up, either, so after a couple rings,
I accepted the call.

"Hey, Mattie," he said.

He looked like his usual self—glasses, in need of a shave, floppy
hair like mine. But his voice sounded a little strained.

"Are you okay?" I said. "You didn't call me back yesterday."

I tried not to make it sound like an accusation, but I had sent
him a text asking him to.

He looked confused. "Did you call?"

"I texted."

"Sorry. I must have missed it. We were working on this piece about—"

"Don't worry about it," I interrupted. "I had another reporting question, but I figured it out myself."

"That's good, Matthew. You're a smart kid."

I expected Dad to ask me about it and then dive into another journalism lecture. Instead, he'd just called me Matthew. Something was definitely off. My chest felt tight.

"Are you sure you're okay?" I said again. "You're not feeling sick or anything?"

I wished there was a way I could reach through the screen and touch his forehead.

"Sick?" Dad laughed. "No, don't worry. I'm fine."

I let out a deep breath.

"It's just . . ." he said, pausing. "I have some disappointing news."

Every muscle in my body instantly tightened. "What?"

Dad grimaced. "It's about your visit this summer. The way things are going, our plans may need to, you know, pivot?"

"You mean like we'll have to stay in Paris and not hike?" I asked. But deep down I had a feeling this wasn't what he meant.

Dad tried to look me in the eye, but no one really can over video.

"Mattie, listen. I've been holding off making a decision and hoping for a miraculous recovery. But the thing is, this virus isn't going away anytime soon. Mom and I don't think it's a good idea for you to get on a plane this summer—"

"Mom? She's scared of everything! This was her decision, wasn't it?"

Dad lurched forward so his head filled up my screen. "No, Matthew! I was the one who brought this up with her. We decided together. She even wanted me to alert you sooner."

"You *decided*! A minute ago, you said we *might* have to cancel; now it's a done deal?"

But he wouldn't answer this. "I know you're disappointed. I'm disappointed, too."

"Just a few days ago, you let me talk about the trip like it was happening!"

"I wish it were. I was looking forward to it, too! But this pandemic is a lot worse than I first thought. I just want to keep you safe."

I knew he was trying to make me feel better. But if it was so dangerous over there, why was it okay for him to stay?

"If it's so bad, then come home," I said.

"It's not that easy . . ."

My leg jiggled frantically. When would I see him again? Last year's school photo of me was on a side table behind him. I didn't even look like that anymore.

"Sure it is! If you really wanted to."

"Mattie, that's not fair," said Dad quietly. Which made me even angrier. How could he be so calm, so unemotional? Maybe it was no big deal to him, but it was to me.

"You're probably happy our vacation's canceled," I shouted. "You've always cared more about work than me!"

Before he could reply, I ended the video. He tried me again, but I didn't accept the call. I muted my phone, stuffed it under my pillow, and jumped down from my bed. Then I ran to GG's room.

GG was watching TV—more blaring cable news about Covid deaths and contact tracing and the latest cancellations. But she took one look at me and switched it off.

"What's wrong?"

I just shook my head. I didn't want to cry.

GG pointed to her sweater drawer.

I dug out the bag of chocolate, handed her a 3 Musketeers, and took one for myself. She inched over to the side. I figured she was making space for the papers and notebooks, but then she patted the bed and said, "Sit." I sat down next to her, and we silently ate our chocolate.

"Tell me," she said.

"My dad. He lied to me."

GG studied me with interest. "What about?"

"He acted like I was going to see him this summer, but he knew the trip was off. He just lied about it."

Dad might not see it that way, but I did. Now what did I have to look forward to? Absolutely nothing. My eyes stung with tears.

I was afraid GG was going to ask more questions. But she just pointed to the box and said, "Mila, May Day 1933."

35

MILA

Kyiv, Ukraine, USSR
1933

How I'd always loved May Day, the holiday celebrating laborers and our great Soviet nation. The massive parade down Khreschatyk, the songs promising to defend our motherland against the enemy, the workers' brigades holding up portraits of Papa Stalin and Lenin, the folk dancers waving sprigs of cherry blossoms, the military trucks and soldiers on horseback, the proud, wiggly Octobrists, and the confident Young Pioneers in their red scarfs waving at the cheering crowds. On May 1, 1933, I still donned my Pioneer scarf. I still marched. I still sang. I still waved. But my heart was elsewhere.

Comrade Gavrilok had finally agreed to let Katya hold her party—a May Day party after the public festivities. I had told Papa that we would head to her apartment directly after the parade. But I had decided to pay a quick visit to Nadiya before the party. Dasha had been in another cranky mood that morning—working herself nearly into tears as she tried to battle my cowlick. Papa, on the other hand, had given me a pound of Bumble Bears to celebrate the holiday, and I wanted to give them to Nadiya.

At the parade route's end, I grabbed Katya's hand, gave it a quick squeeze.

"I'll meet you at your place!"

Katya blinked uncertainly. "Where are you going?"

She was probably nervous about the party and wanted me there to put her at ease. But even the disappointment in her eyes couldn't stop me.

"I need to say hello to a friend!"

I let go of her hand and drifted off as if I was being pulled away. It wasn't a lie, not at all. I kept going, didn't look back until I was far enough away to pretend not to hear. Fortunately, by this time, Nina and several others had surrounded her.

It was easy enough to slip through the crowds and make my way back up the hill, past Mariinsky Park, and over to Anna Mikhailovna's building. I took the stairs two at a time, picturing Nadiya's smile when she saw the chocolates. Grinning with anticipation, I knocked on the door to the studio.

"Anna Mikhailovna!" I said.

I hopped on one foot, then the other. Knocked again.

Could they have gone to the May Day parade? It seemed unlikely. There were no lessons on May Day, but perhaps Anna Mikhailovna herself was practicing and couldn't hear me? I put my ear to the door, listened for the piano. But there was no music. My stomach tightened.

"It's me, Mila!" I said, louder than before. "Are you there?"

I jiggled the doorknob. The door was locked. They could have gone out to get a breath of fresh air. *That's it*, I told myself. But would Anna Mikhailovna risk them all going out together on a holiday, when the neighbors might be home to see them together and ask nosy questions? I tried to push down my growing unease. I knocked again.

A distant sound. Shuffling footsteps. Someone was there! I slumped against the door with relief. Anna Mikhailovna was out, that was it, and Nadiya was sleeping. Olga Stepanovna had been in back with Nadiya and had only just heard me.

The door opened, as I had predicted, on Olga Stepanovna. But the moment I saw her, I knew something terrible had happened. Her eyes were red, and she sagged against the wall.

"What is it?!"

She waved me inside, closed the door.

"The secret police came early this morning," Olga Stepanovna said. "They took Anna."

"Why?!" But I already knew. A wave of nausea shot through my stomach. I raced into the back bedroom. The beds were unmade; papers and clothes were strewn across the floor. I stumbled back into the studio. "Where's Nadiya?"

The old woman was weeping now. "They took her, too."

I couldn't breathe. "Where?"

"I don't know. But they said she couldn't remain in Kyiv."

I flung my arms around Olga Stepanovna. We both sobbed as she held me tight. I pictured Nadiya in the back of some military truck headed out of Kyiv and Anna Mikhailovna on her way to Siberia or worse.

"It's all my fault!" I cried. "I should never have brought her here. I've ruined you!"

"Nonsense, Mila."

But she let go of me, and I knew that deep down she blamed me or at least regretted my dragging her and Anna Mikhailovna into this business. What had I done? I couldn't bear to think about the pain I had caused, so I turned my attention to another question.

"How did the police find out?"

Olga Stepanovna shrugged. "Someone told. They didn't say who."

"I was careful," I whimpered. "I truly was—"

"It could have been anyone."

But as she said this, I couldn't help thinking of how Katya had looked at me when I'd told her I had to go see a friend. Had it really been disappointment that I had seen in her eyes—or guilt? She hadn't liked keeping my secret—she'd made that clear. She could have told someone—her father, my father—about my secret sessions with Anna Mikhailovna. Her betrayal could have led to this.

Everyone is a possible enemy!

Papa's words echoed in my head.

"You need to go," Olga Stepanovna said, interrupting my

thoughts. "Anna told them I was a half-witted old lady, that she'd lied to me that Nadiya was one of her students from Kyiv. But they may come back to interrogate me yet. You don't want to be seen here."

My heart hammered at the thought of the secret police. I could almost hear their boots on the stairs. But instead I stumbled over to Anna Mikhailovna's piano, ran my fingers silently over the keys. I needed her now more than ever to tell me what piece to play to make sense of what I had done. I closed my eyes, squeezed them tight, tried to conjure my teacher beside me. But the only sound was silence, a silence that told me I would never see Anna Mikhailovna or her studio again.

No! I couldn't let that happen. I would beg Papa to save her, to save Nadiya—beg him like I'd never begged for anything else.

"Forgive me," I said to Olga Stepanovna then dashed out to spare her the lie that there was nothing to forgive.

I meant to run straight home to make my case to Papa, but Katya's apartment was on the way. I found myself hurtling up her steps, pounding on her door. I needed to hear it from her own lips, that she was the one who had told, who had betrayed me. Her housekeeper, Varvara, opened the door, and I blew in like a wind, whirling into the party. From the other side of the room, Katya saw me and grimaced. Guilty! I shoved my way around my classmates till I reached her. Her arms were crossed over her chest, her lips set in a pout.

"You—" I started.

But she cut me off. "You missed it!"

This took me aback.

"Missed what?"

"I recited my ode to Papa. But you're late! So you missed it. You always put yourself front and center, but when it's time to show up for me, you disappear! Maybe you don't want me to get any attention, is that it? What friend were you saying hi to anyway? That was more than a hi. Was it a boy? Is that your big secret? Have you been going to see him?"

My mouth gaped like a fish's. She had no idea.

"Everyone liked the poem," she continued. "They applauded. Even Papa. You should have been here, Mila."

"I'm sorry," I whispered.

"You look awful by the way. Did you just run here? Your hair's a mess."

"I don't feel well."

Katya's face softened, though her eyes were still hooded with suspicion. "Do you need to lie down?"

"I need to go home," I croaked.

"Motherless Daughters don't abandon each other."

Katya had nothing to do with this.

"I'm sorry," I said.

She shrugged and turned her back on me.

I stumbled out of the Gavriloks' apartment. If Katya hadn't betrayed me, who had? *It could have been anyone.* That was what Olga Stepanovna had said, and she was right. A neighbor might have seen

Nadiya, or the parent of a student. But the neighbors were used to seeing different children going in and out of the apartment, and the women had been so careful, keeping Nadiya hidden when students came by, hardly allowing her out. My suspicions turned to Dasha. But she had pitied Nadiya when she had arrived at our door; she had given her extra food. Even if she knew our secret, she wouldn't turn against her—or me. There was only one person with a motive to get Nadiya out of Kyiv and send her back to the countryside: Papa.

36

MILA

Kyiv, Ukraine, USSR
1933

I found Papa in the parlor reading *Pravda*, his face hidden behind headlines celebrating May Day and blaring the dizzying success of Stalin's Five-Year plan. I marched up to him, and he lowered the paper, greeted me with a grin.

"How was Gavrilok's celebration?"

"I don't want to talk about that!"

My voice was shaking.

Papa folded up *Pravda*, patted the seat next to him.

"What happened, little fox? Did you and Katya have a fight? Let me guess . . . you both like the same boy?" His eyes twinkled.

"Papa," I hissed. "It was you, wasn't it, *you* who had them arrested?!"

Papa's smile dissolved. "What are you talking about?" He spoke quietly even though the only person who could possibly hear us was Dasha, and she had the rest of the day off. "Was Gavrilok—"

"Not Gavrilok!" I interrupted. "Anna Mikhailovna and Nadiya!"

Papa stared at me blankly. "Anna Mikhailovna has been arrested?"

What an act! His darting eyes told me more than his false words. "You know she was! You had her arrested so you could send Nadiya away and continue to hide who you are!"

Papa jerked upright, openmouthed. "You had Anna Mikhailovna hide the girl?"

"'The girl'?!" I shouted. "Her name is Nadiya! She's your niece and my cousin and you know it! I found the letter her mother sent begging you for help. Her two little brothers died of hunger. You could have saved all of them, but you did nothing!"

Papa collapsed back against the couch, his face pale. What was he feeling? Guilt? I hoped so. But his gaze was focused completely on me. He held out his hand.

"Mila, my soul, you don't understand—"

He had always seemed so powerful, but now I noticed the wrinkles around his eyes and grooves in his forehead, a missed spot in his shave, the gray at his temples. He looked like a pathetic old man.

"I understand all right! You're no orphan; you had a family! How could you lie to me?"

Papa rose to his feet, began to pace.

"They were ignorant, backward people! They didn't understand Lenin or the Revolution. They called me a radical, threw me out!"

"So you punished them by turning your own niece away at your door! She was starving to death!"

"I wasn't punishing the girl! I was protecting you! When you were younger, it was simply easier to tell you I had no family than to explain all this. But now, having kulak origins is dangerous . . . I had to hide. I could do nothing for them—"

"Don't you dare say you had them arrested for me!"

"I didn't—it wasn't me."

"I don't believe you!"

He tried to touch my shoulder, but I lurched away.

"Please, Mila. You have it all wrong."

"Get away from me!" I shouted. "I'm tired of your lies. People are starving in the countryside, entire villages, and here in the city, too—"

"These are kulaks," Papa said, but his voice was weary as if he no longer believed his own arguments. "The thing you need to understand about kulaks—"

"*You* are a kulak! The son of kulaks! Nadiya's your niece, your flesh and blood. She likes stories and chocolates, like me. She just wants to survive!" I fell to my knees before him, clasped my hands. "Please, Papa, you have to save her and help Anna Mikhailovna! Please, it's the only thing I ask. I'll forgive you everything!"

"There's nothing to be done. Anna Mikhailovna will likely lose her ration card and some of her students. But they'll release her."

"And Nadiya?"

He turned away, shook his head.

"I'm powerless."

"Stop," I sobbed. "Stop lying to me! You just don't want to help!"

Papa pulled me to his chest so fiercely that I couldn't pull away. "I'm telling you the truth, Mila! There's nothing I can do for her. Especially now! She shouldn't have come here. But you . . . you're my happiness! Whatever I've done, it's been for you, to protect you. You must understand that—"

I pounded on his chest. "Let me go!"

But he held me fast, his fingers squeezing my shoulders so tight I knew they would later leave bruises. "You need to listen to me—"

"Leave me alone!"

With a sharp elbow to his ribs, I twisted myself free and ran upstairs to my room, slamming the door behind me. I threw myself on my bed, weeping into my pillow. I heard his footsteps, heavy on the stairs, and braced for his knock. But they shuffled off in the opposite direction, and his bedroom door closed.

My tears finally subsided, but not my anger—it spurred me to resolve. Papa wasn't going to stop me; I would figure out a plan. I wasn't going to give up on finding Nadiya. I had promised her I would do everything I could to protect her. But I had no idea where to even start.

For dinner, Dasha had left Papa and me cold borscht and bread. I considered staying in my room to protest, but my gurgling stomach drove me down to the kitchen. I found Papa waiting at the kitchen table, which he had set for the two of us. His shoulders were slumped, and he wore a faraway look.

"Milachka," he said softly, as if using my pet name could make it all better between us.

I refused to look at him, though, and ladled the borscht into my bowl, sloshing it carelessly onto the table. Papa didn't scold me or ask me to clean it up, and so I left it there, like splotches of blood. I dropped a spoonful of sour cream into my soup and balanced a slice of black bread on the rim then lifted my bowl. I wasn't going to sit here with him. As I turned to go, I could feel Papa's eyes on me, but he didn't order me to stay.

"I know I can't make you listen to me," he said.

I stopped but didn't turn around. I only let him speak to my back.

"You have your own mind, which is actually a wonderful thing," he continued. "Use it to find your way out of trouble. I hope that someday you will come to see that everything I did, I did for you. I love you, little fox, with all my heart."

But I couldn't let him in, wouldn't, not after what he'd done to Nadiya. All his flattery and love meant nothing to me. I let him know that by walking away without a word.

I was anxious for Dasha to return. She would dutifully take Papa's side—I was sure of it. But she had nursed me through sickness and scraped knees, soothed me with her tragic stories of how much worse life could be. She also knew what Papa was like. She would feel some sympathy.

I didn't hear the door open till late, her footsteps as light on the floorboards as Papa's were heavy, creeping up the stairs to her room. I sprang to my open door.

"Dasha," I whispered.

She leapt backward like a surprised cat.

"Dasha," I said. "It's just me!"

She steadied herself against the wall, her face pale.

"I didn't mean to frighten you," I whispered.

She frowned. "Go to bed, Mila, it's late."

"I've had the most horrible day," I said. "Everything has gone wrong."

"I'm tired, Mila. Can't you see that?"

She did look exhausted, her face drawn, the shadows under her eyes hollowed and dark. But I needed her to know I wasn't just some moppet, Papa's darling pet, that I was a serious person who understood the kind of cruel man he could be.

"It's about Nadiya, my cousin, the girl who showed up at the door starving—"

Dasha stiffened then put up her hand, cut me off. "We all have starving relatives. We all want to help them."

"You mean in Obukhiv?" I hadn't thought about this before, but it made perfect sense. Dasha's grumpiness whenever I asked about her village, the increasing sadness with which she seemed to recall her life there. "Dasha, I'm so sorry!"

But she was already moving away from me, her face turned to the darkness.

"We'll talk in the morning, Mila. It's late. Go to sleep."

She was at her door before I could protest. I trudged back to my bed, ashamed, once again, by my own selfish lack of awareness.

Dasha had been suffering all this time, no doubt worried about her nieces and their families. But I was bothered by her lack of curiosity about Nadiya. Had she known my secret? Or was she simply afraid to hear me speak of things Papa wouldn't approve of? I mulled these questions in my mind until, exhausted by the shocks of the day, I fell into a fitful sleep.

I awoke to banging downstairs. Someone was at the door. *Where is Dasha?* I thought sleepily. *Why won't she answer?* I opened my eyes, expecting morning light, but it was still dark.

"Open up!" came a shout from downstairs. "OGPU!"

It was the secret police.

37

MILA

Kyiv, Ukraine, USSR
1933

They had come for me! But this made no sense. Papa wouldn't turn me in. *I love you, little fox!*

I jumped out of bed, raced to the top of the stairs as three men barged through the door and surrounded Papa. Although it was the middle of the night, he was dressed in his *stalinka* and pants, a coat hung over his shoulders. I desperately hoped they had come to escort him to an emergency meeting—perhaps war had been declared or Stalin was dead?

"Lomachenko," the tallest of the three said, not even addressing him as *comrade*. "You have been denounced as a class enemy."

At the same moment, I noticed the small black suitcase by the side of the door. I clutched the banister. I couldn't breathe. The faraway, sad look he'd worn at dinner. The serious way he'd addressed me. I'd read it all wrong, as if he was just trying to convince me he was right. Papa had known they were coming to take him away! This was the trouble he'd wanted to prepare me for, the reason he hoped I would someday remember he loved me. The clues had been there—every single one of them—but I'd been too blinded by my anger to see them.

"No!" I shrieked. "You've made a mistake!"

The men ignored me; only Papa looked up. "Be calm, Mila," he said. Then he turned back to the men as leisurely as if they had just been chatting about the weather. "What is the charge?"

The tall man brandished a piece of paper. "It has been reported to us that you have been hiding kulak origins. In addition, it has been reported that you were using your influence to house a kulak relative illegally here in Kyiv at the home of your child's piano teacher."

I rushed down the stairs. I had to fix this. I had to give us more time. "You've got it wrong!" I cried. "That was me!"

"Quiet, you fool!" Papa snapped.

I stopped short, wounded, even as I understood that Papa was trying to protect me.

The tall man shrugged as if our little drama hardly interested him.

"How do you plead to these charges, Lomachenko?"

I whimpered. Papa fixed me with a hard look.

"Guilty," he said.

But the opposite was now clear to me: Papa was innocent. For once in his life, he had told me the truth. He hadn't known about Anna Mikhailovna and Nadiya. He hadn't turned them in. Someone else had turned them in, and Papa, too.

Who?

I looked around frantically. Where was Dasha? There was no way Dasha could have slept through this commotion. The truth was dawning on me, but I pushed it away, my focus on Papa. I had been so cruel to him, shoved him away, turned my back on him. All that time he must have known that the game was up, that we were about to lose each other. But I couldn't lose him. For all his faults, he was still Papa, the only parent I had. He loved me more than anyone in the world, and I him.

Papa's "trial" over, a squat man with jowls who reminded me of a bulldog grabbed him roughly by his elbows and marched him to the door. But Papa twisted back, and I ran to his side and threw my arms around him. Papa's eyes filled with tears, and he kept closing them, as if trying to hold them back.

I had no such control. "Papa!" I sobbed and hung on to him with every ounce of strength I had. "Forgive me!"

"There is nothing to forgive," Papa murmured under his breath. "Moscow has been purging the Ukrainian Party since New Year's. It was only a matter of time . . ."

But I had still given his enemies cause to arrest him.

"I'm sorry, Papa," I repeated over and over. "I'm sorry—"

"Let go, let go!" the bulldog said impatiently.

The other men pried me off, dragging me away. Papa jerked

around best he could toward the tall man. His voice wavered. "What will happen to Lyudmila?"

The tall man appraised me with a cold eye. "The State will take care of her. But you know this already, Lomachenko—you've ordered enough arrests yourself. Why ask foolish questions?"

Then he opened the door, and the other man pushed Papa out into the night. I could see the headlights of a waiting car parked in front of the curb.

"Papa!" I cried as they dragged him down the steps toward the car.

"I love you, little fox!" I heard him call back.

The tall man opened the back door of the car, and the bulldog man shoved Papa in, wedging himself beside him.

I ran down the steps after them, but before I could say *I love you too*, a voice shouted behind me.

"Come! Inside!"

I turned to find the third man waving me back in. I hadn't paid him much attention before. He was younger than the others and wore a sour look as if he didn't relish being left behind with me. Car doors slammed, and the motor revved to life. I turned my back on my guard and ran toward the street, shouting, "Papa, I love you!" only to be yanked back roughly by the shoulder.

"Stop making a scene!"

The car carrying Papa rolled away down Lypska. My legs collapsed under me; the officer dragged me up the steps and back inside.

"The car for us will be here momentarily," he said, depositing me in a heap on the floor of the parlor.

I pushed away the shock and fog. *Think, Mila!*

"May I get dressed?" I asked. My voice was shaking, but I tried to sound polite. "Pack a few things?"

I was still in a nightgown. But try as I might, I didn't actually care what I was wearing, nor could I think clearly about what I should bring. All I wanted was an excuse to go upstairs so I could burst into Dasha's room and force her to look me in the eye.

The officer seemed to read my mind.

"No," he said. "Stay here."

"There's chocolate in the kitchen," I said. "Bumble Bears. I know where they hide them. You can have some. No one will know."

I faked a smile to show we could be partners in crime.

My guard gave a snort. "You're as much of a hooligan as your father," he said and pulled out a cigarette. "Stay put." Then he stood in the open doorway, his eyes fixed on the road as he smoked.

I was about to tell him I had to go to the bathroom in hopes he'd want to finish his cigarette and let me go myself when I heard the creak of the stairs. I looked up, surprised to see Dasha carrying down my suitcase. Her eyes avoided mine, her gaze fixed on her feet as if she feared she might miss a step and tumble down, breaking her neck like one of the villagers in her own unfortunate stories.

"Sneaking out with my suitcase?" I hissed.

The officer turned around. The familiarity in his eyes when he spotted Dasha confirmed everything I'd already guessed. She was the traitor.

"Go back upstairs, Daria Petrovna," he said.

"I've packed her a few things," Dasha said, setting down my suit-case in front of me.

"So nice of you!" I said to Dasha, my voice choking with rage.

"There's our car," the officer said with undisguised relief. "Come!" He picked up the suitcase and carried it outside to the car. But I didn't follow. I glared at Dasha. My voice cracked. "How could you?"

For the first time, she met my gaze. "This wasn't about you, Mila. Not everything is, you know. My family needed help. They were starving. In reward for my loyalty, the authorities are granting per-mission for them to join me in Kyiv and giving them ration cards."

"Surely Papa would have—"

Dasha snorted. "Your papa wouldn't lift a finger to save anyone but you. Not even his own family!"

I wanted to argue, but I couldn't—not after Nadiya.

"*I* would have helped you."

"You're just a child, Mila, and a spoiled one at that. You bossed me about and treated me like a country fool. Your father was even worse."

I felt the uncomfortable sting of truth. I could hear myself order-ing her to fetch me chocolates, Papa berating her for letting me open the mail the day I found the lice. These memories shamed me. But I wasn't going to let her off the hook.

"I defended you against him!" I shouted. "I loved you!"

Dasha looked away, unable to meet my eyes. But then her face hardened, and she turned back to me. "Nadiya's own family signed your father's arrest warrant when they sent her here to find him. It was only a matter of time. Anyway, what do you know about love, Mila? *You*, who've known nothing of hunger or sacrifice."

"I know a lot more than you think! I helped Nadiya, and I would have helped your family, too. I was changing, Dasha, but you didn't see it, and now you've ruined everything, destroyed everyone I loved!"

Dasha's face paled.

"Lomachenko!" the officer shouted from outside. "Come on!"

"Wait!" she said, her voice frantic.

"What?!" I snapped.

"Your father packed your suitcase, begged me to give it to you. He said to let the guards think I packed it myself. You see, I'm hardly against you. I even slipped some chocolates inside."

What did she expect? A thank-you?

"You'll be all right," she added hopefully.

"Maybe I won't be." I stared straight at her. "Maybe I'll die."

Then I turned my back on the woman who'd raised me and walked out of my home for the last time. It seemed fitting to leave it wearing nothing but a nightgown, as if my life had passed into an afterlife, or a dream.

Nothing felt real anymore, not the cool night air, not the ridged upholstery beneath me or the hum of the motor as we drove. Only the dark emptiness of the back seat, where I sat alone. I didn't ask where they were taking me. Perhaps I already knew, but I couldn't change the car's path. As the headlights illuminated the way, I could only take in the familiar landmarks—Khreschatyk, the Golden Gate, the children's home.

That's what they called it when they pulled up. But I knew the hulking sandstone and brick building by another name.

The Collector.

38
MATTHEW

Leonia, New Jersey, USA
2020

For dinner that night, Mom made tacos, which is usually my favorite meal. But I kept thinking of Mila watching the police drag away Papa.

Mom had forgotten to buy salsa, so I ended up using ketchup instead, but the bottle was almost empty, so it made this farting noise every time I squeezed it. In the background, a TV news reporter droned on as we ate: "Today, coronavirus deaths reached another record high. Area hospitals are at full capacity, and visitors remain prohibited, even for those at the end of their lives. Death-bed farewells conducted over FaceTime are a haunting reminder of the toll this virus has—"

Before I could stop myself, I chucked the ketchup bottle across the room. It hit the wall and splattered.

Mom leapt to her feet. "Matthew!"

"You ruined my summer with Dad!" I shouted. "I hate you!"

Then I ran to my room and slammed the door behind me.

Real mature, I know. But Mom had already taken away my Switch. What could she do to me now, ground me? I was already stuck at home. Ha! I curled up in my bed, closed my eyes tight against the hot tears stinging my eyelids, and tried not to think of people saying goodbye forever to their dying relatives over screens.

A few minutes later, Mom knocked on my door. I knew she was coming to have A Talk. I wasn't interested.

"What?!" I snapped.

"Josh is outside," she said. "He wants to say hello."

I'd forgotten all about Josh! I grabbed my phone, which I'd forgotten to unmute. Alongside a new message from Dad, I love you, Mattie. Talk tomorrow, were two others from Josh:

Be there in 10

Here

I swiped at my eyes, hoping I wouldn't look like I'd been on the verge of crying. Then I barreled past Mom. I didn't even look at her in case she tried to stop me to say we needed to talk later, and I was still in trouble. I was almost out the front door when she yelled after me.

"Grab a mask, Matthew. And not too close, okay?"

I grabbed a mask and put it on, but she didn't have to worry. The moment I saw Josh, I skidded to a stop. I'd expected his whole family. But instead standing at the end of my walkway was just him and his dad. Mr. Cohen was nothing like my father: He worked at a bank and played golf; I couldn't imagine him talking about people's stories or owning a bow and arrow. But it didn't matter. He was there, by Josh's side.

"Hey," Josh said through his mask.

"Hey," I managed to choke out through mine. "I can't really come closer because of my great-grandma."

"That's okay," said Mr. Cohen, readjusting his glasses over his mask. "Josh just wanted to see you. He's been begging me to walk over here for days."

"Dad!" Josh said and gave him an elbow.

They were talking face-to-face, not through a screen. And touching. Even an elbow counted.

"What?" Mr. Cohen said. "It's true, isn't it?"

Josh ignored him, turned to me.

"Did you get your Switch back?"

"No."

He shook his head sympathetically. "You must be so bored."

"It's okay," I said.

"Maybe Matthew reads books," Mr. Cohen said. "You know what those are, right, Joshie? Paper? Ink?"

He ruffled Josh's hair, which had grown out like mine but in curls. Josh ducked away. But his eyes crinkled up, and I could tell he was smiling under his mask.

I couldn't stand being out there even another second.

"I actually have to go. Sorry, I just . . . um . . . I was, um, helping Mom with GG. We were in the middle of something . . ."

Josh's eyes widened with a mix of horror and concern; I was not only Switchless, I now appeared to be working as a nursing aide.

"Tell your mom to call Rachel or me if she needs anything," Mr. Cohen said.

Just then, Mom popped out herself—she'd probably been listening at the door—and she and Mr. Cohen began shouting across the lawn about how crazy life was and whether Covid would ever end. I took the opportunity to slip back inside. I could see Josh through the window, standing there, looking confused and a little disappointed. I hadn't even said goodbye. But he had his dad. He'd walk home with him. He'd see him before he went to sleep and when he woke up in the morning. I could feel that weight on my chest, heavier than ever. I could barely breathe.

I ran back to my room, grabbed the notebook, and flipped it to a fresh page. Then I wedged myself into the darkest corner of my bottom bunk and started writing:

> I miss Dad so much. I don't know when I'm going to see him again. I don't know when this pandemic will end. What if it never ends? What if something happens

*to him and he dies, and I don't get to see him ever
again? I don't want to say goodbye over FaceTime. I
can't lose him. I'm scared.*

Tears ran down my face, hit the page, smearing the ink.

"Matthew?"

Mom opened the door. I slammed the notebook shut.

"Can't you knock?!" I shouted.

I expected her to yell back, bring up the ketchup or my rudeness
to Josh. But she didn't do any of that.

"Matthew, I'm so sorry about the trip."

Of course. Dad had texted her.

"I don't want to talk about it."

But she just stood there. "I know you're disappointed—"

"Leave me alone," I said through gritted teeth. "Go."

I realized I was acting just like GG when she was upset, and I
knew it was probably making Mom feel just as badly. But if she didn't
get out of my room, I was going to lose it completely. She must have
sensed this, because she left. The moment she did, though, I felt a
thousand times worse. I didn't write in the notebook anymore.

39

MILA

Kyiv, Ukraine, USSR
1933

My hair fell to the floor in clumps. I watched it through wet lashes, shivering on a stool in my underwear.

"Why?" I asked, gulping back a sob. "I'm not dirty! I didn't come from the street."

"It's for your own good," Irina Ivanovna, the night matron, told me, switching out scissors for a razor. "You don't want a head full of lice."

I longed for sleep, the only escape from the nightmare I was trapped in. But the moment the door of the Collector had closed behind me, I had been taken to this room to be stripped and scalped. My hand flew up to touch the stubble where my hair had been, but Irina Ivanovna batted it down.

"Keep still!"

I craned my bare neck around to look at her. "I don't belong here!"

Irina Ivanovna roughly jerked my head forward. "All the ones like you say that." Her voice became high, mocking. "'There must be some mistake!' 'Papa is a good Communist.'" She gave a short, hard laugh. "There's nothing special about you."

She might as well have taken her razor and plunged it into my heart. That's how much her words wounded me. But it wasn't being special I cared about; it was losing the people who had made me feel that way: Papa, Anna Mikhailovna, Nadiya.

Irina Ivanovna put down the razor. "Finished. Let's see what you have in here."

She squatted down, opened my suitcase, and began to rummage through it as if it were her own. Anger launched me off the stool, but the sight of my own shorn head reflected in the darkened window made me lose my purpose. I stared in shock at this alien face. By the time I recovered, I noticed Irina Ivanovna pocketing the Bumble Bears Dasha had left in between the carefully folded clothes. For a moment, I didn't know who to be more furious with: Dasha, for thinking that a handful of chocolates would make up for what she'd done to me, or the matron brazenly stuffing them into her pockets.

"Those are mine," I said.

I expected her to pretend she wasn't stealing them, but she didn't even bother. She looked me straight in the eye. "I'm letting you keep your fancy coat—it should be disinfected, but you likely wouldn't see it again. Keep it with you so it won't be stolen."

She handed me my woolen winter coat—that Papa had packed it for me even though it was nearly summer made my heart sink further. Then she handed me a different set of clothes—a gray dress with a worn hem, underwear, and stockings. "Get dressed and I'll show you where you'll sleep," she said, then went back to pocketing the rest of my chocolate.

Minutes later, she led me up a flight of stairs and down a dark hallway. I wrinkled my nose: The air smelled of human bodies mixed with the sharp tang of urine. Irina Ivanovna banged open a set of double doors into a barracks. Children lay on cots arranged in tight rows—some had curled into balls, others lay as pale and straight as cadavers, and others shifted and twitched restlessly. I had expected the door banging open to awaken them, but no one reacted. The room, I realized, was noisy in its own right—full of coughing, sniffling, and whimpering.

Irina Ivanovna marched over to a cot in the far corner and pointed. "This is yours."

I sat down on the thin, lumpy mattress. There was no blanket, but several of my neighbors didn't appear to have blankets, either. I supposed this was why Irina Ivanovna felt she was doing me a favor by letting me keep my coat. I lay down and pulled it up over me.

"I wouldn't get too comfortable," she said. "The morning bell goes off in fifteen minutes."

Fifteen minutes?! I closed my eyes, tried to block out the coughing, the rustle of bodies, the pitiful sighs. I felt a tickle near my brow and reached up to pull the hair out of my eyes, only to realize I had no hair, only stubble, like a boy.

Papa, I thought, *get me out of here*. But Papa's lies had made him powerless to help. I imagined him in jail or on a train to Siberia. *Goodbye, little fox*, he said.

I was on my own.

The next thing I knew, a bell rang, clanging loudly. I must have fallen asleep, but those few minutes of unconsciousness left me even more exhausted than before. I lay on my lumpy mattress watching dozens of girls—their heads shaved like mine—scramble to line up in front of a large bucket. One by one, they washed their hands and faces, all in the same dirty water, then headed out the door. I had no intention of sharing their makeshift washstand and felt only relief when a tall girl hauled the bucket away.

I dragged myself to my feet and followed some other stragglers down the stairs to a canteen. The walls were a drab yellow; the only decoration was a poster of Stalin, grasping the steering wheel of a boat and looking away from us. It was titled, *The captain of the Soviet Union leads us from victory to victory*. There were boys here, too, though they looked much the same as the girls—thin and pasty, with shaven heads and dripping noses. I could tell they were boys, though, because they jostled more in line—here and there a fist flew, or someone pushed.

My stomach rumbled, and I couldn't help sharing their desperate anticipation for food. A sweaty onion smell flavored the air.

"Take a mug," said a voice behind me.

A pair of brown eyes met mine, and I recognized the tall girl who had carried out the wash bucket. She pointed to a wall of tin mugs hanging from hooks. A girl knelt below, rinsing out the used ones in the same wash bucket.

I hesitated, but what choice did I have? I took the driest mug I could find. The inside was streaked orange with rust. I blinked hard, trying not to cry, and slipped back to my place in line.

When it was our turn, the tall girl gave me a gentle shove toward a kerchiefed worker who filled my mug with a thin cabbage-and-onion soup. It was the color of dishwater, and I knew it wouldn't stop the rumbling of my stomach. But worse than the soup itself was the animal way the other children devoured it. They hunched over their mugs, guzzling with elbows raised and a hostile look, as if they feared someone might snatch it away before they could finish. I wanted to take them home, seat them around a table covered with cakes, like in the May Day book I'd read to the Little Octobrists. But I no longer had a home, and there were no cakes for the children of class enemies. My eyes blurred with tears.

"Mila?! Is it you?"

I spun around, my heart leaping at the familiar voice. A girl was running toward me across the canteen. Her hair was shorn like mine, but I recognized her in an instant.

40

HELEN

Brooklyn, New York, USA
1933

"When do you think Nadiya will come?" Peter asked.

We were walking back from Highland Park on a Saturday afternoon. I had originally dragged Peter to the Arlington Avenue library so I could skim through past issues of the newspapers for any mentions of the famine or survivors who'd come to America. But I'd found nothing, and Peter had grown bored and begged me to take him to the park.

"I don't know," I said. "Soon, hopefully."

But the weeks had dragged on, and there was no update from Mr. Kaminski. He had cautioned that it would take time to get permission, especially from two reluctant governments. We had sent a letter directly to Nadiya at the address she'd written us from to let her know we were trying to help, but we had yet to receive a reply.

"Patience," Pop said whenever I asked.

But he didn't sound patient—at least with all my anxious questioning.

"Do you think she'll like me?" Peter asked.

I stopped, wondering why he was worried. "Of course she'll like you! Why wouldn't she?"

"She'll like you because you're a girl and you're the same age. But she's never had a brother."

Pop had told Peter the basic facts, that Nadiya might come live with us, that her parents had died in a famine. But he'd left out that she'd had little brothers who'd died, too. I didn't blame Pop. Each time I thought of those boys, I wanted to give Peter a squeeze and buy him a malted. He had just turned eight, and I still wanted him to believe the world was a kind place, filled with love, not one where children died cruel, unnecessary deaths. But I also wanted him to know he had cousins, to remember them. When Nadiya came to us—I still had faith she would—I wanted him to be able to understand her grief, not be blind to it the way I had been to Pop's.

"Actually," I said. "She had two little brothers."

Peter's eyes widened. "What happened to them?"

"They also died in the famine."

"How old were they?"

"Nine and five."

Peter didn't say anything, but his little brow furrowed.

"Nadiya must be very sad," he finally said.

I put my arm around him. "I'm sure she is. But we'll help her."

Peter nodded, but his face was still clouded with worry.

"What is it?"

Peter looked down at the sidewalk. I wondered if I had made a mistake by telling him about the boys. What if now he was afraid of dying, too?

"I don't want to be an orphan," he murmured.

It took me a moment to understand his logic. Then it hit me: Nadiya's story had made him worry about Pop.

"Have you been worried about this all along?" I asked.

He nodded shyly. I realized that if I'd never told him about Nadiya's brothers, he might have kept this secret fear to himself.

"Pop's okay now. He's even working again. You're not going to become an orphan."

"But I heard Mom tell Mary he's working too hard. What if he dies and something happens to you and Mom?"

I turned him toward me, looked him in the eye.

"Nothing's going to happen to us. Nadiya's family died because the Soviet government doesn't care about its own people; it didn't give them enough food. But we don't live in the Soviet Union. We're safe here in America."

I was afraid he'd ask more questions, tougher ones, like why the Soviet government would starve its own people. But he just looked relieved.

"I want to light candles for our cousins this Sunday in church," he said.

"Me and you," I said. "We'll do that."

Peter sighed. "I wish Nadiya wasn't an orphan."

"Well, she won't be when she gets here," I said. "She'll have us."

"Like Little Orphan Annie," he said.

It was one of our favorite comic strips, the story of an innocent girl with red hair adopted out of a cruel orphanage by a wealthy family.

"Except Pop's not exactly Daddy Warbucks."

Peter considered this. "No. He has too much hair."

I laughed. "And no fancy mansion with a butler and house-keeper."

"Nadiya's not in an orphanage, is she?" Peter said.

"No, she's with kind people," I said. "They're taking good care of her."

The rest of the way home, I was filled with optimism. Peter and I would help Nadiya feel loved. We'd treat her not just like a cousin, but a sister. I'd always wanted one. I imagined us lifelong friends, dancing at each other's weddings, becoming godmothers to each other's children, laughing together at our memories when we were old. If only she would come soon! At least my battle with the *New York Times* offered a distraction. As I raced Peter up the stairs, I decided to ask Pop if I could go through his stack of *Novoe Russkoe Slovo* newspapers for famine stories. But when I opened the door, I noticed he wasn't in his usual chair in the living room and the door to his bedroom was closed.

"Shhh!" Mom said, coming out of the kitchen and wiping her hands on her apron. "Pop's resting."

"I'm going back out," Peter whispered.

But I stayed inside, followed Mom to the kitchen. She was making *kholodets*, or pigs' feet in gelatin. It was Pop's favorite dish, and I liked it, too, though in the past I'd only eaten it at home for fear of what Irene might say. If there were leftovers, though, I decided to ask Mom if I could take them to school on Monday.

"Where's Pop?" I asked in Russian.

"He's resting." Mom didn't look at me, she kept her eyes on the bowl where she was straining broth to make the gelatin. But I still felt the weight of her silent blame. Even though Pop was working again, Mom was still sewing for Mr. Grushko, the tailor. She claimed we needed the extra money for Mr. Kaminski, but I knew she was also afraid that Pop would get sick again. I thought of what Peter had told me, how she worried about Pop working too hard.

"He wanted to go back to work," I said.

"It's not just work," she said.

"What then?"

Mom tasted her broth, salted it, tasted it again. She seemed to be deciding on something much more than just the flavor. My stomach tightened.

"What's going on?" I said. "Is Pop okay?"

Mom put down her spoon, looked up at me.

"Mr. Kaminski says they can't find Nadiya. She's no longer at the address she wrote from."

"What?! Pop didn't say anything—"

"He just found out a few days ago. He didn't want to worry you."

I pulled out a chair and sat down hard.

"Mr. Kaminski's still looking for her, though? Someone must know where she went."

"He's doing what he can. But who knows if the government wants to tell where she is? Or even knows?"

"She'll write again," I said. "She'll tell us where she is."

"Perhaps."

"What? You don't think she'll write?"

Mom sighed. "I don't know, Lenachka. She could be . . . unable."

I tried not to think of what would make her unable to write. What if Peter was right and she was in an orphanage? Or on the street? Sick? Dead? I pushed away this last possibility.

"If she's in trouble, she'll write," I said. "She did it before."

Mom shook her head, gave the strainer a vigorous shake. "I knew this would come to grief."

I could feel the tears pooling in my eyes. "Pop needed to know! I did the right thing."

Mom just shrugged. "We'll see."

41

MILA

Kyiv, Ukraine, USSR
1933

Over her mug of soup, Nadiya told me everything that had happened to her since the secret police had shown up at Anna Mikhailovna's apartment. After taking away Anna Mikhailovna, the secret police had threatened to drop Nadiya back in the countryside, but instead they had driven her to the Collector.

"It's Dasha's fault!" I said.

I told her about Dasha's betrayal, Papa's arrest. As I was nearing the end of my story, the tall girl who'd helped me get my mug interrupted us.

"You must be sisters—"

"Yes," Nadiya said before I could correct her. Then she introduced us. "Vera, this is Mila."

I liked that Nadiya wanted to pretend we were sisters; I didn't realize there was a purpose to it until after breakfast, when we were divided into work brigades. Siblings were allowed to stay together, and when Nadiya introduced me as her sister, our shared last name and resemblance were proof enough for the matron in charge. As we carried bundles of dirty sheets down to the laundry in the basement, Nadiya explained that if the staff believed we were sisters, we were also less likely to be separated and sent off to different orphanages. "We have to stay together, no matter what."

I admired her quick thinking; I certainly wasn't capable of it myself. I was hungry and tired, and kept feeling that the situation around me couldn't be real. But then my shock would clear like a fog, and the horror of my surroundings would set in.

"Shouldn't we just get out of here now?" I whispered.

"And go where?" Nadiya said. "The street?"

"Papa thought they'd release Anna Mikhailovna. We can go to her."

"Release her with no punishment?"

Nadiya sounded skeptical.

"He said they'd probably take her ration card."

"She'll starve!" Nadiya said.

Compared to the punishments in my head—exile in Siberia, jail—losing a ration card hadn't seemed so bad. Only now did I think how ordinary people were dependent on their ration cards for bread.

"They have the Torgsin at least."

"They already traded most of their gold for me," Nadiya said.

"No, no, we can't go back and put them in more danger. Besides, we'd have nothing to eat."

I tried to think of someplace else. But none of Papa's friends would help us now that he'd been unmasked as a class enemy, and even if she wasn't still furious over my lies, Katya would never take the risk of hiding us.

"The street's better than this place," I said.

Nadiya shot me a skeptical look. "I know this seems bad to you. But at least here they give us something to eat, a place to sleep—"

We had reached the entrance to a large steamy room in the basement where under the direction of another matron, children mixed enormous boiling cauldrons of bedding and clothes. The heat from this room added to my desperation to flee.

"You don't understand," I said. "I know all about this place. After Papa sent you away, I came to look for you here. They were bringing out the bodies of dead children."

Nadiya froze at the door. I could tell I'd surprised, even shocked her, and I was glad. Now she'd agree with me and we could sneak out of the Collector, go someplace safer.

But when she finally spoke, she didn't say at all what I thought she would.

"You came all the way here to find *me?*"

This wasn't the point I was trying to make. "Yes, but don't you understand? Kids are dying here—"

Nadiya dropped the wash in her arms into a bin then swung around to face me.

"Oh, Mila," she said. "You think they're not dying on the street?"

My heart sank. Of course, she was right. There were bodies under Besarabsky market. There were bodies littering the countryside. There was nowhere safe for the child of a class enemy. I heaved my load into the bin then leaned against the side, dizzy from the steam and my own gnawing hunger. I didn't have the strength to be like Nadiya, to pick myself up after losing everything and keep going. A sob escaped me.

"Shhh," Nadiya said. "You're going to get through this. I'll help you."

"Why?" I choked out. "I'm the reason you ended up here!"

"What are you talking about? If it weren't for you, I would have died. You got me to Anna Mikhailovna's. You *saved* me, Mila, and sacrificed everything. It's my turn now. I'm going to write Yelena, our cousin in America, the one who sent me the cross. Tell her where we are—"

"Did her family even get your last letter?"

"I don't know. But maybe our uncle could bring us both? I'll tell them all about you. I didn't before—I was worried about getting you in trouble. Too late for that now. I'd like to go to New York, wouldn't you? See the Statue of Liberty?"

She smiled, trying to lift my spirits. I attempted to smile back but only because I was too exhausted to argue. This was a fantasy, at best. And even if her latest letter could get past the censors and my American uncle could pull off such a feat, he had been trying to save Nadiya and her family—not me. I didn't even want to go to

America. Kyiv was my home. Papa was my home. What if he came looking for me? But I had to admit that Nadiya was right about one thing. If anyone was going to come looking for us, it was probably best to stay put, even at the Collector.

That night, we shared a cot even though we each had our own. Nadiya spooned against me, and I pulled up my coat over both of us. My head ached from hunger—dinner had been a piece of bread and another mug of watery soup. All around me, I could hear coughing and sniffling, moaning and sighing, the door banging open and shut. I could smell whiffs of urine. But the feeling of Nadiya's warm body next to mine, like a twin question mark, lulled me to sleep.

I woke in the darkness to the same tickling sensation of hair on my forehead that I'd felt earlier that morning. Like before, I automatically brushed away the ghost strand, but before I could fall back to sleep the spot started to itch. I sat up to scratch it and felt a small raised bump.

Nadiya looked up at me. "What is it?"

"Something bit me."

"Probably a louse," she murmured. "The place is infested."

I frantically swiped at my forehead, trying to flick away the invisible bugs I imagined swarming my head.

"What if they make us sick?"

"There's nothing to be done," Nadiya said. "Just try to sleep."

I lay back down, but I couldn't settle my mind. Instead, I thought about the day when the lice had tumbled out of the envelope, how Papa hadn't let a single one bite me, how he had stomped them out. The irony didn't escape me—I was now one of the lice-infested kulak children he had taught me to fear. But I missed him with a physical ache, a rising panic.

"Nadiya?" I whispered in the darkness.

"What?"

"Will I ever see my papa again?"

She didn't answer right away, but her pause told me more than the words that followed.

"You never know."

I closed my eyes as tight as I could, curled into a ball. But it didn't help. I could barely breathe with longing for him.

Nadiya curled her body around mine, protective, like a shell.

"What do I do?" I whispered.

It was a stupid question. There was nothing *to* do. Papa was gone—he would be exiled to Siberia, starved, worked to death. There was no getting him back, just as there was no getting Nadiya's parents or brothers back. I hardly expected an answer.

"What he'd want you to do."

"What's that?"

Nadiya sighed deeply.

"Survive."

42

MATTHEW

Leonia, New Jersey, USA
2020

"Mila got that disease, the one that lice have, that her father was all worried about!" I interrupted. "Typhus, right? That's what happened to her . . . She was bitten . . ."

I looked at GG. Her eyes were brimming with tears.

"No!" I cried. "It's not fair!"

I was mad at myself for being as upset as I was. Hadn't GG warned me from the beginning that something terrible had happened to Mila? It was already a miracle that GG herself had survived the famine, then this horrible orphanage. There weren't going to be two miracles. But I didn't want Mila to die. I wanted her to grow up and grow old, like GG.

GG's hand clasped mine. Her fingers were cold, her skin soft and loose around the bones. "Life's not fair," she said.

She pointed to one of the boxes still against the wall. "Open it."

I dragged over the box, slashed at the tape, curious and half-afraid of what might be inside. It was a stack of photo albums. I pulled one out and opened it up to a color photo of GG—her face younger but her hair still white—holding up a baby to the camera. A pretty woman with long brown hair parted in the middle and a dimple in her cheek grinned beside them.

"Is that Mom?" I asked.

GG shook her head. "Anna."

GG pointed to the baby I had assumed was me. "Your mom."

It turned out all the photos in the albums were of my grandma Anna. I had seen a few of her before—Mom had some in her room—but never this many. There were photos of her as a toddler, face smeared with pie; dressed as a witch for Halloween; at her high school graduation in a cap and gown, her arms around friends; in a wedding dress, holding a bouquet of purple flowers that had to be lilacs; leaning against a cane as she stood in between a skinny girl with braces I recognized as Mom and GG. In this last photo, Anna's hair was stubbly, her face hollowed out. She looked almost as old as GG.

Tears escaped GG's eyes, dripped down her wrinkled cheeks. "Before she died."

GG had made her point. Life wasn't fair. People you loved died. People you loved were taken from you. I thought of Dad, pushed away a fresh wave of fear.

I brought her a tissue. "Has Mom seen these?"

She blew her nose. "Long time ago."

I flipped through the albums again until I found the photo of smiling, young Grandma Anna with GG next to her holding baby Mom. "Can I borrow this?"

GG nodded.

I arranged the albums on a shelf next to her record collection then told her I had some homework to do. She helped gather the notebooks and papers, which I carefully placed back in their box. I had a feeling she was relieved that I hadn't asked her to tell me the rest of the story. After looking at all those photos of Anna, making GG talk about Mila's death seemed cruel. But it was more than that. I didn't want to say goodbye to Mila, either.

I knocked on Mom's bedroom door. I half expected her to snap at me for interrupting, but the door opened, and she stood there, looking so much like Grandma Anna that I felt as if that photo had come to life. Behind her on the desk, I could see a bunch of people in a Zoom meeting on her laptop.

"I'll come back later," I said.

But she'd already stepped out into the hall. "I stopped my video. They won't even notice I'm gone."

"Are you sure?"

"It's the world's most boring meeting. Really. I should be thanking you."

We stood there for an awkward moment before I could get it out. "Sorry," I said. "For the way I acted last night."

Mom smiled. "It's okay," she said. "Hungry? I could use a snack."

I was suddenly ravenous. "Sure."

I followed her into the kitchen and sat down at the breakfast bar. I thought she'd open the drawer where she kept Mom-approved healthy snacks like granola bars and packets of nuts, but instead she began digging around in the pantry. Even before I heard her mutter, "Where are they?" I knew what she was looking for.

"Um, Mom?"

"What?"

"GG and I—"

"Wait, you can tell me what the two of you've been up to in a second; let me just find—"

"The chocolates," I said.

That brought her out fast. She narrowed her eyes, one hand on her hip. But her lips were curving into a grin, so I knew she wasn't really angry.

"She was pretty sick of prunes," I said. "And chocolate-flavored Ensure just isn't the same as Hershey's."

Mom laughed. "GG loves her chocolate, that's for sure. She always had some hidden in her house when I was little. When my mom brought me over, I used to steal a few pieces. I guess we're even now."

"We found some pictures in one of her boxes today of Grandma Anna." I pulled the photo out of the pocket of my hoodie and slid it across the counter to her. "I brought you one."

Mom sat down next to me at the breakfast bar and picked up the photo. "Oh!" she said, and her whole face brightened.

"I thought it was you," I said. "She looks like you."

Even though she was smiling, her eyes were wet, and I was afraid she might cry. But she just kept grinning at the photo. "That's a compliment. She was very pretty."

"Mom," I said softly. "What was it like when she died?"

Her smile faded. She put down the picture, took a deep breath. "Hard, really hard. I wasn't much older than you. My parents were divorced, and my dad had moved away and remarried. GG became my second mom."

But this wasn't exactly what I was asking. I knew these details. My throat tightened, and my voice came out high and tight. "How did you stand it? Missing her that much?"

Mom sighed. "You just do. It never goes away, but each day it gets a little easier."

I tried again. "When did you know that it would be the last time that you'd see her? I mean, I know she got sick, but then it was like, one day she was gone?"

Mom looked at me, confused. "What makes you ask?"

I looked down. "I don't know. It's just that Dad's so far away . . ." My words trailed off.

"Matthew, I know you miss Dad. But you're going to see him again."

"But what if I don't?" My voice cracked. "What if he gets Covid and—"

Mom put her hands on my shoulders, tilted my chin so I was looking straight into her eyes. "Your father is being very careful not to get sick. So am I. But if something were to ever happen to him or to me, I need you to know you're strong. You'll be all right."

That heavy weight was crushing my chest again.

"I'm not! I won't!"

"Matthew, trust me. I know this from experience. You'll put one foot in front of the other. You'll survive."

I blinked. "Who told you that?"

"GG."

It was the same advice she'd given Mila. Except Mila hadn't survived. What if Dad didn't survive, either?

Mom pulled me in for a hug.

"I'm scared," I whispered.

Mom hugged me tighter. "We all are. That's why we snap at each other."

I sniffed. "You snap at me a lot."

"I know I do. I've been trying to do everything and just doing it all badly. I haven't been there for you enough. I'm sorry."

I relaxed against her. "I'm really sorry, too, about the ketchup bottle. And for being rude to Josh. It's just when his dad—"

"You don't have to explain." She smoothed back my hair. "Maybe just text Josh you were having an off day. Just so he doesn't think it's him."

"Okay."

"Okay? Now let's see if we have some ice cream instead."

I was still mad at Dad for not being straight with me, but I didn't feel quite as panicky about not seeing him. Just knowing Mom and

GG had survived a lot worse helped. My thoughts turned to what Mom had said about her trying to do everything.

"Hey," I said when she came back from the freezer. "Maybe you can have the groceries delivered so you don't have to go out? It would probably be safer for GG and give you a little more time to work. I could prepare the order."

She froze, ice cream scooper in hand, and studied me like I was someone new.

"That's really considerate, Matthew."

I grinned. "It's the only way to make sure I get salsa."

Mom jabbed me in the side with her elbow, then we both ate too much chocolate fudge brownie ice cream and she told me more about Grandma Anna—how she always read the last page of a book first, kept a cat, and loved the ocean, how she'd asked Mom and GG to scatter her ashes there.

Finally, Mom checked her watch and said she had to check in and make sure she hadn't missed anything in her meeting. After she left, I scooped out one last bowl of ice cream. But it wasn't for me. I was finally ready to hear the rest of Mila's story—including the sad part.

43
MILA

Kyiv, Ukraine, USSR
1933

"**W**ake up, sleepyhead!"

Nadiya stood over me, shaking my shoulder. The morning bell was clanging and, judging from the clamor of footsteps and voices, had been for a while. After nearly two weeks at the Collector, I knew the value of grabbing a spot at the front of the queue before the wash bucket water had turned gray. But my head ached, and my arms and legs felt heavy. Fear tugged at my chest. I wasn't sick—I couldn't get sick. I was just tired.

"Are you okay?" Nadiya asked.

I forced myself upright. I wanted to say yes. But my face felt hot and tears stung my dry eyes. Nadiya rested her hand on my forehead. Worry flitted across her face.

"Lie back down," she said. "I'll ask Masha for some broth."

Masha was a server at the canteen whom Nadiya had befriended and who sometimes slipped us extra soup. The broth revived me enough for Nadiya to drag me with her to the large assembly room where every morning we divided up into our work brigades. To my relief, I wasn't assigned the worst job—spreading lime across the reeking, open-holed toilets—but scrubbing the canteen floor. All the kids hoped for this job because it held the possibility of finding a fallen scrap of cabbage or potato skin. But I had no energy for the hunt. Nadiya scrubbed the floor around me to make it look as if I'd done my part.

"Good work, Mila!" said the matron in charge, confusing Nadiya for me.

Then she went back to poking around the kitchen for bread she might steal for herself. But nothing escaped Vera.

"What's wrong with your sister?" I heard her ask Nadiya.

Nadiya's plan had worked—by this time, everyone at the Collector believed we were sisters. With our similar size and stubborn insistence on sharing a cot, some of the matrons even mistook us for twins.

"Headache," Nadiya said.

She tried to sound as if it were nothing serious, but Vera eyed me darkly.

"Don't bring her to the infirmary. The doctor's a drunk."

"I'm fine," I said, giving a half-hearted scrub of the floor wavering in front of me.

But I wasn't. At dinner, I took one look at my slice of bread and my stomach heaved. Nadiya rushed me over to the bathroom, where I threw up the watery remains of the broth. When I finally stopped vomiting, my face pulsed with heat. Nadiya put her hand to my forehead, winced, disguised it with a smile.

"Back to bed," she said cheerily.

Tears ran down my hot face. "You need to find another cot. I'll get you sick."

"Too late for that," she said. "Besides, I feel fine."

I scanned her face, which was thin and hollowed out again. But now so was mine. Her large blue eyes shined brightly, though. Gratitude toward Anna Mikhailovna coursed through me. Those six weeks of meat and milk had strengthened Nadiya, were keeping her alive. But what had they cost my teacher? Was she starving now herself along with her kind old mother? Normally, when I had these thoughts, I tried not to think about them for too long. But whatever sickness had taken hold made me weepy, and I fell forward into Nadiya's arms.

"Don't cry," she said, stroking my feverish cheek. "We'll get you well. We just need to bring your fever down."

I nodded miserably.

"A clean cloth," she murmured, half to herself. "We need something clean—"

Her eyes dropped to my coat, which she was wearing. We passed it back and forth during the day, lay under it together at night. It had turned out to be well worth the loss of the chocolates. Nadiya flipped up the bottom, touched the silk lining.

"It's cleaner than anything else we have—"

She looked at me questioningly.

"Go ahead," I whispered.

She wedged her finger into the stitching then tore out a square of the coat's lining. She helped me back to our cot then dashed off, returning with a bucket of water. Perching beside me, she dipped the square of lining into the bucket, squeezed it out, then placed the cool, wet cloth on my forehead. I sighed, closed my eyes.

"Dasha used to do this when I was sick," I murmured.

There was silence, then Nadiya said, "My mother did, too."

"Your mother loved you, though. For Dasha it was just duty."

"Shh," Nadiya said. "What was that piano music you played for me at Anna Mikhailovna's?"

"'Sweet Dreams.'"

But everything sweet seemed like a lifetime ago.

"'Sweet Dreams,'" she repeated, stroking my shorn hair. "Tchaikovsky, right? Think of that."

But the fever made me babble on. "Dasha used to do that— stroke my hair when I was sick, when I had hair." I was crying again. "She made it look like love."

"Maybe it was."

"Then her betrayal is even worse!"

I shifted restlessly, my body aching.

"I was never her family."

"No," Nadiya agreed. "But you're mine."

I gripped her hand with my clammy fingers. "What if I die?"

Her brow set and her eyes burned, a stubborn Lomachenko look if I ever saw one. I almost laughed. "You're not going to die," she said.

But the idea latched on and wouldn't leave me. I squeezed her hand.

"Promise me you'll get out of here—"

"Stop talking like that," Nadiya snapped. "We'll get out of here together."

I realized I was speaking the way her mother had, that it was upsetting her.

"I'm sorry. But promise me, please!"

She looked me straight in the eye. "I promise. But you must promise me the same, okay? We live for each other. Now rest! You need to sleep."

She pulled away her hand, checked my compress.

As if to make certain I wouldn't keep talking, she started to sing softly under her breath. She had claimed she wasn't musical. But now I wondered if Anna Mikhailovna's and my own piano skills had simply intimidated her. Her voice was high and reedy but not unpleasant, a voice that made me think of what voices were like long ago.

"*Spi, mladenetz/moi prekrasni*," she sang.

Sleep, darling, my dearest.

It was a lullaby, too old for me to know and yet familiar. Had Dasha sung it? Or had my own mother, in the few hours we'd had together? I'd never know.

I nodded off, found myself alone in a desert, calling for Papa. I had no water, and the sun was beating down on me.

Loud buzzing made me look up. An enormous plane was overhead. The *Maxim Gorky*! Surely it would rescue me. I ran after it, waving my arms, but my feet sank into the sand and I couldn't get purchase. "Help!" I screamed.

Papa waved from the cockpit. Relief swallowed me up. But then the plane continued on. I tried to chase it but tumbled face-first onto the hot sand.

I woke up gasping for breath. Where was I? Why was it so dark?

"Nadiya!" I tried to scream, but a hand clapped over my mouth.

Where was I? What was happening?

I struggled to breathe.

"Hold her down!"

Someone was crying.

A louse was biting me. I tried to slap it away.

Nothingness.

44

HELEN

Brooklyn, New York, USA
1933

"How much longer?" I asked Pop anxiously.

We were sitting on a bench in Tompkins Square Park on the Lower East Side, dressed in our best Sunday clothes, even though it was Saturday. Pop didn't have to pull out his pocket watch; he was already holding it in his palm. He flipped it open.

"Our appointment's in forty minutes," he said. "We'll walk over in twenty."

Pop had arrived home yesterday with exciting news: Mr. Kaminski had called him at the printing press and asked him to come to his office the following morning. There had been new developments in Nadiya's case, but the lawyer hadn't revealed what they were. Mom had offered to go with him, but Pop had insisted she stay with Peter and do her usual Saturday shopping.

We'd started off early, much earlier than we'd needed to, which was how we'd ended up in the park. The neighborhood around it was lively—full of shops and bars. Normally I would have enjoyed watching the people, but all I could think about was what Mr. Kaminski had to tell us. Had he found Nadiya? Was she alive? Safe? Could we bring her home?

Pop's voice interrupted my thoughts.

"The first place I lived when I came to this country was a few blocks from here."

I looked up, surprised to hear Pop talking about the past. It felt like a window had been pushed open a crack, and I rushed in with a question to make sure it stayed that way.

"How old were you?"

"Barely eighteen," he said. He paused, then added, "You know, I left Ukraine to escape the draft."

Pop had never told me his reason for coming to America. I had just assumed he'd wanted a better life, like Mom, whose family had been so poor she wore rags for shoes.

"My mother knew there was going to be a war," he continued. "My father was already dead, and with five boys—"

"Five!" I interrupted. "I thought you only had one brother— Nadiya's father!"

Pop didn't answer, and I was afraid he might not continue. But my interviews about the famine had taught me the value of patience, especially when the subject was painful. I said nothing and waited.

Pop finally spoke.

"Mykola was the closest to me in age. Next were Stepan and Volodymyr, the twins. I was the oldest, so the idea was I would go ahead, and they would follow. But by the time I got settled and could help them, the Great War had already begun. The twins were killed in the war; my mother died soon after. Mykola survived, but he didn't want to leave—our family owned some land, and he wanted to farm it, like our father had. By this time, the Communists had taken over. A few years ago, they arrested him for refusing to give them our land—they wanted to collectivize it, make it State property. They sent him to a work camp in Siberia, where he died."

I knew Pop's brother had died, not that he'd been arrested and sent to Siberia. But it wasn't just Mykola. Pop had lost his entire family. Or almost his entire family.

"You had one more brother," I said. "The youngest."

Pop's face hardened.

"Lev."

"What happened to him?"

"He was swept up in the Revolution."

I pictured a big red wave crashing over the head of this uncle I'd only just discovered.

"The Communists worked him to death, too?"

"Worse." Pop's jaw tightened angrily.

What could be worse than being worked to death? Hung? Beheaded? I cycled through every horrible death I could think of, but I wasn't prepared for what Pop said next.

"He became one of them."

"A Communist?"

"High-ranking, too! He turned his back on our family, pretended not to know Mykola or his wife even when she pleaded to him for help."

"How could he do that?!" I exclaimed.

"He's a scoundrel!"

"He's still alive, then?"

Pop's eyes blazed. "Who knows? Anyway, he's dead to me. Absolutely dead! And he's dead to you, too."

"I wasn't planning to write him," I said gently.

Pop looked down at his lap. I put my hand on top of his. He took it in his own. His nails were stained black from the printing press, no matter how much he washed them.

"I can see why everyone tells you their stories," he said.

I looked up sharply. I'd never told him about my interviews. I had believed Mom that it would anger him, that he wouldn't like me asking his friends about their families back home, making them relive the pain and loss that, like Pop, they were helpless to fix. But there was no note of disapproval in his voice.

"I'm glad you told me yours," I said.

He blinked hard, sniffed. Was Pop . . . crying? I'd never seen him cry before. The thought that he might start weeping made me frantic. What if he got so upset that his heart—

"Lenachka, don't worry," he said. "I'm okay."

Pop was staring at me, reading the fear that must have been written on my face.

"And you'll be, too," he added, "even if we can't find Nadiya or save her. The world is a difficult place; we can only try our best."

"Do you think the news is bad?" I interrupted.

"I don't know. But I want you to be ready, no matter what Mr. Kaminski has to tell us."

By the time we arrived at the lawyer's office, my own heart felt like it would burst, and it wasn't just from racing ahead up the two flights of stairs. I'd tried, as Pop had told me, to prepare myself for anything. But I wasn't prepared for the surprise that met me when I burst into the crowded waiting room.

"Hello," Mom said with a sheepish grin.

She was sitting on a chair in the corner in her blue silk dress, the one she wore to church.

"What are you doing here?" I asked. "And where's Peter?"

"I left him with Mary. I wanted to be here."

I bristled with annoyance. She was probably just worried that Mr. Kaminski's news would upset Pop and I would make the situation worse. I turned to Pop, who had just entered. Surely he knew her motivation and would scold her for turning up out of the blue like this. But his face softened at the sight of her.

Before I could ponder this, the door to Mr. Kaminski's office opened and a man with a downcast expression shuffled out, followed by our lawyer. Mr. Kaminski was shorter than Pop, with a long nose and a limp Pop said was from the war. I raced up to him. His secretary, Magda, shot me a look of disapproval. She liked to announce whoever was up next to Mr. Kaminski, not have his clients rush him in desperation. But I couldn't wait.

"Pop said you have news?"

"Helen!" Pop's tone was scolding, but I noticed he was eyeing Mr. Kaminski just as eagerly.

"I do," the lawyer said. "Looks like the whole family's here." He turned to Mom. "Mrs. Lomachenko, I presume?"

As Pop introduced her and they all shook hands, I studied Mr. Kaminski's face. But his polite smile gave nothing away.

"Come in."

I barely waited till he closed the door behind us.

"Is it good news?"

"Sit down, please."

We all quickly took a seat. He walked to his desk, the catch of his limp slowing him down just enough to add to the suspense. Then he sat down and faced us, his eyes crinkling.

"I don't often have the chance to deliver happy news. But we've located Nadiya at an orphanage in Kyiv and secured the permission of both governments for you to bring her home."

I leapt out of my chair with a shout of joy and threw my arms around Pop. We had done it! We had saved Nadiya! I felt him exhale, as if he'd been holding his breath for a long time. His head sank into his hand.

"Thank God," he murmured.

Mr. Kaminski stood up to hand Pop some papers.

"I would advise you, Mr. Lomachenko, to book passage to Kyiv as quicky as you can before anyone changes their mind."

I'd never allowed myself to think this far ahead, but now, for the first time, I realized that Pop would have to make a long, difficult trip to bring Nadiya back to Brooklyn. I couldn't go with him either—one ticket was expensive enough; there would be the cost of Nadiya's passage, as well. With a sickening feeling, I turned to Mom. Just as I'd feared, her anguished eyes told me she didn't want to let him go. Maybe this was why she'd come, to try to stop him. Surely Pop wouldn't listen to her; he'd make the trip even against her wishes. But why, then, was he staring at her as if waiting for her blessing?

Mom's eyes passed from me to him. They were full of fear—the fear of losing Pop, the fear of not being able to provide for us—all the fears of the last, difficult year. But then I realized what I hadn't seen before in the waiting room, but that Pop must have. They were also full of love.

Mom took a deep breath.

"Of course, Vanya," she said. "Of course you must go. Bring our Nadiya home."

45

MILA

Kyiv, Ukraine, USSR
1933

A demon's face loomed above me—bristly brows accenting a pair of bloodshot eyes.

"Can you hear me, Mila?"

His breath reeked of vodka and cigarettes as if a wild party were underway inside his mouth. I made a face.

He laughed. "Well, at least you can smell me."

He drew back and I realized he wasn't a demon, just a rumpled, gray-haired man. The room around him came into focus: rows of cots, children thrashing and coughing.

"Where am I?" My voice was hoarse and didn't sound like my own.

"Typhus ward of the infirmary," he said.

"How long have I been here?"

The doctor, for that was clearly who he was, pulled a stethoscope out of his pocket. He stuck it in his ears then pressed the circular drum against my chest. "Five days."

"I was out all that time?"

"In and out. Delirium. Shhhh."

I obediently fell silent. It made me nervous to imagine what he heard. My heart seemed to thump in my chest. Was it damaged? Was I dying? I watched his face for clues. But his expression remained neutral.

"Will I survive, Doctor . . ."

I hesitated, not knowing his name.

"Zima," he said.

The Ukrainian word for *winter*. A shiver passed through me. I waited, my anxiety growing, but Dr. Zima didn't answer my question. Instead, he pulled up the sleeve of the fresh nightgown someone must have dressed me in. I gasped—my entire arm was covered with dusky purple spots.

"Natural course of the disease," he said. "Important thing is your fever's broken. You'll survive."

He delivered my life back to me in such an offhanded way that it took a moment to sink in.

"I'm not going to die?"

Dr. Zima stood up. He seemed in a hurry to get to his next patient. But he answered me in a clear, indisputable voice: "No."

I wanted to laugh, shout, dance around. But all I could manage in my weakened state was a teary smile. I had been so certain that this was the end, that I would never turn thirteen or leave the Collector, grow up, fall in love, have children of my own. Only now could I admit to myself how terrified I'd been and how much I'd longed to live—not just for myself, but for Nadiya. Nadiya! I couldn't wait to tell her. She'd told me I'd make it through, and she was right.

"When can I see my sister?" I asked.

Dr. Zima blinked hard, as if the question stumped him.

"Nadiya Lomachenko," I said.

Dr. Zima didn't answer. He just stood there. Then he pulled a flask out of his pocket, unscrewed the top, and took a swig. "Your cousin."

I remembered what Vera had said about him, how he was a drunk. Perhaps he was also someone who liked to make trouble. Why else would he bother to check our records when everyone else, even the matrons, had accepted that Nadiya and I were sisters? I decided to ignore his correction.

"Does she know how I am? Can I see her?"

Dr. Zima wiped his lips with the back of his hand, screwed on the top.

"It didn't make sense your being sisters."

He wanted me to admire how clever he was. But no, that wasn't it. He wasn't gloating. His voice was gentle. My throat tightened.

"What do you mean?"

"Your system wasn't weakened by malnutrition. Hers was. It makes all the difference with typhus. A healthy child can fight it off."

I dragged myself upright, my heart thumping wildly.

"What are you saying? She wasn't even sick!"

But I knew the same lice that had infected me must have bitten Nadiya. I scanned the infirmary beds, looking for her. Every face that wasn't hers increased my panic, deepened my terror.

"Where is she?" I shouted.

"I'm sorry," Dr. Zima said. "She was falling ill herself when she brought you. She died last night."

46
MATTHEW

Leonia, New Jersey, USA
2020

"**W**ait, what?!" I hollered.

GG slumped down, almost melted into her bed.

"Dr. Zima must have made a mistake—" I said.

I looked to GG, but she just stared off into the distance.

I suddenly remembered something else about *Zelda*: The game can trick you. You think you're on the right quest, but you're actually off track. It's supposed to teach you a lesson about using the Quest Menu. But it's also a warning about making assumptions.

"Or—"

A shiver ran down my spine. The second possibility was that freaky. But at the same time, it made perfect sense: the knowing way she had hummed along to that Russian composer's piano music;

how she'd talked about losing her dad—but never her mom; even her obsession with chocolate.

I put my hand over GG's cold, bony one, leaned in, looked her right in the eye.

"Mila?"

Silence.

As it dragged on, I began to feel like an idiot. It was a crazy theory anyway, that my great-grandmother had lived most of her life as an imposter.

But then she answered.

It was just a whisper.

"Yes."

A terrible secret. Changed my life.

GG's terrible secret didn't just change her life. Her terrible secret was that *she had changed* her life! Before I could stop myself, a couple of not exactly Mom-approved words popped out of my mouth. I expected GG to frown or shake her finger, but her watery eyes crinkled with amusement. For a fleeting second, I saw mischievous young Mila staring back at me.

"I don't understand," I said. "Why did you become Nadiya?"

The ghost of young Mila faded as GG's expression darkened.

"To survive."

47

MILA

Kyiv, Ukraine, USSR
1933

I recovered and grew stronger, but I was already not myself. I didn't talk, didn't smile. The matrons, who could never keep straight which one of us was me and which one of us was Nadiya, simply called me Lomachenko, since there was only one of us now. I didn't stop eating—to starve myself in Nadiya's memory seemed terribly wrong—but I ate mechanically without tasting my food. Only Vera knew my name—"I'm sorry about your sister, Mila," she told me—and urged the kitchen staff to give me a little extra "to fatten me up" after my illness. But I hadn't the heart to utter more than a quiet thank-you.

At night, my tiny cot felt as cold and empty as an ocean without Nadiya's body against mine. The matrons had burned her possessions after she'd died—for sanitary reasons, they'd explained. Included in these possessions was the letter she'd written but hadn't yet figured out how to send to our relatives in America, as well their address. There was no way to write them, even to tell them Nadiya had died. The only item that had been saved was our coat, which had been deemed too expensive to burn, and had been fumigated and, out of pity, returned to me. Most nights, I curled into a ball beneath it and cried myself to sleep.

It was a miracle I wasn't sent off to another orphanage. Perhaps they thought I was still recovering and not strong enough; perhaps I looked so hollow-eyed and unlovable that there seemed no rush. More likely I was just forgotten in the chaos. New children arrived daily, were sent away, ran away, died. I hardly bothered to look at them, never mind interact. But one day, herded into the assembly hall, where they sorted out who they would move to other orphanages, I heard my name, "Mila! Mila Lomachenko!"

My heart jumped until I remembered that it couldn't be Nadiya, that Nadiya was dead. I swiveled around and spotted a healthy, round face eagerly staring in my direction. The shorn hair threw me, but just for a moment.

"Katya?"

We pushed through the crowd toward each other and embraced.

"How long have you been here?" I asked.

"Not long. Just a day. I was hoping you were still here, but someone told me you'd died! I saw you before, but I didn't recognize you—"

She stopped, blushed. I could only imagine how I looked to her:

half-starved, pale, weak. Like a street child. The way Nadiya had once looked to me.

"They arrested Papa!" she whispered. "Oh, it was horrible, Mila! He's loyal to the Party; he's done nothing wrong. I'm sure it's just a terrible mistake."

She didn't say it, but I could tell she believed that my papa's case had been different. I should have told her the truth: that our fathers were both guilty and innocent, that the stupid little girl begging her papa for Bumble Bears had been living in a foolish dream, and so was she. But I'd never been a very good friend to Katya—or at least an honest one.

"It'll work out," I said.

She nodded, but her eyes, still fixed on me, remained unconvinced.

She reached up and touched her shorn scalp. "I kept thinking of Mama when they shaved my hair, how now she can't brush it, even though of course she can't . . ."

Her voice drifted off.

I forced a smile, my first in weeks. "At least the Committee of the Motherless Daughters of the Communist Party is reunited."

"Fatherless now, too," Katya said with a deep sigh. "I'm sorry they shot your father . . . Mila, are you okay?!"

I teetered, the room spinning around me. Papa gone, gone forever. I would never see him, never feel his arms around me, never hear him call me "little fox." I imagined his twinkling blue eyes, blank and lifeless. I felt like screaming, but I couldn't breathe.

Katya's voice reached me as if from a great distance. "You knew, right? You must have heard."

"Yes," I managed to blurt. I knew it was possible. Nadiya had tried to prepare me. Besides, there was no point in making Katya feel worse. I was completely and utterly alone. She was all I had.

Katya took my hand. The feel of her warm fingers filled my eyes with tears. No one had touched me since Nadiya. A second longer and I would have told her all about Nadiya and everything that had befallen us, but one of the matrons began shouting out names, and Katya let go of my hand and looked away. It was just as well because a moment later, her name was called, and she joined a group on the other side of the assembly hall. This group was then herded out of the Collector. I never saw Katya Gavrilok again.

A week later, I was on the line for soup with Vera when one of the matrons marched into the canteen and barked my name.

"Lomachenko!"

I turned around but didn't leave. I didn't want to lose my place. "Yes?"

"The director wants to see you!"

There was a stir.

"Lomachenko's in trouble," someone behind me taunted.

I was afraid they were right. The director, Comrade Pavluk, hid away in his office and rarely interacted with anyone, children or staff. When he did, it was usually to scold or punish them.

"But my soup—"

"Now!"

"Give me your mug," Vera whispered. "I'll get it for you."

I passed it to her, my stomach grumbling, then scurried over to the director's office. The faster I went, the faster I hoped to return. If the director kept me too long, the canteen would close, and Vera would have to eat my soup, too, not that I'd blame her for it.

I pounded on his office door with the urgency of hunger.

Comrade Pavluk opened it with a smile, as if we were old friends, although he'd never said a word or noticed me before.

"Nadiya, there you are!" he said.

Her name froze me in place.

"Your uncle is here! All the way from America."

He moved to the side to reveal a man in a dark suit, rising to his feet. His hair was gray, but his blue eyes crinkled just like Papa's.

"Nadiya, dear," he said. "I'm your uncle Vanya."

I stared at him dumbly.

"Would you like to come back with me to America?"

I had to tell him who I was. But what if he couldn't take me with him? What if he didn't want to? This was my chance to escape to somewhere safe, to the only family I had left. I might never have another. I heard Nadiya's voice: *Go on, get out of here! Live for the both of us. It's what you promised me.*

But before I could answer, a voice interjected.

"You don't have to go, Nadiya," said a man I hadn't noticed until then, who sat stiffly in the corner. "This is your fatherland. Papa Stalin will take care of you."

Anger curdled inside me. He was clearly from the government or secret police—probably Uncle Vanya's minder. I wanted to tell him that Stalin had taken care of Nadiya all right, that he was talking to a dead girl. I wanted to see the look on his face. But I couldn't *be* Nadiya and tell him that.

"I want to go" was all I said.

Uncle Vanya rushed over, gathered me up in his arms. My heart was pounding. What had I done? Surely they would figure out my lie. And even if they didn't, it was Nadiya who should be going to America, not me. I buried my head against his chest and burst into tears.

Uncle Vanya disentangled us, pulled out his handkerchief, and dabbed my face. "Hush, hush, Nad'ka," he said gently. "No need to weep."

"She's leaving her homeland; of course she's weeping," the man in the corner said.

"She's been ill," said a voice behind me. "Convalescents are always emotional."

I lurched around.

"Ah, Dr. Zima, there you are!" Comrade Pavluk said. "Mr. Lomachenko wanted reassurance that his niece is well enough to travel."

I had to do something. I rushed up to Dr. Zima, clutched his sleeve, begged with my eyes. "I'm Nadiya, remember? My uncle has permission to take me to America. Please tell them I can go."

Dr. Zima's bristly eyebrows twitched. "Of course, I remember."

Then he turned to the others. Was he going to tell them? He knew who I was—I could see he did. I held my breath.

"Nadiya will be fine on the trip," he said.

Nadiya.

I nearly collapsed to the floor with relief.

"Thank you, Doctor," Uncle Vanya said. "Thank you for saving Nadiya."

"She saved herself," Dr. Zima said with a quick glance in my direction. "I did nothing."

Another lie.

A half hour later, Uncle Vanya and I left the Collector with a medical report signed by Dr. Zima detailing Nadiya Lomachenko's full recovery from typhus. No one seemed to notice that the ink was still wet. I wouldn't be surprised if, at the same time, Dr. Zima made sure there was a record of Mila Lomachenko's death. In any case, no one ever mentioned to Uncle Vanya that there had been another orphan named Lomachenko. Comrade Pavluk likely hadn't bothered to check the records of the dead once the matrons had informed him that the girl the authorities were looking for was alive. And even if the matrons had revealed that there had been another Lomachenko, the director would have realized that no one was looking for her and likely calculated that there would be no advantage in admitting her existence or that she had died under his care to the authorities and a foreigner.

While we waited for the final papers, I asked for permission to say goodbye to a friend. I found Vera in the canteen, still guarding my soup.

"What happened?" she asked. "Did you get in trouble?"

"No," I said. "My uncle found me. I'm leaving. But I wanted to say goodbye. You can have my soup. And this."

I pulled off my coat and draped it over her shoulders.

Vera grinned, clutched it to her. "Thanks! But where—"

"I have to go. But one more thing." I stared at her hard. "I'm not Mila. I'm Nadiya, okay?"

Her brow creased. She didn't yet understand. But she was clever like me. She would.

"Okay—"

"Goodbye, Vera," I said and gave her a kiss on the cheek.

"Goodbye . . . Nadiya."

On the way out of the canteen, I passed the poster of Stalin the sea captain, steering our great nation to victory. He was still looking away from me, from all the people whose lives he'd destroyed. He deserved no goodbye. He loved being in control of that ship more than he ever cared about its passengers. I was glad to chart a different path, to sail away from his grasp. If only there hadn't been such a price. But the ghosts of Papa and Nadiya agreed. I had to abandon myself to survive.

This was the hardest goodbye, whispered in my own mind: *Goodbye, Mila.*

48

MILA

New York, New York, USA
1933

On the morning of our last day at sea, Uncle Vanya took me up on deck.

"There she is," he said in Ukrainian, pointing off the bow.

At first, I saw only her outlines—an enormous, robed figure with one arm raised. Then the mist cleared, and I could see the spikes of her crown and the golden torch she held aloft.

Uncle Vanya took off his hat, as if out of respect for a real lady.

"We're nearly there now, Nadiya."

Her name made tears spring to my eyes. It was Nadiya who'd dreamed of seeing the Statue of Liberty. It was *she* who deserved to be standing on the deck of this ship beside an uncle who loved her. But until I was through immigration and on American soil, I dared not tell Uncle Vanya who I truly was. I was deathly afraid of being sent back. Every step of our journey—from Kyiv to Moscow, Moscow to Riga, where we boarded an ocean liner bound for New York—I feared a telegram would arrive, revealing who I was and demanding my return. If this happened, I planned to argue it was a mistake, that the Soviet government was lying, and that I was truly Nadiya. For this reason, I was careful to play the part, even though it pained me to deceive my uncle. He clearly loved Nadiya and had so wanted to save her.

"We should finish packing up," Uncle Vanya said, interrupting my thoughts. "Immigration won't take long—our lawyer arranged the papers. Everyone will be waiting for us at the pier. Lenachka is probably beside herself with excitement!"

During the long days of travel, he'd told me about the rest of the family, particularly Lenachka, or Helen, as she was called in America. She couldn't wait to meet me, he said. I felt the same anticipation, though for a different reason. Perhaps this girl, my own age, was the person to whom I could reveal the truth.

But a few hours later, it only made it harder to have three more Lomachenkos—the only relatives I had left in the world—cry, "Nadiya, welcome!" and crowd around me on the pier. Aunt Nina kissed me and wept. Helen handed me a giant bouquet of red roses, and Peter thrust a box of chocolates at me. "Maybe you'll share them?" he said hopefully.

"Peter!" Helen said.

She looked like Nadiya—the same pale blond hair, the same watchful eyes—a healthier, rosy-cheeked Nadiya.

My knees buckled.

Helen grabbed me under the elbow. "Are you okay?"

"She's tired," Uncle Vanya said. "It's been a long trip."

I was grateful for his answer. I was afraid to speak, afraid I would start crying.

"Lenachka, Petya," Aunt Nina said. "Take the flowers and chocolate."

Helen took the bouquet of roses then linked her arm through mine. "Don't worry, Nadiya," she said. "You're home."

But she was the one who looked like Nadiya, and nothing felt like home. The buildings were impossibly tall, the sidewalks more crowded than any I'd ever seen, the babble of languages deafening. The packed subway car rattled as it whisked us through a dark tunnel and over an elevated track. I clung to Helen, afraid of being separated and lost in the scrum of strangers. Brooklyn, where they lived, was full of shops with windows stuffed with more types of products than I'd ever seen, even at the Party distribution store. But not everyone looked well-fed; I saw several men in raggedy clothes selling apples on the street.

It was a relief to arrive at the family's apartment. It was a simple flat, nothing like the house on Lypska Street. But it smelled delicious—like onions and frying meat—and almost immediately, Aunt Nina sat me down and fed me. I devoured a plate of stuffed cabbage that was even better than Dasha's and was well at work on my second helping when I looked up to find everyone watching me. Had I taken too much, been too greedy? But then I noticed

Helen grinning at Uncle Vanya and his eyes twinkling back at her, and I realized they were delighted to watch me eat. As far as they knew, I had survived a famine, and I didn't ever want to tell them the truth. But I knew it wasn't right; they were happy because they thought Nadiya was polishing off her second helping, not me.

It wasn't until later that evening that I had an opportunity to talk to Helen alone. We were sitting on the stoop of her building watching Peter and some other boys hit a ball with a broom handle. "It's called stickball," Helen explained. The old me would have demanded a turn. But it was hot, even though the light was beginning to fade, and the air was stifling. The boys were sweating, and so was I—in my case, from nerves as much as from heat. How to begin? How to explain? Before I could figure it out, Helen did it for me.

"I'm sorry my cross didn't arrive sooner . . ."

The sadness in her eyes completed the sentence. She was thinking of Nadiya's brothers. Did she want me to talk about them? I had to end this lie—and soon.

"It arrived in time to save her . . ." I said.

Helen's brow wrinkled. Panic engulfed me.

"I mean it almost arrived in time to save Mama," I said. "But it saved me. It got me to Kyiv. I didn't write you about this, but that's where I met Mila."

It was a relief to say my own name, to creep closer to the truth.

"She's our cousin. Her father, Lev—"

"That scoundrel!" Helen interrupted. "He's the one who turned against our family, who wouldn't help your parents. Pop hates him!"

My stomach dropped. I should have realized that Uncle Vanya would have heard from Nadiya's mother about Papa's horrible behavior. How could I tell the truth now? They had no reason to trust me or believe what I told them. I'd lied to them already. I'd seem dishonest, a bad person like my father.

There was only one way to defend my name.

"Mila was nothing like him," I said. "We ended up together in the orphanage, and that's where . . ."

Helen leaned in, transfixed. But I hesitated. Once I said it, there was no taking it back.

"What?" she asked.

She'd never believe the story if I told it about myself. I had to be the cousin she could trust.

"Mila died," I said. "Typhus. We got sick at the same time—we shared a bed. But she didn't—"

I shook my head. I didn't even have to act, the tears came on their own. The story was true, anyway; it was just the names that were switched.

"Nadiya, I'm so sorry!" Helen said. "I had no idea about Mila. Does Pop know?"

I sniffed. "No. You can tell him. It's too hard for me to talk about."

"Of course," Helen said. "I absolutely understand. You've been through so much, the famine . . ."

She let this word hang in the air, inviting me to share more about my life. But that life was Nadiya's. I had finished off my own, burying myself and my secret forever. I just wanted to be alone.

"I'm tired," I said. "I'm going to go inside."

Helen jumped up to accompany me back to the apartment. Dusk had fallen, and I had the excuse of a long trip, so everyone understood when I asked to go to bed. Aunt Nina had set up a cot for me next to Helen's bed. I was half-afraid Helen would insist on going to bed, too, and continue trying to talk to me, but after showing me where the lights were and bringing me a glass of milk, she promised to join me later. I figured she was eager to tell Uncle Vanya about Mila. At least they would remember me, or rather her, as a good and kind person. And as Nadiya, I'd always be safe and loved.

Still, as I lay awake in the warm darkness, tossing and turning, listening to the unfamiliar noises of the Brooklyn streets, I couldn't shake the guilt of having taken on a life that shouldn't have been mine.

49

HELEN

"One now with just the girls!" Pop said. "Helen and Nadiya!"

My eyes were smarting from the photographer's flash, and I was sweating in my best dress in the August heat, but it was wonderful to see Pop this happy. Although it had been barely a month since he'd arrived back home with Nadiya, he'd insisted on taking "the whole family" to the portrait studio on Pitkin Avenue after church. It was as if having formal photos was the ultimate proof that Nadiya was finally with us and safe.

I took Nadiya's hand and pulled her up to the little stage with the woodland backdrop.

"Hopefully these are the last ones," I said in Ukrainian. "Then we can go to Spitz's and get egg creams."

"It's fine," she said.

Nadiya was always agreeable. She liked all the things I'd hoped and dreamed she would: Coney Island, egg creams (especially chocolate ones), Mom's cooking. But after telling me about our cousin Mila, she never again brought up the past. She never spoke about her parents or brothers, and when I mentioned the famine, she swiftly changed the subject. I knew she thought about it, though, because sometimes when I called her name, she didn't answer, and I'd have to repeat, "Nadiya, Nadiya," until she looked up with a startled expression. "Are you all right?" I'd ask, hoping she'd say no and tell me everything so I could tell her about the *New York Times* and how the world needed to hear her story. But she'd always force a smile and say, "Yes, everything's fine," in a way that made it clear she didn't want to talk.

I couldn't wait forever, though, which is why I'd begged Mom and Pop to take Peter to the park after the photographer's so I could take Nadiya to Spitz's—"just us girls."

A half hour later, Nadiya and I were sitting with our egg creams at one of the tables in the back of Spitz's.

"This is good," she said, detaching from her straw with a smile. "Yours?"

I nodded. "Very."

It was hard to know how to begin this conversation. I wished Ruth could help me, but she wasn't at the shop, and she and Nadiya couldn't really communicate anyway: Ruth didn't speak Ukrainian

or Russian—Nadiya generally spoke the latter for Mom's benefit—
and Nadiya only understood a few phrases of English, though I was
teaching her more every day.

I took a breath. "I need to ask you about something. I know it's
difficult for you to talk about, but it's really important—"

Nadiya's relaxed grin vanished, and the color drained from her
face. "What?"

She looked so upset, I almost didn't continue. But I couldn't wait
any longer.

"The famine."

Nadiya blinked at me, wide-eyed, as if trying to make sense of
what I was saying.

"The world doesn't know what's happening in Ukraine," I said.
"I need your help."

Then I let it all come pouring out, about Mrs. Weber and Walter
Duranty, the stories I'd gathered and sent to the *New York Times*,
the editor's letter back to me. I spoke passionately, confident that
together Nadiya and I could convince the *New York Times* to write
the real story of what had happened to our family and others like it.

"You're the eyewitness I need," I explained. "All you have to do
is tell me about the famine, what happened to you. I'll translate it
into English; maybe you can just sign your name—"

But Nadiya was still staring blankly at me. I figured she'd gone
far away, like when I called her name.

"Nadiya?" I said.

"No."

The firmness of her tone surprised me. I almost wondered if she was responding to some memory in her head. But her eyes were alert and fixed on mine.

"Why not?" I asked.

"Helen, kids died. I almost died. My best friend died. I don't want to talk about it."

"I understand it's difficult," I said gently. "But people need to know what happened."

A tear tumbled down her cheek. I handed her Mom's handkerchief with the red roses.

"All you have to do is tell your story—"

Nadiya dabbed at her eyes. "I can't," she whispered. "It's not my story to tell."

"What do you mean? Of course it's your story."

Nadiya winced, shook her head. "I'm sorry. You saved me, and I'll always be grateful. But I can't tell that story."

"Why not?" I pressed.

She looked directly at me, her eyes hard and haunted. "I'm someone different now."

She was up on her feet before I could respond. Not that I knew what to say or would have felt welcome saying it. Her tone was final.

"The heat," she said feebly. "I'm going to go back to the apartment now."

I stood up. "Wait! I'll come with you."

"No. I know the way."

She rushed out of Spitz's, nearly crashing into Ruth at the door.

I wanted to run after her, but I was afraid this would only upset her more. I collapsed back into my seat.

Ruth hurried over, surveyed the half-finished egg cream and crumpled handkerchief beside it.

"What happened?"

"I tried to get her to talk about the famine. I explained everything, all about the *New York Times*. But it's too painful for her."

Ruth sat down in Nadiya's vacated chair. "She did lose her entire family."

"I know. But that's also what makes her story powerful. I tried to explain that to her, how her story could change things."

"Maybe she'll talk later?" Ruth said. "She's only been here a month."

"Maybe." But I had a feeling she'd made up her mind for good.

"People change," Ruth said. "Try again later."

"The thing is I'm not sure I have the heart to keep pushing her. She's been through so much."

"That's for sure. I'm sorry, Helen."

"Don't be. I'm disappointed, but I'm not giving up. Any luck in the Jewish papers?"

"Not yet," Ruth said.

"Me neither. But there's got to be other witnesses out there. It may take a while, but we'll find them."

Ruth smiled. "If only Mrs. Weber could hear you talk like that—"

I spoke in a haughty voice, wagged my finger. "Helen Lomachenko, who do you think you are?"

I shifted in my seat, pretending to face down my teacher and the editor of the *New York Times* and everyone else in the world who had ever doubted me or made me doubt myself.

"I'm Helen Lomachenko," I said proudly.

Ruth applauded.

"How about a refill on that egg cream, Helen Lomachenko?"

"Thanks," I said. "But I better get back."

I helped Ruth clear the table then stopped by the candy counter. With my last nickel, I bought a 3 Musketeers for Nadiya.

"A peace offering?" Ruth said.

I nodded. But it was more than that. It was a promise that from now on, I would stop bringing up her painful past and help Nadiya's future be as sweet as possible.

"Nadiya may tell her story yet," Ruth said as she walked me out. "But in the meantime, maybe you should write down yours."

"Mine? I didn't survive the famine."

"But you helped someone to."

It was true, Nadiya had said so herself: I had saved her. Me, a girl in Brooklyn who'd once been too scared even to raise her hand in class. Ruth was right: I was worth a story, too.

"Maybe someday," I said.

"Well, don't forget to put me in it," Ruth said.

I laughed. "There's no way I could leave you out."

A few blocks from home, I ran into Mom. She'd left Peter and Pop at the park so she could finish cooking. Mary, Mr. Oleynik, and some of our other friends were coming over for Sunday dinner.

"Where's Nadiya?" she asked.

"Home," I said. "She wanted to be out of the heat. My friend Ruth showed up, so I stayed a little longer."

I felt a twinge of guilt, even though what I'd told her was basically true. But Mom didn't seem to notice. She took my arm, tucked it under her own. "We'll fry her up a chicken liver. It'll help her strength."

These days, Mom fussed over Nadiya more than Pop. She and Mary were constantly cooking and feeding her—it was a wonder Nadiya hadn't become as stout as Mrs. Zelenko.

"Good idea," I said, though I had a feeling she'd prefer my 3 Musketeers.

"All that posing for the photographs must have tired her out," Mom said. "But Pop was so proud. His two beautiful girls."

She squeezed my arm, touched her head against mine. "You did good, Lenachka."

I knew she wasn't just talking about the photos. My heart swelled. "So did you," I said. "Taking care of us when Pop was sick."

Mom's eyes filled with tears. She clasped my hands in her rough ones and pulled them to her lips.

"Don't cry," I said, in the same gentle voice she used with me when I was upset.

But it was too late. The tears were already tumbling down her cheeks. "I was so worried Pop was going to get sick again, Lenachka."

"He's okay now. Pop's a survivor. Lomachenkos are survivors; we're tough—"

"Life can be tougher," she said with a deep sigh.

"You need to have hope."

Mom shook her head, smiled through her tears. "My American daughter."

50

MATTHEW

Leonia, New Jersey, USA
2020

"Did you ever tell Helen the truth?" I asked.

GG hung her head. "No."

I didn't scold her, though. I could tell she felt rotten enough.

"Is that why you didn't stay in touch?"

GG nodded. "Too hard."

Instead, she had doubled down on becoming someone else: marrying a guy with the most American of American names, refusing to talk about her past even to her own kids and grandkids, distancing herself from Brooklyn and her Ukrainian family.

"Did Helen even know about Grandma Anna dying?" I asked.

"No."

It didn't seem possible, but then I remembered there was no internet when Mom was a teenager. But maybe that was for the best.

Despite Helen's hope that GG's life would be full of sweetness, Anna's early death had broken GG's heart and left Mom a Motherless Daughter herself.

"What happened to Helen?" I asked.

GG handed me a manila folder. Inside was a faded newspaper clipping from the *New York Times* metro section from 1988 with a photo of an old woman with short hair. *Mrs. Helen Marchuk, Brooklyn grandmother and secret force behind congressional report*, read the caption. Although her last name had changed, the accompanying photo made me certain this was our Helen; her direct gaze belonged to the girl in the photo with GG in Brooklyn.

"Read it," GG demanded.

Tomorrow, the United States Congress will hear the findings of a report from the US Commission on the Ukraine Famine, a group established in 1985 to conduct a study of the 1932–1933 Ukrainian famine. What many New Yorkers might not know is that oral histories of famine survivors and their families collected over four decades by a Brooklyn grandmother have played a key role in the Commission's report. Mrs. Helen Marchuk, 68, started collecting these accounts as a 12-year old growing up in East New York. "My father's family was personally affected by Stalin's policy of starvation," Mrs. Marchuk said from her home in Sheepshead Bay. "And it troubled me that the paper of record was not reporting it." Mrs. Marchuk said she first reached out to the editor of this paper in 1933 to challenge the reporting of Russia correspondent Walter Duranty, whose coverage of the famine has increasingly come under scrutiny in recent years.

Mrs. Marchuk is not a credentialed historian. She has a bachelor's degree from Brooklyn College and worked as a teacher before retiring to raise her children. But historians have praised her work as both careful and crucial to their efforts. "We've relied on her oral histories both to find living survivors to testify before Congress and to corroborate other witness accounts," said Dr. James E. Mace, Staff Director of the Commission.

"This is amazing!" I said.

GG nodded. "Never gave up."

She picked through the folder of letters, then handed me one. I read it silently.

January 15, 1995

Dearest Nadiya,

I hope you received my Christmas card and are in good health. It's all we can ask at seventy-five, though "old age is not happiness," as my mother used to say. How did the time pass? I look in the mirror and do not recognize the old lady I see there. In my mind's eye, I am still thirteen, waiting for you to arrive.

My dear friend Ruth—do you remember Ruth from Pitkin Avenue?—passed away this summer. She was always encouraging me to write down my own story, so this fall I finally sat down and put in my best effort. Attached is a copy, as well as copies of some of the letters and documents from this time. I thought you and your family might want to have this record of your arrival in our lives and what it meant to us.

I continue to be involved with efforts to recognize the Holodomor and its victims. I know you never wanted to revisit what happened to you and your family. But I still encourage you to consider sharing your story. History is simply that—stories—and it matters enormously who gets to tell them.

My number is below in case you ever want to call. I miss you.

Your cousin,
Helen

I put down the letter, opened the oral history folder even though I already knew what I wouldn't find.

"You never did write down your story, your real story, did you?" I asked GG.

She shook her head.

"Is Helen still alive?" I asked.

GG shook her head again. "Died."

I wasn't exactly surprised—how many people live to one hundred like GG?—but I was disappointed. Helen was the one who should be here, hearing the truth, writing it down for one of her oral histories—not me.

But then I thought: Why not me? Maybe I could help make this right.

"GG, would you let me write down the true story—Nadiya's and yours?"

GG looked at me for a long moment.

"Tell Nadiya's story," she finally said. "Not mine."

"But, GG, how can I tell her story without yours?"

GG shook her head fiercely. "Nadiya can't die."

"But she did," I said gently. "You shouldn't feel guilty because you survived. Everyone will understand why you took her name. GG, it's okay . . ."

She'd covered her face with her hands, but she couldn't hide the tears running down her chin or stop her shoulders from heaving. I wrapped my arms around her. She leaned against me, as light and small as a kid herself. I thought of what Helen had written, how even as an old lady she still felt like a kid inside. It was this child inside my great-grandmother I had to talk to.

"Mila," I said. "Nadiya wanted you to live."

Her hands slid down her face, her eyes full of pain.

"I didn't save her."

"How could you have saved her? You were just a kid."

"Helen—"

"Helen didn't save her, either. You both tried, though. That's why we need to tell the whole story—Nadiya's and yours and Helen's, too. The world needs to know what really happened to Nadiya, how much you both loved her . . ."

She was crying even harder now, reminding me of the first time I'd shown her that photo of the two girls. But this time, I understood where all that sadness was coming from. This time, I was crying, too. I thought about everything she had seen and lived through, everything she'd survived. Would I have been able to get through losing the only parent I'd ever known, then my cousin, then hiding my true identity for nearly ninety years? Considering I'd lost it when Dad told me we'd be separated for a few extra months, it sure didn't feel like it. But then I thought about what Mom had said: how I was stronger than that. I could survive being stuck home with a worldwide pandemic raging. If I had to, I could survive a lot more.

GG pulled on my sleeve.

"Tell the story," she said.

"Whose?" I asked carefully.

She took a deep breath.

"Helen's, Nadiya's . . . mine. All three of ours."

51

MATTHEW

Leonia, New Jersey, USA
2020

With GG's permission, I took her box back to my room. I carefully arranged all the notebooks and papers and folders on my bunk. Then I grabbed my laptop and notebook. Over the next couple hours, I skimmed through the journals, letters, oral histories, photos, and documents. They'd felt like a story when GG had directed me through them and I'd written about them in my notebook. But I couldn't figure out where to begin or how to take all those pieces and string them together. I couldn't decide whether I should tell it from all three cousins' points of view or just GG's and whether I should include myself. I tried it a bunch of different ways, but none of them felt right. Everything I wrote sounded stupid and flat.

This was like the hardest English assignment ever, and worst of all, it actually mattered. GG had said that I could share the story with Mom and everyone else, but I didn't just want to blurt it out. I wanted to tell it carefully, with all the details, so people would understand why GG had kept her secret and what she and her cousins had gone through. But by the end of the afternoon, all I'd done was delete every single attempt. I stared at my cursor blinking at the top of my empty white screen. Panic set in. What had I taken on? I wasn't a writer.

But I knew someone who was, and I owed him a call.

It was almost eleven at night in Paris, but Dad picked up on the first ring.

"Hey, Mattie. I'm so glad you called."

The relief in his voice made me feel guilty about my freak-out.

"Sorry I hung up on you," I said.

"You had a right to be angry. Anyway, I'm the one who needs to apologize. I should have been more honest that things weren't looking great for the summer. I think I was kind of in denial myself. I really miss you, Mattie."

"I miss you, too," I said. Saying it still made my chest ache. "When do you think we'll get to see each other again?"

Dad sighed. "I don't know. That's the honest answer. It's not a great time to get on a plane, and if I leave now, the bureau will be down a reporter since no one is allowed into the country. But I promise you I'm trying to find a way to see you."

I took a deep breath, thought of GG, Helen, Nadiya, Mom.

"I don't need you to jump on a plane, Dad. I'm okay. I can handle this."

Dad spoke after a moment, his voice thick. "I know you can. But I still feel lousy being this far away. You're more important to me than anything, Mattie. I wouldn't have taken this posting if I'd known a pandemic was about to happen and it would be this hard to see you. Now that I'm here, I need to do my job. But it doesn't mean I love you any less—"

My throat felt tight, like I was going to cry. I had to stop him before he embarrassed us both.

"Your job is writing up other people's stories, right?"

"Sure, like we talked about. Why?"

This time, I told him the entire truth.

"GG's letting me write up her life story. But it's not going well."

"Cool project." Dad sounded more relaxed again, back to his old self. "What's the trouble exactly?"

"I have all her old journals and letters and stuff. I even took notes in the journal you gave me on what she showed me. But when I tried to write it . . . it's just a total mess."

"You used the Moleskine as a reporting notebook?"

The shock in his voice made me feel worse.

"I did write a little about my life, too."

"No," Dad said. "I didn't mean it that way. I'm impressed."

"Really?" I wasn't sure he'd feel that way when he saw my pages of scribbled notes about GG and her family. But I was glad to make him happy.

"Really. Anyway, let me get this straight: You don't know where to begin. It seems like a big mess. You've tried it a bunch of different ways and it's not working—"

"Exactly!" Dad seemed to understand what I was up against. "I just suck at this. I'm not a writer."

Dad laughed. "Then I'm not, either."

"But you *are* a writer. People pay you for it."

"Listen, Mattie, everything you're describing? I've been there. I struggle, too—with beginnings, middles, endings, all of it."

"But you write stories every day. You do it fast. I've seen you."

"That's just because I've had a lot of practice. When I started out, the editors would totally rewrite them." Dad chuckled. "Sometimes they still do. Writing's hard, especially if you care. But it's the caring part that makes you a writer—not being 'good' at it. I'm guessing GG's story is pretty important to you?"

"Yeah. So how do you write a story, then? If it's so hard?"

"Well, sometimes I have to get out a really bad first draft, just get it on paper to see what I have. Only then can I figure out how to start making it better."

I glanced at my blank screen. Maybe I shouldn't have erased all those attempts. But even I knew how awful they were.

"What if you can't even get out a first draft? Or you don't know how to tell the story?"

Dad thought about this for a second. "Sometimes I make an outline to try to figure out the order of the story."

I groaned. "Ms. McGruder, my English teacher, is really into outlines."

"They don't work for everyone," Dad said. "Sometimes I try telling someone what I'm writing about: I think our brains are naturally wired to tell stories, so we order them instinctively when we try to describe them to other people."

"I want to write it first then tell everyone about it," I said.

"Fair enough," Dad said. "Sometimes, if I'm working on a longer piece, I use index cards—I jot out different parts of the story. Then I can move them around—"

"That's like this video I saw on the designers who made *Zelda*. They draw out the pieces of the story—"

"Storyboarding," Dad said.

"That was it!"

"Storyboarding is a good way of thinking about it. Video games are stories, especially the kind you and I like. I like movies, too—sometimes I like to think of how I'd tell a story if it were a movie. Stories take a lot of different forms, especially these days—games like *Zelda*, TV shows, podcasts. If you can't write it, maybe think about a different way to tell it, one that feels right for you."

An idea was beginning to form. "Thanks, Dad. I'll let you go. You probably want to get to bed."

"I'd rather talk to you."

"Tomorrow. Zoom call at three?"

"Sounds good. I love you, Mattie."

"Love you too, Dad."

I ended the call, grabbed my laptop, and got to work.

52

MATTHEW

Leonia, New Jersey, USA
2020

I titled my video "The Legend of GG." It was really a bunch of videos. In some of them I read from journals and personal histories. In others, I showed letters, newspaper articles, and photos. I even shared some of my own entries from my journal, including GG's real family tree and my internet research about the famine. Each time I recorded a video, I'd show it to GG—she basically had the director's cut. She'd refer me to a diary or letter or newspaper article when I got a detail wrong, but mostly she approved and rewarded my daily effort with chocolate. Of course, she always took a piece for herself, too. Now that I ordered the groceries and made GG her lunch, it was easier to slip in some extra treats. Mom pretended not to notice.

GG didn't want to be on camera, though. She made a ton of

excuses—she didn't like the way she looked; her speech wasn't clear enough. I told her it was her story and people might not believe it if I did all the talking. She had to show up. Finally, several weeks into the project, she agreed to let me record her, just for a few seconds.

It was May 17. She wore her purple housedress and turban. I helped her to a chair—she didn't want me taping her in bed. On the side table, I'd filled a small vase with lilacs and propped the photo of her and Helen against it. There was no photo of Nadiya. None existed.

I set up the tripod Dad had sent me and snapped in my phone. GG pulled at her hands. I could tell she hadn't slept well from the dark hollows under her eyes.

"You'll do fine," I said. "It's just one sentence."

She had practiced it over and over so it was clear.

"Hard one," she said.

"I know. But as soon as we finish, I'm going to start editing all the videos together. I've been making this outline for how they go—"

"Stop," she said, waving me over.

I stopped fiddling with my phone and knelt next to her. She reached out and stroked my cheek. I expected her to say more, but she didn't.

"You don't have to do this if you don't want to," I said.

"I want to," she said.

But I could see the reluctance in her eyes, or maybe just the fear.

"I know something that might help," I said.

I scrambled to my feet, ran back to the tripod, and unclipped my phone. I had downloaded all the music from GG's story—I planned to use it in the background of my video. So all I had to do was select "Sweet Dreams"—the song from Tchaikovsky's *Children's Album* that Mila had played for Nadiya—and hit PLAY.

As the gentle rising melody sounded, GG closed her eyes and began to hum. But this time, her fingers also began to move, and I realized she was playing. Every finger moved exactly on time with the music as if the song had always been inside her, waiting to come out. I wanted to record her, but I was afraid I couldn't without stopping the music, and there was no way I was going to do that.

The piece was short, too short, just over two minutes. When it ended, GG's eyes were still closed. She wore the hint of a smile, as if she knew the answer to some great mystery.

I didn't ask, though, I just waited. Finally, a car door slammed outside. GG shifted, opened her eyes.

"Ready," she said.

The next morning, Mom couldn't wake her.

It wasn't the virus—we'd kept her safe from that. Sometime that night, GG had had another stroke, a big one. The doctor reassured us that, as deaths go, it was a good one. "We should all be so lucky," she said. "She died peacefully in her sleep."

"She's in heaven with Grandma Anna," Mom said, though it only made both of us cry harder.

I wasn't sure GG believed in heaven and all that. But I think that doctor was right about her finally being at peace. It almost felt as if she had planned it, holding off death long enough to make sure I got the truth down. Or maybe it was just *soodba*, that funny Russian word for *fate*.

53
MATTHEW

Leonia, New Jersey, USA
2020

Mom watched "The Legend of GG" on the deck, where I'd set up target practice just two months earlier. It was a warm, late May night—not yet dark at eight o'clock but dim enough to see the first fireflies. I generally don't like hearing my own voice, which cracks when I get excited, but I felt I'd done a pretty good job editing the video.

Mom didn't look up when I struck a match and lit the citronella candles, though she used to get all touchy about me and fire. She just kept watching, wiping away tears. I managed to keep it together until I heard GG's voice at the end, speaking that single sentence.

"My name is Mila Lomachenko."

Mom closed her laptop.

I sniffed. "Are you okay?"

Mom nodded, but her tearstained face said otherwise.

"I wish she'd told me."

Her voice was sad, but I could hear the hurt in it, too. I had to make her understand.

"GG was sorry for not telling you; I know she was," I said. "But I think she felt she couldn't get out of that lie without hurting people. Don't be angry at her—"

"I'm not angry, Matthew. I'm . . ." Mom paused, trying to figure out the right words. "I'm sad that she felt she had to carry this secret for so long by herself."

"She didn't want to upset you," I said. "Especially after Grandma Anna got sick."

"She was always trying to protect me." Mom sighed, shook her head.

"You protected her, too. You took care of her."

Mom waved her hand in the air, reminding me for a moment of GG. "That was just for a few months, at the end."

"That was a lot of work! All those prunes—"

A smile broke through Mom's tears, then faded. "I didn't do enough. I should have made more time for her."

"I think GG felt guilty about outliving a lot of the people she loved," I said. "But I also think she felt loved, especially by you."

Mom sniffed hard. Her voice wavered. "I just feel like I never really knew her."

"You did know her," I said. "She loved you, and you loved her. Whether her name was Nadiya or Mila doesn't change that."

Mom's face softened, her eyes wet. "How did you become such a wise kid?"

"Video games?"

She'd finally let me play them again.

Mom rolled her eyes. "Come here."

I was almost in eighth grade and officially didn't sit on my mom's lap. I was almost as tall as she was. But when she pulled me onto her lap, I didn't pull away. And when she put her arms around me and squeezed me tight, it even felt good.

"I want to share my video with some of the places that collect famine history," I said. "I'm also working on a written version. That might take a while, though. When I'm done, maybe you could edit it?"

Dad had already volunteered—he was trying to come for a month around Christmas. I'm sure he would be more than happy to spend it giving me writing tips. But I knew it would mean more to Mom. The smile that broke across her face confirmed this.

"Oh, Matthew, of course. I'd be honored."

"Thanks, Mom."

"I could help you draft letters to some historians, too, if you'd like," she said. "But I don't want my name on it, just yours. You're the keeper of GG's story."

Keeper of the Story. It was like some important title: Keeper of the Portal from *Baldur's Gate* or Dungeon Master. I remembered the last time I'd played *Zelda*, after Mom had given me back my Switch. In a single evening, I'd defeated Dark Beast Ganon and gotten back

Link's last missing memory, unlocking the secret ending: Zelda had lost her powers, but together she and Link would rebuild her kingdom.

"Thank you, Link," Zelda said, "the hero of Hyrule."

Except this was real life, and I—Matthew—truly felt like somebody's hero.

EPILOGUE
MATTHEW

On a Friday in the middle of November, Mom and I drove an hour and a half down the New Jersey Turnpike to the town of Jackson. What most people know about Jackson is that it's where Six Flags Great Adventure is—in fact, that's all I knew about it before GG died. But it's also home to St. Vladimir's Russian Orthodox Cemetery.

A cemetery visit on Friday the 13th, Josh texted with a skull emoji.

For a b day party, I texted back and then added emojis of a party hat and streamers, a ghost, and *The Scream*.

I wasn't kidding—it was GG's birthday, and Mom had let me skip school, which was only in person half the time anyway, to celebrate. It wasn't just any birthday, either. Despite the party for her at the nursing home back in January, GG hadn't actually turned one hundred. She had been celebrating Nadiya's birthday, not her own. Today was GG's real one hundredth birthday.

We pulled up in front of the cemetery gates around eleven. Josh would definitely have said there was something creepy about the place. It was on a lonely road, surrounded by pine trees, and there was no one around except for a groundskeeper. When Mom and I had come for GG's funeral, we'd learned there used to be a Russian and Ukrainian summer community up the road—a restaurant, a dance hall, and even a camp where kids could escape the city and swim in a spring-fed pond. Helen's family had been part of that community, and it was during this time that her father had bought a parcel of plots in the cemetery.

Mom had been surprised at first that GG had wanted to be buried here. The place *was* pretty depressing—the restaurant and dance hall were boarded up now, and the pond was filled with mucky green algae. But as we wandered through the rows of gravestones with their three-tiered Orthodox crosses, the wind blew away the clouds and sunlight glinted off the golden dome of the church. It made me think of that old monastery in Kyiv where Nadiya had finally told Mila her story, and I understood why GG had wanted to be buried here—it was as close as GG could get to home.

The Lomachenko graves were side by side in the second section about a dozen rows back. Ivan and Nina Lomachenko, Helen's pop and mom were buried here—their names written on one side of their gravestone in English and the other in Cyrillic. Helen and her husband were buried here, too. Next to Helen's grave was GG's. The stone was shiny and new. Mom and I had talked a bunch about what it should say. I'd like to think that GG would've approved of what we came up with.

Mom put down a spade, watering can, and potted lilac bush then went off to find some water. While she was gone, I lined up a bunch of 3 Musketeers minis on the base of GG's grave.

"Happy birthday, GG," I said. "I'm sure these are not as good as Bumble Bears, but they're all I've got. You can share them with Helen and Nadiya."

I knew this was kind of goofy, but there was no one around to hear me, and I liked to imagine the three of them together, laughing and gorging themselves on chocolate.

"I also wanted to tell you—and Helen, too—that I shared the video of your story with a bunch of historical archives, you know, where they collect stories about the famine so people can use them in books and exhibits and stuff. I'm working on the written version, too. Nadiya won't be forgotten—people will know what happened to her—and to you."

For the second time that morning, the sun broke from behind the clouds. I don't normally believe in mystical stuff or messages from the beyond, but what happened next seemed like more than just a coincidence: A ray of light fell on GG's gravestone illuminating the names we'd chosen—and yes, there was more than one:

LYUDMILA LOMACHENKO JOHNSON
"Our Beloved GG"
November 13, 1920–May 18, 2020
In Memory of Nadiya Lomachenko
January 3, 1920–June 5, 1933

The light didn't last long—the November wind blew the clouds back across the sky—but for that split second, I was certain that GG was there, and Nadiya and Helen, too. I could almost hear their voices, the three of them speaking as one: *Thank you.*

Some of my grandma Natasha's family photographed in Ukraine in the 1930s. Back row, left to right: her sister, Yustina; her niece, Lida; her sister, Anna. Front row, her nieces, Nadiya and Maria. Nadiya and Maria were cousins and I kept looking at their faces and entwined hands as I wrote this book.

AUTHOR'S NOTE

Throughout my 1980s childhood, the letters arrived—airmail envelopes with blue-and-pink-striped edges and marked **АВИА** (*avee-ah*), the Russian word for *air*. Before the internet and when long-distance phone calls were prohibitively expensive, these letters were my grandmother's lifeline to her family—two sisters and a brother—she'd left behind in Ukraine when she'd immigrated to America in 1928 after her mother's death from typhus.

Growing up, I lived with my grandma—she was born Natalia Stepanivna Ostapiuk, but everyone called her by her nickname, Natasha. That she had been able to leave the Soviet Union and come to America when she did was a rare feat. In 1924, the United States Congress passed the Johnson-Reed Act, which banned immigrants

My grandma Natasha and I circa 1981 in Yonkers, New York. I was an egg in a dance performance and she was there, as always, to cheer me on. I grew up in her house and remember the regular arrival of airmail letters from the Soviet Union.

from Asia and severely limited those from "less desirable" regions of Europe, including Eastern Europe and Southern Europe. Even the sponsorship of a relative—in this case, Natasha's older brother, Dmitro, who'd immigrated before the First World War—was not enough to ensure entry. A petite woman in her early twenties traveling alone, Natasha was stranded in Mexico, turned back from the port of New Orleans, and finally ended up in Havana, Cuba, where Dmitro managed to arrange a marriage license that paved her legal entry into the United States.

The journey may have been difficult, but with each passing year, Natasha was reminded of the enormous fortune of escaping her small Ukrainian village when she did. Ukraine at that time was a republic of the Soviet Union, a communist country sometimes referred to as Russia, including by the Western press. In 1928, the year Natasha left, Joseph Stalin, the Soviet Union's ruthless leader, began his policy of collectivization, in which farmers

Natasha and some of her family in Ukraine, circa 1925. From left to right, her sister, Yustina; her brother, Mikhailo; Natasha; an unidentified relative. This is the only photo I have of my grandma before she came to America.

were forced to give their land to the State and join government-run collective farms. Ukraine, a fertile republic that grew much of the country's grain, suffered disproportionately. Ukrainian peasants who resisted collectivization, like Nadiya Lomachenko's father, were evicted from their homes, packed onto trains, and sent to distant settlements and labor colonies where many were worked to death.

Stalin could never have implemented his brutal policies without devout Party officials like Mila's father and a system of propaganda that taught all citizens—starting in early childhood—that the State could do no wrong and that "class enemies" were to blame for their problems. Chief among these enemies were kulaks, the prosperous peasants Stalin claimed were responsible for the country's ills and whom he persecuted accordingly. It was important for me to write from the viewpoint of a child like Mila to show the power of such a system to reduce people to labels, distort the truth, and destroy basic humanity. This period of history is a cautionary tale: Stalin's ability to divide and turn his own people against one another set the stage for the horrors that followed.

In 1932, Stalin kept the State grain quotas at impossible-to-meet levels. Despite widespread reports of starvation in Ukraine, as well as in the North Caucasus and Kazakhstan, the State confiscated grain, sent it to other parts of the Soviet Union, and even sold it abroad. Stalin sought to feed workers at the growing number of factories he was building to industrialize the Soviet Union, but his policies were also motivated by his fears of resistance, especially among national groups such as Ukrainians. The human cost of his orders was enormous: Western historians estimate that the resulting famine killed nearly four million Ukrainians, most of them in the countryside.

When the famine started in 1932, Natasha was married again to my grandfather, John Milosh, whose life story I also drew on to write this book. Like Helen's pop, John (who was born Ivan Petrovich but preferred his English name) fled the Russian Empire at his mother's urging to escape the draft. He was just seventeen when, in 1911, he left his small village in Belarus and arrived alone in America. Like Pop, his brothers died in the First World War, his brokenhearted mother shortly thereafter. Although he was able to help bring over his sister, Anna, my grandfather was tormented by survivor's guilt.

But that August of 1932 was a happy time for my grandparents as they welcomed their first child—my mother, Yelena, or Elaine. Like Helen's family, they lived in East New York, Brooklyn, and my grandfather had a steady job at a newspaper printing press. Their community included other working-class Ukrainians, Belarusians, Russians, Moldovans, and even a few Poles (my grandparents were both also a quarter Polish). As most of the adults were born and raised in the Russian Empire, Russian was a common tongue, but everyone spoke their own native languages as well, especially with others of the same origin. Like Helen, my mother would grow up wanting to be a regular American girl (she really was teased for bringing caviar sandwiches to school).

Throughout her life, Natasha sent parcels—or *posilki*, as she called them in Ukrainian—to her family containing fabric and clothing. Sometimes, according to my uncle Eugene, she would sew money into the hems to hide it from Soviet customs officials. Family memory is unclear on whether she was able to send these *posilki* during the famine, but I adopted her trick for Helen's cross.

My grandpa John and grandma Natasha photographed in East New York, Brooklyn, circa 1936, with their children: my mom, Elaine or Yelena, and my uncle Eugene or Evgeny. John, like Helen's pop, had a weakened heart; he lived to see my mom and uncle grow up, but died before I was born.

What is clear is that many Ukrainian immigrants knew about the famine as it was happening. Letters from the Soviet Union were censored but the Soviet government allowed some basic word to leak out to encourage relatives to send money through its system of Torgsin—or hard-currency—shops. Dollars were worth more than rubles, and the State was happy to give a starving relative a loaf of bread in exchange for foreign money.

By mid-1933, Natasha knew the full extent of the famine from her own eyewitness sources. That summer, her American cousin, Ignat, managed to return to the family village in Ukraine and bring his nineteen-year-old daughter, Anastasia, as well as a new wife, Anna, back to America. (As Helen explains to Ruth, the Soviet government was more reluctant to part with boys, who were valued as future soldiers, so Ignat had to leave behind his son.) Upon their return, the family lived with my grandparents for six months.

Anastasia, or Nastya, as she was called, would end up living to 106, with a sharp mind and memory till nearly the end of her very long life. She always treated me like a granddaughter, and while I relied on numerous oral histories and historical accounts to re-create Nadiya's experience during the famine, it is Nastya's that served as my emotional touchstone. Hers is the haunting description of the silence of the village after its starving inhabitants were forced to eat all the dogs and cats. To survive, she ate tree bark. The experience was so traumatic that she didn't talk to her own children about the famine till they were adults. She could never revisit her memories without crying.

My grandmother's family—her sisters, Yustina and Anna, and brother, Mikhailo—survived the Holodomor—or death from hunger—as the famine came to be called in Ukraine. But, as with Nastya, it left indelible and horrific memories. Yustina's grandson, Ruslan, wrote me that his grandmother told him how starving children would dig up the fields for rotten potatoes, which they boiled with grass; how funeral brigades would collect dead bodies onto a cart and deposit them in mass graves.

Memories like these were not only difficult; for many years, they were also dangerous. As with many dark chapters of its history—including the Great Terror of 1936–38 when Stalin executed an estimated million people, including a quarter of his own Party, as traitors and enemies—the Soviet Union forbade public discussion. Oral histories, passed down in secret between survivors and their descendants, were the chief means of keeping the memory of what had happened alive. It wasn't until the late 1980s that the Soviet Union publicly acknowledged the famine. Even in 2020, when Ruslan paid a visit for me to our family village's library/museum to search its collection of historical records, he could find none related to the Holodomor.

Western awareness of the famine was hampered by the reporting of Walter Duranty and other Moscow correspondents who feared losing access and perks if they deviated from the Soviet Party line. But there were courageous exceptions, chief among them Gareth Jones, the Welsh journalist and political advisor who sneaked into hard-hit regions of Ukraine to provide the searing eyewitness account that Duranty attacks in the article Helen reads in class. Canadian Rhea Clyman was another of these journalistic heroes— and one of the rare women journalists of that time. After working as Duranty's researcher, Clyman—who had lost a leg in a childhood streetcar accident and used a prosthetic one—slipped out of Moscow and detailed the early days of the famine before the Soviets threw her out of the country in late 1932. The British reporter Malcolm Muggeridge anonymously authored several dispatches about the famine in March 1933, and that fall, Harry Lang, a reporter for the Yiddish-language *Jewish Daily Forward*, managed to enter Ukraine and cover the famine especially as it affected the Jewish Ukrainian community.

Lang's colleague at the *Forward*, Mendel Osherowitch, who was born in Ukraine and still had family there, visited even earlier—in February and March 1932. Thanks to his brothers, who were Communist officials, Osherowitch was able to travel freely, and in early 1933, he published a book based on his reporting, *How People Live in Soviet Russia: Impressions from a Journey*. This powerful book was only published in Yiddish, however, and shortly after its publication, Osherowitch fell silent, likely fearing retaliation against his family by the Soviet government. By the time Ruth was trying to help Helen find eyewitnesses, it is doubtful he would have been willing to speak publicly.

While the main characters in this book are fictional, the US Commission on the Ukraine Famine was a real group established by Congress in 1985 to study and present its findings on the famine.

Using both oral histories and survivor testimonies, the commission concluded the famine was entirely man-made and unrelated to drought or kulak sabotage, as the Soviet government had long claimed. The *New York Times* began to acknowledge Walter Duranty's failures around this time as well, and in 2003, the paper issued a statement that I like to think Helen would have approved of: "[Duranty's] taking Soviet propaganda at face value . . . was completely misleading, as talking with ordinary Russians might have revealed even at the time."

Recognition of the Holodomor has continued to increase, especially after the collapse of the Soviet Union in 1991. In 2008, the Ukrainian government built a memorial to the victims of the famine on the banks of the Dnieper River in Kyiv. I visited it in 2016. It's right near Pechersk Lavra, the monastery where Nadiya finally tells Mila her story. Called "The Bitter Memory of Childhood," it features a statue of a frail girl holding a tiny handful of wheat in memory of the child victims of the famine.

On that same visit to Kyiv, I met up with my Ukrainian relatives. When I wrote this book, I never imagined that I would find myself in the same situation as my grandmother, feeling worried about their safety and powerless to help. But just as I received my copyedits, Russia invaded Ukraine. Once more stories of death, including of children, are emerging from Ukraine. And again, the Kremlin is using disinformation and propaganda to justify brutality, painfully dividing the many families whose members live on opposite sides of the Russia-Ukraine border. More than ever since the end of the

Soviet era, the Russian government is also silencing internal voices of opposition and dissent—including closing the last of the country's independent press, as well as human rights organizations such as Memorial, which seeks to restore historical memories of Soviet-era repression.

As the author of another novel for young readers, *Nowhere Boy*, about the 2015 European refugee crisis that I witnessed firsthand from Belgium, I am also deeply concerned about the growing number of Ukrainian refugees. As of this writing, millions of Ukrainians have fled the country, the majority of them women, children, and the elderly. I now write my relatives regularly—not by airmail, but by email—and the anguish and worry at the heart of this work of historical fiction feel all too current and real.

A note on language in *The Lost Year*: After a period in the 1920s during which Ukrainian was permitted to be taught in Soviet Ukrainian schools and was an accepted part of public life, the Soviet government dictated that Russian be the primary language. In keeping with historical accuracy, characters in this novel speak Russian as well as Ukrainian, and in some cases use Russian names. In addition, due to Ukraine's history as part of the Russian Empire and Russia's influence over many aspects of life, there were Ukrainian communities where Russian was spoken alongside Ukrainian, and Russian names were used as well as Ukrainian ones. Geography and intermarriage also impacted language use but did not prevent people from maintaining a distinctive Ukrainian identity. It is important to note that the intersection of language and identity can change over time.

After the Russian invasion of Ukraine, many more Ukrainians—even some from Russian-speaking communities—have chosen not to speak Russian.

My grandmother died in 2002 when I was holding her hand and singing the same nursery song, "The Cossack Lullaby," that she and my mother sang to me as a child, that I still sing to my own children, and that I have Nadiya sing to Mila when she falls ill. She is buried next to my grandfather John at St. Vladimir's, the Russian Orthodox cemetery that Matthew visits in Jackson, New Jersey, with his mom to see GG's grave.

Natasha had dementia at the end, and one day, shortly before she died at ninety-five, she left the house. By this time, her siblings were dead—her brother, Mikhailo, had been killed in the Second World War; her sisters, Anna and Yustina, had died of old age. It was winter, and she wasn't wearing a coat. She was less than five feet tall by then, and half-blind, but she marched off with determination.

"Where are you going?" we called after her.

"Home," she said.

It took us a moment to understand. She didn't mean her home now, or even her former homes in New York City; she meant back to her childhood home in Ukraine.

Katherine Marsh
March 2022
Washington, DC

ACKNOWLEDGMENTS

On a December morning in New York City in 2019, over coffee and bagels, my editor, Jennifer Besser, encouraged me to write something about my family history. Years before that, Ruta Sepetys had encouraged me to do the same. I jotted out some ideas, and my longtime agent, Alex Glass, recognized this story's potential in its earliest form. My incredible critique group—Caroline Hickey, Erica Perl, and Tammar Stein—kept me on track throughout the writing process (and the pandemic) and made every single draft better. Special thanks to Tammar for suggesting the title. Jennifer Besser and fellow Macmillan editor Kate Meltzer pushed me to take this story to a deeper level and didn't let anyone—even me—stand in the way of my best work. The talented Ukrainian artist Maria Skliarova drew the incredible cover and chapter illustrations for this book from the middle of a war zone. Thanks also to the incredible team at Macmillan supporting this book including Molly Ellis, Teresa Ferraiolo, Chantal Gersch, Samira Iravani, Morgan Kane, Nicole Schaefer, Emilia Sowersby, Mary Van Akin, Kathy Wielgosz, Janet Robbins Rosenberg, Veronica Ambrose, Peter Mavrikis, and Melissa Zarr.

Dr. Matthew E. Lenoe was my first Russian teacher and accompanied my high school class on a memorable semester to the Soviet Union. He is now a Russian history professor at the University of Rochester specializing in the Soviet era and served as a trusted advisor and reader on this book. Dr. Daria Mattingly, a native Ukrainian, Holodomor expert, and lecturer at Cambridge University, read and critiqued the history in this book not only once, but twice, as drafts evolved. I highly recommend her YouTube video "Holodomor: The Ukrainian Famine of the 1930s" as an introduction to this topic. Dr. Kathleen Smith, a professor who specializes in memory and Russian history at Georgetown University, also read the book and shared her expertise, including deep diving into Soviet chocolate. Thanks to former Russia correspondent Maura Reynolds for connecting me to her as well as to our book group of female journalists, the Chick Hacks, who remind me every month of the importance of journalism. Dr. Serge Cipko, of the Canadian Institute of Ukrainian Studies, patiently answered my questions about correspondence between families during the Holodomor and the workings of the Torgsin system. My former journalism colleague Julia Ioffe, who is working on her own book on women and Russian history, was another helpful sounding board. Dr. Steven E. Harris at the University of Mary Washington shared his expertise on Soviet aviation. Dr. Mateusz Świetlicki at the University of Wroclaw also provided a helpful pre-publication read. Any errors in this book are my own.

My mother, Elaine Milosh, told me many of her childhood stories over the years; through them, she brought a community to life and gave me an appreciation and love for my Ukrainian and Russian, as well as Russian Orthodox, heritage. My uncle, Eugene Milosh, also shared his memories of life in East New York. My late grandmother Natalia Ostapiuk Milosh brought the old country to the new through her stories and cooking. My Ukrainian cousin, Ruslan Mihal, shared family memories of the famine. Our American cousins, Paul Zoltanetzky and Mary Vukosa, discussed their mother, Nastya's, memories of the famine and how it shaped her life. Nastya's granddaughter, Andrea Zoltanetzky, did the same and helped me gain insight into intergenerational trauma. Her husband, translator Paul Beason, gave a copyedit of this book. A group of ninety-year-old to one-hundred-year-old women—Millie Bonsignore, Ray Botvinik, Judy Fogelman Sennett, and Janice Levy—helped me recreate early 1930s Brooklyn by sharing their childhood memories. Maggie Tai Tucker, SueAnn Partow, and Judith Meltzer helped me find them.

Orli Wildman Halpern served as my first kid reader on early chapters of this book while undergoing chemo and modeling the strength and spirit of a survivor. My son, Sasha Barnes, and my daughter, Natalia Barnes, also served as readers and advisors on Matthew's text messages while helping me see the pandemic through a kid's-eye view. My father, Kenneth Marsh, makes me proud, like Ruth, of my Jewish heritage; his declining health as I wrote this book gave me a deeper appreciation for the act of caring, especially for elders, at the heart of this story. There would be no book without Julian E. Barnes: husband extraordinaire (doing the housework as I write this), very best of newspaper reporters, and kind and loving father.

Last, but not least, I'd like to thank the DC Commission of the Arts and Humanities for their financial support during the pandemic and the writing of this book.

Keep reading for an excerpt
from Katherine Marsh's
Nowhere Boy.

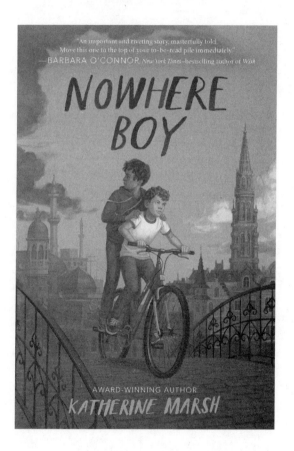

"A resistance novel for our time." —*The New York Times*

CHAPTER ONE

◆

They had purposely waited for a cloudy, moonless July night. It was less likely, the smugglers had said, that the Greek Coast Guard would spot them.

But now their invisibility was a problem. The top of the inflatable rubber dinghy bobbed barely ten centimeters above the Aegean, several centimeters lower than when they had started. There was no land in sight. The captain struggled to restart the motor while the silhouettes of eighteen men, three women, and four children huddled together. Some had ill-fitting life jackets; only a few knew how to swim.

"If the motor doesn't start, we will drown," one of the women said, her thin voice rising in panic.

No one disagreed.

Ahmed Nasser hugged his life jacket against himself. It was too small for a boy of fourteen, especially one nearly as tall as his father. He remembered the stories he had heard in Turkey of smugglers selling defective life jackets that made people sink instead of float.

A hand touched his shoulder. "Ahmed, my soul, don't be afraid."

Ahmed looked at his father, his large frame crammed against the side of the boat. A black inner tube was slung over his shoulder and he smiled calmly, as if he knew they'd be okay. But the smell of bodies, unwashed and sweating, the terrified gazes, the sickly toss of the sea, told Ahmed otherwise.

"The lady is right," Ahmed whispered. "The boat's deflating. If the motor won't start—"

"Hush," his father said.

His voice was commanding yet gentle, as if he were soothing a child. But Ahmed was old enough to know the powerlessness that lay behind it. He thought about his mother, his sisters, his grandfather—would his death be worse than theirs had been? His father had assured him theirs had been painless. Surely theirs had been quicker than this. There had been no time for false words of comfort.

Less than ten kilometers separated the coast of Turkey from the Greek island of Lesbos. Ahmed tried to make out lights from land or even from another boat, but he could spot nothing. Where was Europe? Where was the rest of the world? There wasn't even a star to promise a better elsewhere existed. The sky was as dark as the water below it. He could barely see the face of the stainless-steel watch his father had worn until earlier tonight, when he'd fastened it around Ahmed's wrist. It had been Ahmed's great-grandfather's Omega Seamaster, a name that seemed ironic now.

"Baba, you know I can't swim," Ahmed whispered.

"You won't have to," his father said.

But water was soaking Ahmed's sneakers. He could feel it rolling back and forth across the bottom of the boat. People tossed bags into the sea, trying to lighten the load. Ahmed watched the bags bob, then float away or sink. A few people tried to bail the water out with plastic bottles, but it hardly seemed to make a difference. The woman in front of them started crying. For the first time, Ahmed noticed she was holding a baby in a sling.

"Don't cry," Ahmed's father said to her, his tone light. "There is already enough water in this boat."

But this only seemed to make the woman cry harder.

"*Allahu Akbar*," several people prayed.

"Baba—"

"The woman is right," his father interrupted. "We must keep this boat moving. But you will not sink. Nor will the others."

Ahmed noticed him glance at the woman and her baby, then at the rest of the desperate, frightened strangers in the overcrowded boat. Baba pulled the inner tube off his shoulder and slipped it over Ahmed's head and around his torso. Then he leaned over and whispered in his ear.

"Forgive me, my soul. For a moment, I must leave you."

"Leave me? Where?"

But his father had already turned away.

"Baba!"

Ahmed tried to reach for him, only to realize that his arms were pinned to his sides by the inner tube. By the time he'd freed them, his father's leg was already over the side of the boat.

Ahmed lurched forward to grab him, but it was too late. His father slid into the dark water like an eel. A moment later he reappeared, treading water.

"What are you doing?" Ahmed shouted after him.

"We need to pull the boat." His father's eyes searched the passengers. "Can anyone else swim?"

They were from a medley of places—Syria, Afghanistan, Iraq—but Ahmed realized from the helpless way they looked at one another that they had one thing in common: none of them could swim.

But then a voice behind him said in Iraqi-accented Arabic, "I can."

Ahmed turned around. A slight, wiry man took off his jacket, then his shirt. He handed them to the woman beside him, who folded them neatly, as if to make a point that she expected him back. A little girl sat between them, half swallowed by her life jacket.

"I can, too," said the captain. He looked ashamed about the motor, but Ahmed felt it wasn't his fault. He wasn't even really a captain. He was just an engineering student from Homs whom the smugglers had chosen from among the refugees to pilot the boat. This thankless duty had earned him an oblong orange buoy. He tossed it into the sea, then dove after it.

Ahmed tried to give his father back the inner tube, but he refused to take it, claiming it would slow him down. The men swam to the front of the boat and, as a passenger shined a flashlight across the dark water, they looped the boat's towrope around the buoy, conferring in tones too hushed for Ahmed to hear. Then each grabbed onto the rope with one hand, kicking with their feet and paddling with their free arm. Ahmed's father swam in front, the two men behind him.

The boat jerked forward, as if a giant hand had given it a shove.

Cheers and shouts of "Praise be to God!" rose up from the passengers. Those in the center of the boat scooped water from the bottom into bottles and passed them to those on the edge to pour out. As he emptied bottles, Ahmed felt his fear ebb, replaced by pride that it was his father leading the swimmers. It reminded him of long-ago weekends before the war, when his family had barbecued and picnicked with friends outside of Aleppo. Late at night, his father would lead the *dabke,* whirling the line of dancers as they held hands and stamped their feet to drum and tambourine. Ahmed would stare up at the star-filled sky and let himself be dragged along wildly, knowing Baba was in charge.

But a half hour later, he was jolted from his memories as the wind picked up and choppy waves rocked the dinghy. Occasionally they spilled over the sagging sides, and Ahmed could hear the water slosh in the bottom. He looked anxiously out into the beam of light that illuminated his father and the other swimmers.

Whitecaps broke over their heads, slowing their pace, but their free arms continued to pinwheel around.

A hard summer rain began to fall. Within minutes, Ahmed was drenched. He told himself that rain this heavy never lasted long, but it stirred up the sea even more. The swimmers pulled the dinghy straight into the waves. It pitched and bucked, pulling the swimmers' rope taut, but it stayed afloat.

Then came the sideways wave.

Ahmed didn't see it, but he felt it. It tipped the dinghy to one side and seemed to hold it there, as if considering the worth of those inside. Ahmed sucked in air, expecting to be flipped. But the wave let the dinghy slide down its side and instead swept over the swimmers so that they vanished completely. Then it ripped the buoy off the rope and tossed it into the darkness.

There was a second of silent shock before everyone started shouting, shining their phones' flashlights across the water.

"Where are they? Can anyone see them?"

The captain sputtered to the surface. The Iraqi popped up next with a gasp, his hand still clutching the rope.

But where was Baba?

Far in the distance, through the driving rain, Ahmed thought he saw his father's head bob to the surface.

"Baba!" he shouted.

But there was no response, and when he looked again, all he could see were the endless whitecap waves.